The Cowboy Wins a Bride

By Cora Seton

To Jennifer G. – my friend and sister – for your support, love, and laughter.

Author's Note

The Cowboy Wins a Bride is Volume 2 in the **Cowboys of Chance Creek** series, set in the fictional town of Chance Creek, Montana. To find out more about Cab, Rose, Hannah, Mia, Fila, Ethan, Autumn, Jamie, Claire, Rob, Morgan and other Chance Creek inhabitants, look for the rest of the books in the series, including:

Look for the **Heroes of Chance Creek** series, too:

The SEALs of Chance Creek Series:

A SEAL's Oath

A SEAL's Vow

A SEAL's Pledge

A SEAL's Consent

Sign up for my newsletter HERE.

www.coraseton.com/sign-up-for-my-newsletter

Chapter One

"**W**HY DON'T YOU ASK HER TODAY?**" Ethan Cruz said, hauling a pile of folding chairs for the wedding out of the Party Plus Event Rentals delivery truck. In his jeans and t-shirt, his dark hair standing up every which way, you'd never know he was getting married in a few hours. He looked like he'd climbed out of bed a minute ago.

Jamie Lassiter snapped the velvet box shut, hiding the tasteful diamond ring he'd just showed to his friends, and shoved it back into the pocket of his jeans. He grabbed an armful of chairs, too, and followed Ethan toward the front lawn of the Cruz Ranch's Big House—where he was helping to set up for Ethan's wedding to Autumn Leeds, the city girl who'd only come to Chance Creek a month ago, but now was here to stay.

"It's not time yet," he said. He wasn't in a rush like Ethan and Autumn were, and he never jumped into things the way those two did. The only reason they even met was because of a practical joke. By all rights they should have taken one look at each other in the Chance

Creek Regional Airport and gone their separate ways.

Instead, they'd fallen head over heels in love, and rumor had it Autumn was pregnant with Ethan's baby. Talk about taking chances. Jamie liked Autumn, and he figured she and Ethan might just make a go of this marriage, but when he proposed to Ethan's sister, Claire, he wanted to be sure of everything ahead of time—including her answer.

He definitely wasn't sure of that yet.

"For heaven's sake, you've carried a torch for her for what—ten years? Twelve?"

Try twenty. Jamie had decided to marry Claire back when he was eight. He'd practically grown up on the Cruz ranch, since he loved horses and his family lived in town. Ethan's father, Alex Cruz, welcomed his interest and even nurtured it. Jamie learned to ride alongside Ethan and Claire, did chores with them, worked just as hard as they did to build the ranch by their father's side. Sometimes Alex felt more like a dad to him than his own father did.

"Why you'd want to marry my sister is beyond me," Ethan said, breaking into his thoughts, "but if you're going to do it, it might as well be soon. Heck, if you'd hurried up a bit we could have had a double wedding."

Rob Matheson came up behind them, hauling another load of chairs, his blond hair falling into his eyes. "Yeah, Jamie, you should have planned ahead. That way we'd only need to lug these chairs around once."

"What about your wedding?"

Rob snorted. "I'm never getting married. Plus, if I

ever did—which I won't—I'll be married from my own spread. Not Ethan's."

"So? Why not ask her today?" Ethan pushed. "Weddings are romantic. You might have a better shot getting the answer you want."

Cab Johnson lumbered up behind them, carrying more chairs than the rest of them combined. The large, quiet sheriff had obviously been listening to their conversation. "Jamie's got a plan," he said. "And the plan doesn't call for any proposals today."

Jamie knew he was laughing at him. They all were. But his careful planning had taken him from hired hand on the Cruz ranch to part owner, and it would lead him to the rest of his dreams as well—he was sure of it.

"What does Jamie's plan call for today?" Rob said wryly.

"Planting the seeds," Jamie said. "I've taken the first steps. I always knew Claire wouldn't look twice at a man who wasn't a rancher, so here I am—a legitimate rancher now."

"Amen," Ethan said. Jamie had only bought into the Cruz ranch a week ago, but by doing so he'd saved Ethan from losing it all. He knew Ethan was more grateful than words could say. He didn't want his friend's gratitude, though. He just wanted a steady business partnership that would last for the rest of their lives.

"That's all fine and dandy," Rob said. "You're part owner of a ranch. But Claire still lives in Billings and she hasn't wanted anything to do with this place for years."

"She will—you wait and see," Jamie said, but he had

to acknowledge the truth of Rob's words. When he was fifteen and Claire seventeen, he was just working up the nerve to ask her out when she fell head over heels for Mack Mackenzie, the Cruz's much older horse trainer. When her mother pointed out that no thirty-year-old man was going to look twice at a little girl, they'd had their biggest fight yet, screaming at each other so loudly they frightened the horses out in the corrals. Claire left in a raging huff, and so far she hadn't shown any sign of moving home, even after her parents died in a car accident last year.

"Planting seeds, huh?" Rob said. "You know, if I was going to plant something in Claire, it wouldn't be…"

Jamie dropped his chairs on the lawn and turned on Rob, his fist raised, but Cab stepped in between them. "Wedding," was all he said and both Rob and Jamie backed off. Rob wasn't worth getting worked up over anyway. The man ran off his mouth without ever thinking first. He bent down, grabbed the chairs and hauled them closer to the piles they'd dropped off on earlier trips.

"If you ever so much as touched my sister I'd deck you," Ethan said, putting his chairs down, too, and starting back toward the truck.

"So Jamie gets to touch her but I don't?" Rob complained, as he dumped his chairs and followed Ethan.

"That's about the size of it."

Jamie appreciated that his friend didn't mind the crush he had on his sister. He couldn't remember ever telling Ethan about it in so many words. Somehow

Ethan just knew, and Jamie knew that he knew, and they both knew that it was okay.

Claire was the only one who had a different opinion.

A few years ago, just after New Year's, he thought she might be coming around, though. Finally. As if she'd made a resolution to patch things up with her mother, she'd begun to make the two hour drive from Billings almost weekly, staying over in her old room in the Big House, spending whole weekends at the ranch. She'd been friendly to him. Smiled at him sometimes. Even flirted with him a little.

"She doesn't want a rancher, she wants a hot-shot city guy," Rob said when they reached the truck again. He lifted his cowboy hat, and swiped his arm across his brow.

Jamie tamped down his anger and grabbed another pile of chairs. Rob knew all too well how to get under his skin. Growing up on the spread next door, he was here on the Cruz ranch almost as much as Jamie was. He was right, though; last time Claire did pass him over for a city guy. After a month of her weekend visits to the ranch, he'd decided this was his chance. He'd dumped his current casual fling, Hannah O'Dell, and readied himself to ask Claire out the following weekend when she arrived in town. Valentine's Day weekend.

Unfortunately she didn't come to town on Valentine's Day, and soon after that Ethan let him know—as tactfully as he could—that she had a new boyfriend in Billings. Her boss. Daniel Ledstrom of Ledstrom Designs, the interior decorating business where she worked.

The English language didn't contain words to describe what Jamie felt then. To have been so close—to let himself picture what it would be like to finally hold her in his arms, to finally make love to her—and then to have that dream yanked away from him again...he'd almost despaired of ever carrying the day.

But when Daniel Ledstrom ran off with his secretary, Edie, last May, clearing out the business's accounts and making headlines in the Billings papers, Claire hardly seemed to care.

She may have dated the guy for a couple of years, but apparently she wasn't in love with Daniel, after all.

Once again he prepared to ask her out, but fate intervened against him a third time. When Claire came home to the ranch next it was for her parents' funeral. And his plans went on hold again.

He was beginning to think they'd never work out.

"Bet she shoots you down when you do ask her," Rob said, catching up to him.

"Bet you she doesn't," Jamie said, even though secretly he thought Rob might be right.

"How much? Hundred bucks?"

"You got it."

"Good luck winning that bet," Cab said, overtaking them. "Seeing as how Jamie isn't asking her anytime soon."

Jamie frowned. "I'll ask her soon."

"Bet you can't marry her by Labor Day," Rob said.

"If you're getting married in ten weeks, you better

hurry up and pop the question," Ethan said from behind them.

"I'm not marrying Claire on Labor Day," Jamie said. His plan called for using the summer to build her interest in the ranch. At some point, he'd ask her out, and in the fall he'd suggest they move in together. Maybe he'd propose at Thanksgiving. Sure, he'd bought the ring early, but experience had taught him to be prepared. Like Ethan said, some occasions were more romantic than others. If things should move faster than he expected, he didn't want to be caught short.

And…well, he was looking forward to being engaged to Claire.

"You admitting she'll turn you down?" Rob said. They reached the stack of chairs again, and added the new ones to the pile.

"No. I'd just like to go on a few dates before I ask her." Jamie straightened up.

"Chicken."

"I ain't…"

"If you haven't asked her out in the past decade, you aren't going to ask her now. You're blowing smoke up your own ass if you think you're ever going to marry her."

Jamie shoved his hands in his pockets to keep from balling them into fists and punching Rob. "I ain't chicken and I am going to ask her."

"Hundred bucks says that come Labor Day, you're still single," Rob said. "Safest bet I ever made."

Cab, joining them, laughed out loud. "Got that

right."

"He's got to think it over for another twelve years," Ethan chimed in. "Doesn't do to rush these things."

Jamie bristled at this group attack on his cautious personality. "Hundred bucks says I'm married to Claire by the end of the summer."

"Deal." Rob grabbed his hand and shook it before Jamie had a chance to reconsider. He pointed across the lawn. "There she is, tiger. Go on and ask her. Just keep your distance from her right hook. You know how cranky she gets."

Already regretting the bet, Jamie turned and spotted Claire. In shorts and a t-shirt, her dark, glossy hair reflecting the morning sun, she made quite a picture as she stood counting tables on the far side of the yard. He wouldn't propose to her, as much as the ring was burning a hole in his pocket.

But he figured he might as well start planting those seeds.

CLAIRE CRUZ WAS COUNTING THE CIRCULAR TABLES set up on the lawn of the Cruz ranch Big House, but there was only one number that stuck in her mind. *Six hundred thousand dollars.* She could finally start fresh and no one— *no one*—had to know she'd let a bastard like Daniel Ledstrom take her to the cleaners. Her relief made her weak in the knees, and just about made up for the stupid practical joke Rob had played on her this morning.

She refused to be angry at anybody today—her brother Ethan's wedding day—now that her bank account was out of danger. To have the whole weekend stretching in front of her here at the ranch was a gift she planned to thoroughly enjoy. It had been too long since she'd spent any real time here—too many years since it had been her home—and she was ready to let its beauty heal her soul. Soon she'd leave it behind again—if not for good, at least for a good long while—so she needed to make the most of this opportunity.

As Ethan's only living relative, it was up to her to take charge of the festivities—with help from Autumn's mother and sister and a few other family friends, of course. Later in the morning she'd cover the tables with the freshly pressed white tablecloths the event rental outfit had dropped off, and decorate each one with an arrangement of candles and flowers. For now, she intended to savor this moment of peace before the chaos of the wedding celebration set in.

She raised a hand and touched her face, which still felt warm from the scrubbing she'd had to give it. Rob had replaced her moisturizer with some sort of goop that stained her skin a violent orange. It'd taken her half an hour to get it all off and now her skin stung under the heavy layer of foundation she'd applied. Pressing her lips together she remembered the note he'd left pinned to her wash cloth. Once she'd seen the horror of her orange face in the mirror, shrieked and reached for the cloth to clean it off, she'd felt the paper, unpinned it and read his message.

Claire—you are the beautifullest girl ever. Marry me?
Your secret crush—Jamie

Idiot. She'd recognize Rob's handwriting anywhere. And Jamie wasn't going to propose to her, as much as she'd once hoped he would, because he was too busy sleeping with everything in a skirt.

No. She wasn't going to let Rob's jokes ruin her morning, and she wasn't going to waste any time thinking about what might have been with Jamie. She'd been hurt too many times to be interested in marriage to any man—at least not one from Montana. When she took off on her round-the-world cruise, however...well, some handsome European might just be the ticket.

Better get these tables counted.

One, two, three...

"Forty-five, eight, one hundred and nine," Jamie Lassiter said, coming across the lawn toward her.

Speak of the devil. Dressed in the cowboy uniform of jeans, a t-shirt, and a pair of battered boots, he looked far too handsome to be the same scrawny, wiry little kid whom she used to tower over. Now he filled out his clothes nicely and the top of her head barely reached his shoulder.

"Damn it, you made me lose count," she said, plucking at her collar. It was already hot at nine in the morning. *Six hundred thousand dollars.* Plenty of money for whatever she wanted to do. She planned to close down Ledstrom Designs as soon as possible. Then she'd forget Daniel Ledstrom. Forget Jamie. Forget Mack Mackenzie and all the other men who'd ever given her grief. Take her round-the-world trip. After that—who knew? Make a home where people didn't lie or cheat or steal or walk out on her.

Wherever that might be.

Too bad it wasn't right here on this ranch.

Jamie stuffed his hands in his pockets, leaned against a table, and looked at her, his cowboy hat cocked back the better to see. With a deep breath, she forced herself to focus on the task at hand. *One, two, three…*

"You figure out yet what you're going to do with all that money?"

She should have known he'd bring up the cash. When Jamie bought into the ranch, he and Ethan were able to re-mortgage it. That, in turn, allowed them to buy her out. Hence the six-hundred-thousand dollars soon to be deposited in her bank account.

"Yep."

His eyebrows shot up. "Really? What?"

Surprised you there, didn't I, cowboy? "I'm closing down Ledstrom Designs and taking off."

"Taking off? Where are you going?"

He sounded angry, which confused Claire. It wasn't like he gave a damn where she went. Sure, he flirted with her now and then, and he'd even invited her to celebrate with the rest of the crowd the night he and Ethan became partners. She'd gone along with it, but made sure they were never alone. And she'd made sure to leave in plenty of time to drive back to Billings. She wasn't going to be another one-night-stand notch on Jamie's bedpost. "Wherever I choose." She moved away from him, beginning her count again.

"For how long?"

"A year. Maybe two." At this rate she'd never figure out if she had enough tables set up for all the wedding guests.

"Damn it! You can't do that!" Jamie's fist hit the table and made her jump. When he took her arm and pulled her around to face him she could only stare.

"Why the hell not?" Once she was over her shock, anger flooded her. What was he playing at, scaring her like that? She tried to shrug him off, but he tightened his grip around her bicep. He looked furious, too.

"Because...because you're marrying me on Labor Day," he blurted out. He fished around in his jeans pocket and pulled out small, velvet box. Letting go of her arm, he opened it, yanked out a ring, grabbed her hand and shoved it halfway onto her finger before she could react. She tried to pull her hand away as the ring's setting dug into her skin, but he gripped her wrist with iron fingers and pushed it farther over her knuckle.

"What are you doing? Stop it!" Claire struck out, batting at his arms and chest. She'd had enough of Ethan's friends' stupidity today. It was one thing to switch the contents of her moisturizer and leave her a dorky note—she expected that kind of crap from Rob—but for Jamie to play along with the gag and take it to this level? She wouldn't stand for it.

"No, I won't stop it," Jamie growled. "I've got everything planned out and you're not going to screw it up again! You're not going on any god-damned trip around the world, because you're going to stay here and become my wife." He rammed the ring the rest of the way onto her finger, then pulled her close, slid one hand around her waist and kissed her, hard.

When he released her, she rocked back on her heels, too stunned to speak. Clapping from across the lawn alerted her that Ethan, Rob and Cab had witnessed this whole debacle—hell, they were in on it, too, weren't they? Heat surging into her cheeks, she shoved Jamie as hard as she could, and when that didn't work, she went to peel the ring off and throw it in his face.

It didn't budge.

"Shit." She pulled and tugged, but the ring refused to slide back over her heat-swollen knuckle. "Jamie, I'm going to kill you!"

"You can do anything you want to me after we're married. Until then you'll shut up and act happy."

What had come over him? Normally Jamie was laid back. He might laugh at Rob's antics, but he didn't participate in them. He'd picked a hell of a time to start. Outrage filled her until she thought she would burst with it. Of all the tricks he could think of to play on her, this was the cruelest one he could ever dream up. He'd already broken her heart once, but she'd gotten over it. Now he was going to pretend to care for her? Pretend to propose?

"I'll bet I'll kick your ass before sundown." Trust Jamie to make her sound like she was seventeen again. If only she was. Things were simple back then. He crushed on her and she ignored him. She was too close to him then to see him for the catch he was. It took her years to realize Jamie was the one for her.

By then it was too late.

A few years back, she'd made a New Year's resolution to stop fighting with her mother and spend more time at the ranch. As soon as she came home to visit, though, it was Jamie who caught her attention. She hadn't been able to stop watching him. She loved the way he moved, the way he did his chores. The way he lavished attention on the Cruz ranch horses even though he was only a hired hand back then. The way he was always present, how he offered his two cents when her father asked him for it, and kept quiet when he didn't. How he attended to the day to day problems of running a ranch even when they weren't his job to solve.

His words to her on those weekends were kind and teasing, and more than that. They started a fire within her she'd never felt before. When he wasn't flirting, he was fun, warm, intelligent, a man who thought things through before he allowed them past his lips. She wanted to work with him, ride with him, build a life with him based on their shared love of the ranch. She wanted to be with him, too. Watching his hands when he worked made her buzz with longing to feel them on her skin. She fantasized about his arms around her—his mouth on hers.

Then one Friday night in early February, after another long, lonely week in Billings, she couldn't stand it anymore. She'd packed a weekend bag, driven the two hours from the city to Chance Creek, parked down the drive and crept past her parents' house to the path that led to Jamie's cabin. Swallowing all her pride, she knocked on his cabin door and prepared to confess her feelings for him—confess that she was finally ready to be his girl.

But he didn't answer. And when she walked around to the cabin's back door, she saw why. He was too busy undressing Hannah O'Dell to hear her knock. Too occupied to even close the drapes on his bedroom window. She remembered all the other women she'd seen him flirt with over the years and finally understood.

His attentions meant nothing—they never had. They were just the ramblings of a man who couldn't help but act interested in every woman in easy range. How had she fooled herself into thinking she was special? Now she knew she wasn't—not to him, anyway.

The shock yanked her budding desire for Jamie and for ranch life up by the roots and tossed it to the wind, and she'd never allowed herself to consider it again. She'd redoubled her efforts at her job, and soon was promoted to lead designer at Ledstrom Designs. Then she began to date Daniel.

"I'd like to see you try to kick my ass." Jamie leaned in, and for a moment she thought he might kiss her again.

Wanted him to despite everything.

"Don't think I can't." Seriously. Were they ten? If memory served, she'd scuffled with Jamie right about here one day when he'd squirted her with a watergun and she'd wrestled it away and beaned him over the head with it.

"I'll be happy to prove you wrong after you agree to

be my wife," Jamie said.

"Ha ha hardy har har." She turned to Ethan and the rest of them lined up on the far side of the lawn. Raising her voice she called, "Very funny, guys. Now you've had your practical joke, can we get on with getting ready for the wedding? I don't need this shit today." She tugged at the ring again and winced when the diamond's setting pricked her.

"Hey—did she say yes?" Ethan hollered from across the yard. Claire was going to kill him.

"I'm not joking, Claire. I'm part-owner of the ranch now. I intend to breed horses and help Ethan and Autumn with their business. I want you here with me."

Something inside Claire snapped. She didn't need this kind of baloney on a day that already had her emotionally wrung dry. Her mother and father should be here at Ethan's wedding, but they were gone, killed in an accident last August. She hadn't had the chance to set things all the way right. Hadn't seen either of her parents for months before they died, and it was all Jamie's fault.

"Quit fooling around," she said, trying to brush past him. He wouldn't let her go.

"Jamie—what'd she say?" Ethan hollered again.

Tears pricked her eyes and she blinked them back. She was not going to cry. She couldn't. Not in front of all of them.

Jamie's tone softened. "I'm sorry, honey—I meant to do this right. Just…stop, Claire and listen to me. I'm as serious as I've ever been. You know I've wanted this all along. I worked and saved so I could become a man worthy of you. I'm building a house, I'm going into business. I have everything I need, except you. Claire, will you be my wife?"

He actually dropped to his knees as if he was going to propose for real, except if he was serious, he would have mentioned the word *love* somewhere in the last ten minutes. She blinked harder, her throat aching with the injustice of it all, until she thought she would scream. Maybe Jamie was a god-damned flirt who couldn't even take marriage seriously, but that didn't mean everyone was that way. Some other man might actually want to marry her. She was hanged if she was going to let her first proposal be a damned joke.

She glanced at the rest of the pranksters standing across the yard. Was Rob Matheson filming this mock proposal with his phone to use against her later? Was Ethan in on this, too? A tear spilled over.

Damn it!

She kicked Jamie square in the chest, her rage lending her strength. Over he went, landing flat on the ground. "Get off your knees and get the hell out of my sight. I don't deserve this, Jamie."

"Hey!" Jamie lurched unevenly to his feet and swayed, one hand raised to the dirty footprint on his white shirt. "What are you doing?"

"Telling you exactly what I think of your little joke."

"It's not a…"

"Stow it!" She was shouting now. She didn't care who saw them or if Rob got it on film. "I wouldn't marry you if you were the last man on earth."

He stiffened, glared at her, all trace of softness gone. A chill ran down her spine at the intensity of his gaze—she couldn't remember ever seeing Jamie this angry before. When he spoke his voice was calm. Implacable.

"Wanna bet?"

Chapter Two

FIVE HOURS LATER, Jamie stood next to Ethan under a latticed trellis watching Autumn process along the aisle between the rows of guests, as radiant as a movie star in her striking wedding gown. He knew Ethan could barely breathe for love of her, and he was happy for his friend, but try as he might he couldn't keep his eyes on Ethan's bride.

Instead, his gaze kept sliding over to a certain sister-of-the-groom who sat in the first row, her flowered sundress and cowboy boots a whimsical combination that was a far cry from the dark, severe suits she normally wore these days. She sat ramrod stiff on the plastic seat, her black bob shaking with every move of her head. She was still furious, but he could tell she was trying to put on a good show for Ethan and Autumn's guests. It wasn't working. That fake smile could cut someone if she wasn't careful.

He'd blown it. All his careful plotting and planning were smoke up a chimney now. Forget about planting the seeds of friendship in her mind. Forget about getting her involved in the guest ranch operation, and soliciting her help designing the interior of the log house he was building on his plot of land. Forget inviting her to ride the horse he'd hand-picked for her and taking her all over the land and reminding her just how much she loved this place.

He had intended to walk her step by step through a process of falling back in love with the ranch, with horses, and with him.

Instead he'd demanded she marry him and shoved the ring on her finger with all the suaveness of a caveman bludgeoning his woman.

He was an idiot. But Rob was a bigger one for not telling him what he'd done: leaving that note in Claire's bathroom, making sure she was furious before he ever had a chance to open his mouth. He knew now that she interpreted every word he said this morning as a personal attack rather than a proposal. He had a lot of ground to cover if he wanted to get things back on the right track.

But he was determined to marry her, and now that he'd broached the topic he wasn't stepping back. Claire would bolt for Billings the second the wedding was over and who knew how quickly she'd shut down her business and leave for her tour around the world.

He needed more time with her—time to do all the things he'd meant to do before popping the question.

How could he keep Claire on the ranch for a few weeks—maybe even a month—so he could convince her this was where she wanted to stay? How did you get a stubborn, unreasonable, competitive terrier of a woman to admit she's wrong and you're right?

He glanced at Rob, standing next to him in the line of groomsmen. Rob rubbed his thumb and first two fingers together—a not-so-subtle reminder that he thought he was going to win their bet.

That stupid bet.

He stiffened, a crazy idea forming in his mind.

Jamie began to smile.

ETHAN AND AUTUMN took turns repeating their vows. They exchanged rings. The ceremony wound down.

Claire did her best not to look at Jamie, but she couldn't help it—he was standing right up there with Ethan, Rob and Cab. As Ethan's best man, he stood beside the groom. Rob came next, his blond hair glinting in the sunshine. Cab was last, having walked Autumn up the aisle, standing in for the father she hadn't seen in years. With the backdrop of ranchland sloping down toward the creek, and mountains in the far distance, the wedding looked straight out of a fairytale. Claire's heart ached at the thought of leaving all of this behind again.

For the first part of the ceremony, Jamie's face was stony and she knew he was still angry. Because she'd ruined his game? Certainly not because he'd been serious. As the ritual came to an end, however, some silent message passed between him and Rob. Then Jamie smiled suddenly—a wicked, triumphant smile.

It made her insides flip, and then tighten with the realization that she'd been right—Jamie and Rob were in cahoots. Once again she tried with all her might to pull the engagement ring off her finger, inadvertently nudging Autumn's friend Becka, who sat beside her. Becka peered down at her hands to see what she was doing, and Claire quickly covered up the ring. What was Jamie planning now? Had he decided to humiliate her further?

Why?

Because she'd left his house last Saturday and driven home rather than spend the night with him? Was he that pathetic? Did he really need her particular notch on his bed post to feel like a man?

She glanced at the thin silver watch on her wrist. Five hours at least until she could make a break for it. No matter how badly Jamie behaved she couldn't ditch Ethan on his wedding day. He was depending on her. Her gaze slid back to Jamie. He was still smiling.

The former hired hand had been full of surprises lately, and she didn't want to guess what he'd do next. He must have saved every penny he earned since he came to work on the spread. And done incredibly well with his investments.

Maybe she shouldn't have been surprised he wanted to buy into the ranch. He respected Alex Cruz, her father—worshipped him, in fact. He stuck closer to Alex than even Ethan did, and that was saying a lot. She guessed Alex was the father Jamie wished he had, instead of the dour man who pressured him through four years of business school when all he wanted to do was live and breathe horses.

Jamie was born a cowboy the way other people were born athletic, or smart, or pretty. Every move he made around horses was a symphony of understanding of the beasts. Claire always appreciated that about him, because she loved horses, too. Adored them.

Of course, she hadn't touched one in thirteen years.

Damn her mother. Damn Mack. Damn Jamie, too.

Jamie—sensing her agitation, perhaps—lifted an eyebrow.

She fought to keep her ragged emotions in check. The cowboy had soothed the jangled nerves of many a mare with a touch or a murmured word, but he wasn't soothing her at all. Instead, she felt all too exposed in her thin, cotton sundress—a new, pretty one she'd bought especially for the wedding since her usual severe suits didn't fit the occasion. She felt silly, too, in her old cowboy boots, but she knew the combination would garner a smile from Ethan, and after this last year, she'd do anything to make her brother smile.

But the damn engagement ring made her feel most conspicuous of all. It wouldn't come off—her knuckles were swollen from the heat. She tugged at it again.

Under the lattice archway, Autumn lifted her veil and Ethan leaned in to kiss her soundly on the mouth. The crowd cheered and clapped as the kiss went on and on, and when the happy couple pulled apart, Autumn was flushed and Ethan grinning ear to ear.

They will be happy, Claire thought, surprised at how sure she felt. *They really are in love.* A pang of deep loneliness followed that thought. Would she ever experience that kind of connection?

As the wedding party filed out, Jamie stopped next to

her chair, bent down, and before she could push him away, he leaned in and kissed her cheek softly. "Look at them," he said in his husky, velvet voice. "We could be like that." He kissed her again. There was nothing she could do about it and he knew it—not in this crowd. Not without making a scene. She was trembling with rage when they stood up along with everyone else as Ethan and Autumn paced up the aisle together.

Jamie took her arm. "I like the way that ring looks on your finger. I hope you never take it off. You'll need a wedding dress like Autumn's before too long," he murmured as the crowd surged around them. "Better start looking."

She confined her answer to an unladylike snort, turning the ring around so only the band showed. "Fat chance."

"Wanna bet?"

Those two words again. That knowing look. What did it mean? And why did his low, confidential tones make her hum all over?

Before she could question him, she realized Autumn's mother was watching her with raised eyebrows.

Right.

Since she was the only other remaining member of the Cruz family besides Ethan, and the marriage was taking place on the Cruz ranch, it was her place to keep this shindig going smoothly.

"Okay, everyone," she called out in what she hoped was a happy, steady-sounding voice. Heaven knew she was a master at masking her emotions. "The barbecue will be ready shortly and the bar is open. Please help yourself to appetizers and drinks and we'll call you to dinner in a few minutes. Thanks for coming and celebrating with us!"

Autumn's mother headed over to check on the buffet table, and Claire knew she was off the hook for the moment—at least as far as her wedding duties went. Autumn and Ethan disappeared into the Big House for a moment to themselves. Once they returned, the wedding party would have to take photos while hors d'oeuvres were served to the waiting guests. The bulk of the crowd meandered slowly toward the area of the lawn where tables and chairs were set up for dinner, stopping to chat with each other and exchange news. Claire knew all the guests, of course. How could she not, growing up in a small town like Chance Creek—population 7865? That's why she moved to Billings—for the anonymity a city afforded you, even a relatively small city.

She knew her father and brother didn't understand why she left home and why she didn't come back. No one but her knew about her mother or what she'd done. First Aria had made fun of her schoolgirl crush on Mack, the man who trained the Cruz ranch horses. Claire had put up with that, spending every possible moment in the stables or corrals watching the much older man work with the animals. But when she came home early from school one day and found Aria and Mack in the barn—together—she couldn't stand to stay.

The apology she hoped for never came. In fact, nothing changed between her and her mother even after she moved out. Just like always, Aria Cruz came and went from the ranch like a hummingbird—beautiful, lively, and incapable of standing still. Surely she spent more time in Europe than she ever spent at home. How her father bore her escapades she had no idea.

Claire tried to push away her memories as she moved toward the photographer, noticing Autumn and Ethan had reappeared and were heading his way, too. But how could she not think of her mother—both her parents—on her brother's wedding day? As for weddings in general, if she had her way she'd never go to another one.

"First we'll take pictures of the bride and groom," the photographer said as he led the wedding party to an open-air pagoda her mother had had built on the property years ago. As she watched Ethan and Autumn pose on the pagoda's steps, she knew she'd never be the one wearing a wedding dress. Whatever romantic notions she'd once had, her mother, Mack, Jamie and Daniel had long beaten out of her. Daniel's betrayal had nearly killed her. Just when she'd convinced herself she was over Jamie, and pinned her hopes on him instead, he'd taken all her money and left town with another woman.

Ninety thousand dollars.

Gone.

"Mother of the bride, sisters, join us, please." Claire moved stiffly to stand by Ethan's side, with Teresa and Lily Leeds taking their places next to Autumn. "Smile."

She tried her best, but knew her attempt was a dismal failure, as memories of Daniel's desertion swirled in her mind. She hadn't reported the crime to the police. She had no proof. When she brought up signing a contract, Daniel had blown her off. "It's just for a couple of days. By the time we get the paperwork drawn up and signed, I'll have the money back to you. Plus interest, and maybe something else." He smiled at her and took her hand. "Something sparkly to put on your finger."

Marriage. She'd actually thought Daniel wanted to marry her. Like any man cared about her that much.

There wouldn't be any justice for her—just the humiliation of the whole world knowing how gullible she was if word got out. Bad enough the whole office was talking about how she'd been dating Daniel when he ran off with Edie. At least they didn't know she thought he was about to propose to her.

"Groomsmen and bridesmaids, come on up." It took several minutes for the photographer to arrange everyone this time. Jamie grinned at her as he took his place and she scowled back.

The day she realized she was back to square one— less than $5,000 in her bank account, betrayed by the man she thought would be her fiance—was devastating, but she didn't shed a tear. Nor did she high-tail it back home, although if she had she would have gotten to see her parents one last time before they died. No, she'd dealt with the police as a representative of Ledstrom Designs since Daniel had cleaned out the business accounts, too. She'd handled their clients and her coworkers in a calm and professional manner, and she hadn't missed a single day of work. When one of the other designers suggested that Claire should take over all the open accounts and keep the business running, that's exactly what she did.

To her surprise, it worked—barely. She used her multiple credit cards to fund the supplies she needed for the current contracts, and when those jobs were finished and paid for she had earned enough money to do it all over again with new ones. She was managing to get by— just.

"Smile for the camera. Big smiles." The photographer's flash went off again and again. The more Claire smiled, the more she wanted to cry.

Then came Ethan's phone call in August, telling her their parents died in a car accident, followed soon after by the news of the ranch's debt.

She couldn't help Ethan even if she wanted to, since she was barely scraping enough cash together each month to make payroll and rent. She thought he would have to sell the ranch. There was no other way, or he'd end up in the same situation she was—running, running, running as fast as she could and still barely getting by.

But he found another way. Who would guess Jamie Lassiter, hired hand, would save the day? Together, Ethan and Jamie remortgaged the ranch and bought out her share—to the tune of six hundred thousand dollars.

She was rich.

Her ordeal was over.

"All right—I want a few more photos of the bride and groom. The rest of you can go."

Thank God. Claire walked to the house as fast as she

could, shrugging Jamie off when he came to take her arm. "Not now, okay?"

To her surprise he actually let her go. Five minutes in the bathroom was time enough to splash water on her face and get her emotions under control again. She wouldn't think about the past anymore. Time for a new start.

Just as she walked out of the front door, a cheer went up from the crowd as the happy couple rejoined them on the lawn, and people rushed to offer their congratulations. Jamie joined her and nudged her toward them, too, and she let herself be led over, playing with the ring on her finger once again. Get married to Jamie on Labor Day? A sudden image entered her mind of the two of them boarding an airplane, flying off to their honeymoon on an island shore where they could make love for days…

For heaven's sake—what was wrong with her? If she was ever so stupid as to marry Jamie, she'd just find herself single again a week or two later when another woman turned his head.

She forced another smile to her face as she hugged first Autumn, then Ethan. She was happy for them—really. It was just that all of this—the wedding, the guests, even the ranch itself—made her feel as lonely as the sole survivor of a shipwreck trapped on a desert isle. She would never trust a man enough to marry him. Certainly not Jamie.

"Let's get on with the eating so we can get the band going," Ethan said.

"You got it," Claire said, hoping her voice sounded normal.

Ethan tugged her closer. "Stop it—you'll hurt someone with that fake smile. Why didn't you just say yes to Jamie? You could be as happy as I am. Wait a minute—are you wearing his ring? Did you say yes?"

Claire gaped at him, her eyes stinging once more. She couldn't believe Ethan was in on this joke and would carry it to such an extreme—on his wedding day. She and her brother had their spats over the years, but he'd never been cruel. She opened her mouth to tell him so, but he pulled Jamie into a man-hug, pounding him on the shoulder.

"Congratulations! When's the happy day?"

He was in on the joke, wasn't he? But he was doing an incredible job acting like it was real. She couldn't remember ever seeing Ethan this happy—especially not since their parents' deaths.

"Labor Day," Jamie said emphatically and grinned at her, daring her to deny it.

She looked from one to the other, at a total loss for what to do.

"You're getting married?" Autumn shrieked, grabbing her hand and pulling it close to see her ring. "Oh my gosh, Claire—it's beautiful. I'm so happy for you!" She threw her arms around Claire and gave her a stifling hug.

This can't be happening, Claire thought, waiting for Jamie to tell them it was all a joke—waiting for Ethan at least to let Autumn in on it. Her stomach twisted when she realized both of them were going to play it straight. Ethan was beaming, and Jamie...he looked like the cat who'd swallowed the canary.

Damn it, she wasn't a helpless bird.

But as she turned to set Autumn straight, her new sister-in-law cupped her hands to her mouth and called out, "Everybody! Everyone—can I have your attention? Yoo-hoo!"

The crowd immediately quieted, all eyes turned to the bride.

"I just have to share the happy news—I'm so excited!" Autumn's face was flushed and her eyes shining. She pointed to Claire.

"Wait..." Claire began, but Autumn rushed on.

"Claire and Jamie have just gotten engaged—they're getting married on Labor Day, so everybody better save the date! We'll all be right back here in a couple of months to do this all over again."

As the crowd cheered and clapped, Claire turned to Jamie, begging him silently for help. He just threaded an arm around her waist and kissed the top of her head. As people surged in to offer their congratulations, she once more pasted a happy expression on her face.

She would be a laughing-stock when September rolled around and no wedding took place.

If she survived this day she would never speak to any of them again.

"CAN I GET YOU A DRINK?" Jamie asked a few minutes later, touching Claire again—just because he could. Hell, he was having a hard time keeping his hands to himself. When Ethan kissed his bride, it was all he could do not to stride across the lawn, pull Claire close and kiss her just as long and hard. Now that Autumn had announced their nuptials to all and sundry he didn't have to hold back. He knew Claire; she wouldn't spoil her brother's wedding day, and that gave him time to recover from his earlier tactical error. Why, oh why had he blurted out that proposal this morning? Given a chance, she'd bolt from the wedding early, get a jeweler to cut the ring off her finger and he'd never see her again.

"Whatever."

Uh oh. That didn't sound good. It didn't sound good at all.

"Something wrong?" He stopped and turned her to face him, ignoring the throngs of guests around them all heading for the buffet where trays of appetizers had been laid out by some of the local ladies who'd volunteered their help.

"Of course something's wrong." Her eyes blazed up at him and he knew that if they weren't in the middle of a crowd, she'd be tearing him a new one.

"Relax. Enjoy yourself."

"Like that's possible now that everyone thinks we're engaged. With this on my finger." She waggled her hand and the ring sparkled in the sun.

"Okay. I get it—I blew it. I should have spent a lot more time with you before I proposed. Maybe taken you on a date once or twice. I'm sorry—the romance of the occasion turned my head."

"You shouldn't have proposed at all. It's mean, Jamie. I'm not part of your little…gang," she waved a hand at where Cab and Rob stood next to Ethan. "I don't play practical jokes and I don't like it when you do."

Jamie swallowed the urge to march over to Rob and knock him upside the head. His stupid joke this morning had done some serious damage to his chances with Claire. "Hold on. This isn't a joke."

"Of course it is. What else would it be?"

Jamie hesitated. He had one chance here to turn things around. If he tried to explain and kept apologizing, she'd walk away from him, disgusted. If he kept up the caveman act, she'd probably punch him. Time to get those competitive juices flowing. He hoped the brainstorm he'd had during the wedding ceremony worked.

"It's not a joke. It's a bet."

He could have laughed out loud at her expression. Frustration, anger, and something that looked an awful lot like desire crossed her face in swift succession. Maybe he was getting to her. He sure hoped so. Maybe he'd finally found the key to her heart.

All-out competition.

"Would you stop saying that word?"

No, he didn't think he would. "The foundation for my house is being laid this week. Pretty soon it'll be framed up and ready to finish."

"So what?" His change of topic had her voice rising.

"I also need help with the horses when the guest ranch gets going."

"And?" She looked ready to explode, crowd or no

crowd.

"Here's the bet. You put off your round-the-world trip for six weeks. Design the interior for my new house and then help me out with the first batch of guests that come to stay."

"That's not a bet. That's a request. And the answer is…"

He cut her off. "At the end of six weeks of us living and working on the ranch together, you tell the truth— which do you want; city life and world travel or marriage to me? I bet you choose to be my wife."

CLAIRE OPENED HER MOUTH to tell him he could shove his bet where the sun didn't shine, but before she could say anything, Becka approached with a wide smile. "Hey, congratulations, guys," she said. "Wasn't the ceremony beautiful? I wanted to thank you, Claire, for all you've done for Autumn."

"I've hardly done anything," Claire said automatically. "You helped out far more. Without you and Autumn's mom and sister, there wouldn't be a wedding."

"I guess everyone helped out," Becka said happily. "I'm having such a good time here. Who knew Montana was so beautiful?"

"We did," Jamie said. He smiled at Becka and the young woman noticeably brightened.

There he went again, Claire thought. Flirting—even now.

Becka moved closer to him. "Yeah. Well, you have certainly done a great job keeping it a secret. I had no idea what to expect when I got on the plane. But as soon as I got here I understood why Autumn fell in love with the place."

"Fell in love with Ethan, you mean." Jamie laughed, a sound that tugged at Claire's heart despite her fury. From Becka's expression, the girl was entranced.

"Well, you know—no one can resist a cowboy, right?" Becka said.

Claire frowned. Suddenly she didn't like Becka so much; the girl was flirting with Jamie right in front of her eyes—and they were supposed to be engaged. An emotion she couldn't identify had her moving closer to him, putting her hand on his arm so the ring caught the light. "Good thing there's lots of them here at the wedding. You should be able to find one of your own if you look hard enough."

A smile lit Becka's face and Claire felt her own cheeks heat. No doubt about it, Becka heard her message loud and clear, and thought it was hilarious.

"I guess I better get started on my hunt since this cowboy's taken already," she said. "Congratulations, again!" She headed off toward Autumn's sister.

Jamie chuckled and slid an arm around her waist again, resting his hand on her hip. "Damn, Claire—glad you changed your mind. I thought you said you wouldn't marry me if I was the last man on earth. Now I know you can't wait to be my bride."

"Yes, I can." What the hell had she just done? Was she losing her mind? She pulled away and hastened toward the buffet, grabbing a plate and filling it with appetizers.

She hoped he would take the hint and leave her to her mortification, but he didn't. As he took the plate from her and loaded it with more food than she could ever eat, she wondered how this day had gone so far afield. She wanted to climb on top of one of the flimsy rental tables and shout to everyone that the engagement was a fake, but instead she allowed Jamie to take her hand and lead her back up the lawn to the porch, where a sturdy swing hung in the shade. He sat down and patted the slatted seat beside him. "So how about it? Are you on board for my friendly wager?

Friendly wager?

"Let me get this straight. You want me to put off the trip of a lifetime to stay here and design your interior and run trail rides for Ethan and Autumn? All because you think that's going to convince me to marry you?"

"Yep."

"Give it up—the joke's over, for crying out loud."

Mary Needlebaum, entering the house with her young niece, looked over at her raised voice. Claire smiled and waved, then scowled at Jamie again. "I'll play along for this one day because I don't want to spoil things for Autumn. But as soon as the last guest goes home, this ring comes off and goes in the trash. You got that?"

"No—I don't get it. I know you want me—we've got chemistry, Claire. You can't deny it."

Chemistry? Hell, yeah. They had that in spades. And now she understood perfectly what this was all about—

Jamie's desperate attempt to get in her pants. He was mad about last weekend. He did want her notch on his bedpost. And he'd go through all this rigamarole to get it.

Sonofabitch.

She sat back and stared at him. "You really think that spending six weeks with you will make you irresistable?"

"I hope so." He grinned his lazy, knockout grin. "You spend six weeks here with me, working at all the things you used to love and then you tell me you'd rather travel the world than get married. If you still turn me down, I'll pay for your cruise around the world and I'll never propose again."

He was unbelievable. They all were. It was high time someone showed Jamie, Ethan, Rob and Cab just what they could do with their practical jokes. "Okay," she heard herself say slowly, a desire to turn the tables on Jamie and the rest of them growing within her. They weren't the only ones who could play games. She'd take the opportunity Jamie was handing her to make his life miserable. And if she could figure out a way to get back at the other men, she'd do that, too. When her six weeks were up, she'd hop on that boat—free of charge. Not like she'd planned to leave tomorrow, anyway. "I'll take that bet. Under one condition," she added when he began to smile.

"Anything," he said.

She fixed him with a triumphant gaze. "You can't touch me during those six weeks—not one touch," she said. His smile disappeared. "And you can't flirt with or touch any of the women guests who come to the ranch, either—or I automatically win."

"I DON'T FLIRT," Jamie said, indignation sending him to his feet.

"Are you kidding me? You flirt with everything that moves," Claire said. She speared a mini quiche with her fork and cut it in two. Judging by the smirk on her face, she thought she had him by the short hairs.

Actually, she did.

"It doesn't mean anything," he tried again. She had to know that. Flirting was like breathing to him—people expected him to act that way.

"Whatever. Those are my terms."

"But…there's bound to be women among the guests. How do I talk to them?"

She put down her fork and raised an eyebrow. "Really? You don't know how to talk to women without flirting with them? No, why am I even surprised? Of course you don't." She shook her head. "Just talk to them. Pretend they're men."

Jamie turned away. Hell, she had him this time. He didn't mean to do it, but flirting came as naturally as the beating of his heart and it made life a hell of a lot easier. A smile and a look, and women just took care of your needs. It wasn't his fault God gave him a handsome face. He wasn't stuck up about it, either. He knew what he had and he used it to make other people happy, and if that meant flirting with a pretty girl at the local takeout place or an older woman manning the desk at some office in town, why not? It didn't hurt anyone.

And if he'd slept with women from time to time during the years, so what? He wasn't a monk. He'd always known the minute he got Claire's attention all that would stop. And so it had. Except she'd instantly gone off with that Daniel guy.

Claire watched him, her sharp blue eyes taking in all the arguments he wasn't speaking out loud. If he couldn't touch her, then how was he supposed to convince her during their six weeks' time together that she belonged with him back on the Cruz ranch?

By letting her figure it out all by herself.

He considered that notion and nodded. She couldn't tell him that she didn't itch to be back among the Cruz horses, training them, riding them, living and breathing those magnificent beasts. Claire rode like the wind and understood animals better than she did people—just like him. Five weeks on the ranch while she designed his interior, and one week helping him run the trail rides and she'd be hooked all over again.

He hoped. Because if she left Montana to travel the world he didn't know what he would do. All his plans depended on her marrying him. Besides, he didn't think world travel was the answer for her, either. A few years ago when she'd started hanging around the ranch again, she'd been happier than he'd seen her in years. Then she'd quit coming. These days she looked so pale and drawn he knew she was miserable. She was doing a good job keeping that fake smile plastered on her face anytime Ethan or Autumn or one of the guests wandered by, but her eyes gave her away. Maybe a trip around the world would bring the bounce back to her step, but he doubted it. Something was really wrong with Claire and his gut told him she needed to come home—to the ranch, to her family—to her horses, or she might get to a place where she couldn't be healed.

"Deal," he said aloud and her eyebrows shot up.

"Really? You think you can handle six whole weeks without flirting with or touching a woman?" Her playful tone was at odds with the coldness in her eyes, and for one second Jamie thought he was getting close to the truth behind the mystery of her defeated expression. Some man had hurt her—bad. Ledstrom? The thought made him clench his fists.

"Easy," he forced himself to say. Well, not really, but hell—he should be able to survive it. Most guys did, right?

She laughed, a sound too bitter to suit him. "Well, this I gotta see. Okay, I'm in, too." She put out a hand and he shook it, reveling in touching her. He pulled her in and stole a kiss, not surprised when she pushed him away roughly.

"See—you can't even last a minute."

"Our bet hasn't started yet."

"When does it start?"

"Tomorrow. And you have to keep that ring on until the bet's done."

She pulled her hand back and wiped it on her dress, then tugged at the ring he'd put on her finger. He hadn't meant it to be so small she couldn't get it off, but he liked seeing it there. Liked that she was stuck with it. "And if I lose?" she asked.

"If you lose, that ring stays on your finger forever, and we get married on Labor Day. I happen to know the lawn will be free that day." He waved a hand to encompass the wedding festivities in front of them.

"This is ridiculous."

He sat back and gazed at her. "Are you afraid I'm capable of not flirting for six weeks or are you afraid you actually want to marry me?"

"Neither."

He crossed his arms. "If it's neither, then you shouldn't be worried about the bet."

"You're such a pain in the ass." Her sharp face had grown even paler.

"Yeah, but I'm a pain in the ass who's completely in control of my libido. Ah, you didn't think I knew fancy words like that, did you? I'm a surprising guy." He grinned again, and watched her fight her reaction to it. Fury, desire, and for one split second, anguish. Then she forced her face into its familiar pleasant expression.

"Your libido is in no way under control," she said. "You'll lose before we even hit the trail with those greenhorns, and I'll laugh myself all the way back to Billings and onto my round-the-world tour. And even if you don't, nothing can convince me to marry you."

Jamie smiled as she walked away. He might be facing the toughest six weeks of his life, but, oh, the reward was going to be sweet.

Chapter Three

S HE WAS LOSING HER MIND.

How else to explain the seesaw of emotions she'd felt during this endless day? Happiness for Ethan mixed with the ache that came from knowing no man had ever loved her the way he loved Autumn. Fury at Rob's stupid trick. Sadness that her parents weren't here on the most important day of their son's life. Dread of her own future.

All mixed up with the swirl of lust and anger Jamie's fake proposal and bet stirred up within her. Libido was certainly the word for the day. She didn't know if it was Ethan and Autumn's tangible love for each other, the romance of the wedding, or Jamie's talk about getting married but she wanted to feel his hands on her body, and she more than anyone knew that desire led to nothing but heartbreak.

Although she tried to put some distance between them, Jamie sat next to her at the head table when the real dinner started, and took advantage of the situation by brushing her arm, bumping her shoulder and re-filling her champagne glass at every opportunity. When she confronted him angrily, he smiled his slow smile and reminded her that their bet didn't start until the next day. As more and more people stopped by to offer their congratulations, Claire realized how hard it was going to be to undo this farce.

Thank God she already planned to travel for at least a year. Maybe by the time she came back, gossip would have died down.

As dusk set in, the Cruz lawn was lit by fairy lights and the band began to throw in some slow songs among all the popular dance tunes. When Jamie appeared by her side again and pulled her to the dance floor, Claire threw caution to the wind and actually let him draw her in close. After all, everyone thought they were engaged.

She scanned the crowd, noting Rob dancing with Autumn's friend, Becka, and Cab Johnson squiring Rose Bellingham around the floor.

"See, this isn't so bad," Jamie said.

She made a face. "It is now that you're talking." But he was right; it felt good to be in his arms. Too damn good.

"You know you belong here."

On the Cruz ranch or in his embrace? "Never. Get that in your head right now. I'm not marrying you and I'm not coming back here to live."

Jamie abruptly stopped swaying to the music. He took her hand and pulled her through the couples.

"Where are we going?" She tried to tug free, but he gripped her tighter, probably guessing she wouldn't make a scene. He nodded at friends and acquaintances as he dragged Claire across the lawn, around the back of the house and toward the stables.

When she saw their destination, she dug in her heels. "No. No way."

"Come on, quit squirming. You've been in the barn before."

"Not in a hell of a long time." She pulled him to a stop. "I don't want to do this. Not now." She wobbled slightly where she stood. Too much damn champagne.

"Too bad. You're going to do it." Wrapping an arm around her waist, he practically shoved her into the stable, flicking on the light by the door.

The pungent smell of the horses took her immediately back to the long days of her childhood spent mucking out stalls, oiling saddles, and curry combing manes. Overwhelmed by memories, she looked for Starshine. But no, the mare she'd ridden as a teenager in countless rodeos was long gone, sold by her father when it was clear she wasn't coming home. Tears pricked her eyes and she forced them back. She missed her horse desperately when she moved to Billings. Cried for her every night for weeks. What had the mare thought when Claire disappeared?

"Come see," Jamie said softly, and led her down the center aisle. She heard the mounts shifting in their stalls, saw heads stretch over walls to see who had come to visit. Snuffling for treats. She hardened her heart. No way would she touch any of them.

Jamie opened a stall at the far end and crooned to

the grey quarter-horse within. "This is Storm," he said, maintaining his soft cadence.

"She's beautiful," Claire heard herself say. She was drawn forward against her will, wanting so badly to run her hand along her glossy coat. Storm turned and looked at her from one long-lashed eye.

Claire was a goner.

Later, she barely remembered stepping to the mare, barely remembered stroking her, pressing her cheek to hers, and feeling the acquiescence of the horse, the subtle shift that told Claire this animal would consent to bear her. She breathed in the warm, straw scent of the beast, and something unhitched in her heart, a little give like a crack in a dam. She ignored it, talking to Storm as Jamie saddled her, then took over from him, buckling buckles, tightening straps, her fingers going through the motions as if she'd never left the ranch.

"Let's go," Jamie said, and wonder of wonders, she was in the saddle, riding Storm, her dress bunched up around her thighs, thankful she was wearing her old boots. She followed Jamie, who rode a bay gelding he'd introduced as Walter. Dusk had deepened into night while they were in the stables, but she didn't care. She knew all the trails around the ranch as well as the streets of Billings. Besides, all she cared about was Storm. The way she paced, the way her muscles shifted under Claire's own.

To be back on a horse…

Jamie headed northwest, past outbuildings, pastures and onto open range, winding through the rolling land for nearly half an hour before he came to a stop. Claire finally took stock of her surroundings and her heart squeezed. Damn it, she should have known.

"No."

"Yes, Claire. You can't let the past control your life." He dismounted and turned to face her. "We'll only stay a moment."

After a second, she, too, slid down from her horse and dropped the reins to the ground. Cautiously, she followed Jamie the final few steps to her parents' gravesite. The Cruz headstones stood plain and matter-of-fact in the desolate ground. There were no trees to shade them, no flowers, no bench. Her mother and father laid to rest together for all eternity.

"I came to the funeral," she said.

"Have you come back to visit their graves since?"

"No."

"Why not?" Jamie moved to her side, but didn't touch her.

She shrugged.

"Are you still angry at her?"

She thought about that. "I don't know."

"Still carrying a torch for Mack Mackenzie?" His tone was ironic, but she sensed the question was real.

"Of course not. What an ass."

"Then maybe it's time to forgive your mom for putting an end to all that," he said.

She closed her eyes. Jamie didn't know the half of it. He thought she left the ranch because her mother found out about her crush on Mack. He had no idea she'd walked right in on them. Mack and her mother, right in the stables.

"Was it all her traveling? Did you mind that she didn't take you with her?"

"Hell, no. I liked it when she was gone." Claire hugged her arms across her chest, the lie sitting heavy in her throat. "She was miserable here and she made all the rest of us miserable. She wouldn't have wanted me on those trips of hers anyway. I would have cramped her style."

"In what way?"

"Not you, too." Claire shook her head. "I don't know if all of you just play dumb or if you really are dumb."

"Whoa, slow down there. I assume you mean Ethan and me."

"And my father."

"None of us are dumb."

"You sure act like it." She blew out a breath. "What exactly do you think my mother was doing in Europe?"

"Shopping, I guess. She sure spent a lot of money."

Claire turned to him. "So you were paying attention. Sure, she shopped all right. Spent us all into debt. But that's not the half of it." She waited expectantly.

"I'm not following you."

"She had affairs, Jamie. Lots of them, I bet. How do you think she blew all that money? Buying dresses? Uh uh—she was supporting lovers over there. Putting them up in expensive hotels, wining and dining them, doing God knows what. Then she'd get guilty, I guess, come running home and pretend to be the loving wife and mother for a few months before she went off and did it again."

Jamie stepped back. "How on earth do you figure that?"

"Because she did it here, too."

"You can't know that," he said.

"I saw them," she blazed. "Up against a stall, Mack's hands braced against the wall, my mom's arms around his neck, her legs around his waist. Do you want to hear more?"

"Shit." Jamie shifted uncomfortably. "I'm sorry, Claire."

"Well, sorry doesn't fix it."

He rubbed a hand over his face. "No wonder you left. Did you ever...say anything?"

"To my father? No. I couldn't. I never looked him in the eye again, either. He had to know." She shook her head. "I was so angry at him, too—angry that he didn't stop her, or leave her, or something."

"You hardly ever came home after that."

"How could I?"

"And now they're gone."

A sob nearly escaped her at his plain-spoken words. Now they were gone, and she couldn't ask her mother why, or tell her father how sorry she was that his wife betrayed him, or tell either one of them good-bye.

"Let's ride." She moved toward Storm, who'd wandered off a few paces in the darkness.

"Claire, wait. Just a minute." His hand on her wrist

held her in place. "You have to forgive them or it'll tear you apart."

She tried to speak. Couldn't. This time when she tugged, he let her go.

SHE FELT BETTER once she was back on Storm. Jamie took the lead again, retracing their steps and as the gravesite receded, she was able to breathe. Jamie was right—her parents were gone and there wasn't anything she could do to fix the past. Despite everything that happened she missed them both horribly.

Would spending more time here on the ranch make that worse or better? It felt so good to ride again. Could she return to Billings after six weeks on the ranch? Could she take off to travel around the world after spending so much time at home? Would she be able to carry off her revenge or would she fall for Jamie's charm? She snorted and Jamie looked back over his shoulder.

"You okay?"

"Yeah."

"You want to go back or go on?" Jamie asked.

Scanning the terrain, she saw the lights of the Big House to her left, the open range ahead of them. A flicker of a memory set her nerves alight. She knew one way to leave the past behind.

"Race you to the lookout!"

Storm responded almost before she issued her command, bunching her muscles and bursting into an all-out gallop that made Claire cry out in joy. Her hair whipped back behind her as her own muscles responded, naturally lifting her into a crouch over the saddle as Storm picked up speed. She gripped the reins firmly and moved with Storm until she felt it was her own legs running, her own heart pounding fit to burst as they flew over the ground. Her laughter pealed out as they raced on and on and she didn't even look back to see if Jamie was following. She didn't care.

This was freedom. This was living. How had she forgotten?

"Come on, Storm," she urged and the horse responded, going even faster. Just as she had as a teenager, she was flying toward a ridge that overlooked the river valley, with a moon climbing the sky and the whole world to herself. She was invincible on the back of a horse. She could do anything.

"This way." Storm knew what she wanted. They veered off down a slope and then up again, skirted a stand of brush. It was her own way to the ridge, the one Jamie had avoided last time they took this ride together. They'd been fourteen and sixteen then, before all the trouble with Mack started. Before her family fell apart. They'd snuck out one night onto the range, stole two of the ranch's best racehorses and galloped over the terrain like they were chased by the hounds of hell.

"Claire!" he called now, but he was too far behind to stop her. She knew he'd divert her from this trail if he could. No one took this jump.

No one but her.

She rode flat out, skimming the ground, Storm's stride so long she flowed like the river water so far below.

"Claire! No!"

Too late.

As one, horse and woman leaped out over the abyss, cleared the wash of logs an old creek had pushed together and jammed up against an outcropping of rock making an obstacle so high and wide that most horses would balk rather than go over it.

Storm cleared it like an eagle swooping to the sky with its prey.

Claire raced up the ridge, then slowed Storm to a canter, then a walk. Jamie caught up, flung himself off his horse and strode toward her, grabbing the reins out of her hands.

"What the hell are you thinking?"

"I knew she could do it."

"It's dark, Claire. That jump's stupid in the light. You have no right to risk…"

"I knew she could do it."

Claire gave Storm one last caress, pressed her cheek to her mane and hoped the horse knew half of what she felt at this moment. She slid down and faced Jamie.

"I knew…I got on her and I felt…I felt…" She couldn't put it into words. "Oh, God, Jamie—"

His scowl turned into a reluctant grin as she grappled for words. "You forgot what it feels like, didn't you?"

He was right—she'd forgotten everything about riding horses. What it felt like to work as one with an animal, to streak over the ground, to break free from the every day into eternity.

Her nerves on fire, pulse still racing in her veins, she felt a hunger for life she hadn't felt in months.

Years.

And Jamie looked so good.

She took a step toward him, wanting something—wanting…

With a groan he pulled her to him, bent to cover her mouth with his, tangled his hands in her hair, devoured her. He tasted so good she forgot her reasons for keeping him at bay. She wanted more. She wanted to be closer to him, pressing against him. His hands sliding over her skin brought every nerve alight and she stood on her tiptoes, the better to crush her mouth against his. Jamie groaned, an animal sound, and she leaned into him, covering him with kisses. The bristles of his beard scraped her lips and she relished the feeling; it let her know this was real—this was happening.

She ripped at the buttons of his shirt, pushed it off him, smoothed her hands over his hard chest.

"Claire," Jamie breathed. He worked at the buttons of her dress, searching for a way to get it off of her. Claire dragged him to his knees and he cradled her in his arms.

It wasn't enough.

She knew she would regret this, but she didn't care. She'd wanted this for so long—wanted Jamie for so long, whether he was good for her or not. Whether he'd stay with her or smash her heart to smithereens. With one hand she brushed the ground free of sticks and pinecones, then lay back and pulled him on top of her, kicking off her boots.

"Claire," he said. "Are you sure?"

"Yes." How had she waited this long? How had she thought she could resist him? Intoxicated by the night, the moon, the ride, the champagne, all she felt was the burning desire that pulsed within her—the desire only he could fulfill.

"You ready to lose our bet right now?" he said.

"That doesn't start until tomorrow."

She fumbled with his jeans and he pushed her hands away, doing the job for her with the ease of long practice.

"You think one time with me is gonna do it for you?" Together they slipped off her dress and she unclasped her bra. Suddenly shy, she waited until Jamie's calloused hands slid the straps off her shoulders.

"Let me see you," he said, his voice husky with emotion.

She let it fall, leaned back and watched his face in the moonlight. She saw wonder in his eyes, his own hunger. Then he moved forward and covered her with his lean body. She had no idea if one time would satisfy her for a minute or a lifetime and she didn't care. All she wanted was Jamie. Inside of her. Loving her.

"Protection?" he breathed.

"I'm on the pill." She let out a ragged moan as his hardness pressed against her core. "Please, Jamie—now."

He pushed inside her with one strong stroke and she arched back, crying out. Sliding out and pressing back in again they soon found their rhythm and she gripped him, pulling him against her, gasping when her nipples bounced against his chest, matching his pace as his movements lifted her higher and higher, closer….

"Yes. Jamie, yes!" They moved faster, Jamie pumped harder within her and anticipation built until with one final stroke she fell over the edge of desire and cried out again, clinging to Jamie, digging her nails into his skin until she shuddered to a stop, sinking back against the rough ground.

Jamie collapsed on top of her, nuzzling her neck as she stared up at the blaze of stars that covered the sky. She wanted to stay here for all eternity. Wanted to hold her breath and forget everything.

Please don't let this end. Please don't let me think…

Too late.

As her breathing slowed, reality came crashing back, leaving her emptier than she'd been before. Suddenly sober, horror washed through her. Jamie's trick had worked. He'd stuck a stupid ring on her finger and she'd spread her legs. Now Jamie had what he wanted, he'd be on to the next woman before she could blink. Hadn't she learned anything? Now she could never come home again, because there Jamie would be, watching her, laughing at her, swapping tales with the others of how he'd bagged her.

What had she done?

"Ah, Claire," Jamie said. "Forget the bet. Let's go find that preacher and get married right now."

She lay still while he kissed her cheek, her jaw. An hour ago she'd felt so alone. Now she'd connected—

with Jamie. With Storm, too.

With her old life.

And she had to leave it behind again. All of it behind. A wordless agony built within her at the thought of turning her back on it all again. How would she find the strength this time? Fury at her mother, fury at Jamie had kept her at bay before. Now she was just tired. And sad.

And alone.

Tears pricked her eyes as the ring's glitter in the moonlight echoed the stars dotting the sky above her. No matter what words he said to her now, tomorrow morning the joke would be on her. Jamie wasn't capable of staying with one woman. He'd propose tonight, and take it all back tomorrow. Just like Daniel making his empty promises.

She couldn't stand it if she said yes to Jamie and he cast her off.

Meeting his gaze as he slid off her and touched her cheek, she realized she had to stop this right now. She sat up and began to gather her clothes.

"What's the hurry?" he said, his voice warm and caressing. He looked at his watch. "We still have time. We could go another round."

"No, we can't," she said, fastening her bra and tugging up her panties.

He stilled. "Something wrong?" He stood up, too. God, he was magnificent in the moonlight. Claire ached to toss her clothing to the wind and jump him again.

"This. Us. We can't do this," she forced herself to say, turning her back to him as she shrugged into her dress.

"Hell, you're kidding, right? Tell me you're kidding, Claire." He stalked around to face her. "This ain't no one night stand."

"Yes, it is. I'm sorry—I got carried away."

"Came to your senses finally is more like it."

Tugging on her boots, she stalked off toward Storm. Jamie followed. "Hey, we're not done here."

"Yes, we are." She tried to keep going, but he refused to let her, drawing her into an embrace she knew just might be the end of her resolve.

"You can't tell me you don't feel something for me. Hell, you're the one who started this."

"I shouldn't have had sex with you. That was wrong." So wrong. It had pried the lid off the feelings she'd managed to clamp down inside her for months. Suddenly she was blinking back tears for the third time tonight. She was never setting foot on this stupid ranch again. Knowing it was fruitless, she tugged at the ring again. Stuck.

"Well, I'm not sorry," he said and stepped away. "And I'm holding you to our bargain. You said you'd help me with my house and with the trail rides."

"Oh, come on," she said, her voice cracking. She folded her arms across her chest, cold now away from Jamie's embrace. She just needed to live through the next few hours—see the happy couple off on their honeymoon, clean up a bit, and retire to the room she was occupying in the Big House for the weekend. She could do it—she knew she could.

"No, I'm serious. Unless you've turned into the biggest liar west of the Mississippi. You can stand there and tell me you regret making love with me, but I won't let you go back on your promise to help me out."

Why wouldn't he let her go? He'd gotten what he'd wanted—did he really need to drag her through the rest of this farce? To prove what? That he held all the cards?

He was right. She was lying to him, but how could she tell him the truth? That she wanted nothing more than to be with him, to chuck everything to the wind—everything—and just make sweet love to him all night long, but she couldn't—wouldn't—because she couldn't trust him or any man after what she'd been through. Because she'd been privy to far too many of the practical jokes he and Ethan and his friends played, and she couldn't stand knowing she was the victim of another one of them.

"Fine, I'll help you." Anything to get away from him now. She had to get home before she lost her composure for good. Before she started crying and couldn't ever stop again.

Jamie brushed past her to reach his clothes. He leaned close and spoke into her ear. "And you'll marry me before we're through."

LONG PAST WHEN they'd brought the horses back to the stable, wiped them down and put away their saddles and tack, long past when he'd walked Claire back to the bunkhouse and left her there after kissing her softly despite her stony resistance, Jamie lay awake, sketching their future out in his mind.

Working together to design an interior for his home. Leading guests on trail rides and helping build the guest ranch business. Getting married and having babies....

Things hadn't gone exactly according to plan today, but he wasn't entirely dissatisfied.

He'd been with Claire.

He'd made love to her.

Man, oh man. It had been everything he'd dreamed of—and that was only the first time. He had no doubt they could rock the rafters when they really got down to it. He should have found a way to get her on a horse sooner. She just never made it easy.

All those years grinding through school, working, saving his money. It had all paid off. She wanted him. She wanted to come back to the ranch.

She just didn't want to admit it yet.

CLAIRE BENT OVER the sink in the bathroom off her old bedroom in the Big House, lathering her hands furiously, her tears mingling with the water running down the drain.

She'd made love to Jamie, and it had felt so good. And now that it was over—well and truly over—she thought her heart would tear in two again. No matter how hard she tried, she couldn't forget the way he'd felt inside her, the way his mouth had trailed kisses down her neck. The way he'd looked into her eyes as ecstasy ripped through her core. Baring herself to him had felt as right as slipping into Chance Creek on a hot summer afternoon.

She loved him.

After all this time and what he'd done, she still loved him.

It wasn't fair—he was playing a game and she was losing her mind. And, damn it, his stupid ring wouldn't come off her finger.

Swiping hot tears away, she flipped open the medicine cabinet doors and searched through the products she'd put there the preceding evening. Hand lotion. Maybe that would do the trick.

She squirted a big dollop on her finger and worked it in. Tugging on the silver band once again, she groaned when it still hung up around her knuckle.

She hated Jamie for doing this to her—reducing her to a sniveling, shaking, furious mess. She had to get the ring off. Had to show him she wasn't buying his tricks. Wouldn't be a victim of his games.

The ring popped off.

Claire half-laughed, half-sobbed as she slid down to sit on the bathroom floor. Cool tile reminded her she was still in her sundress. Her bare feet poked out from under its long skirt.

She studied the ring, a ring she'd be proud to wear under different circumstances—if Jamie really loved her, and if he was capable of sustaining that love. Her finger felt bare without it and she felt empty, too—as if she'd shucked off her connections to her old life on the ranch when she'd taken it off.

In a way that's what she'd done, wasn't it? She was

choosing a trip abroad and then life in Billings over trying to build some kind of a new life here on the ranch. She thought about how it might have been to go through with the wedding; working together, having children someday, sharing the property with Ethan and Autumn, being surrounded by all their friends.

Making love to Jamie every night.

She leaned her head back against the wall, closed her eyes, and a tear slid down her cheek. It was the life she'd dreamed of growing up. The man she'd dreamed of these past two years.

Now it was time to put all of that behind her. Time to cut all her ties to the past and march forward into a new and brilliant future. So why did the thought of purchasing that round-the-world-cruise make her want to cry?

Because she wanted to come home. Needed to come home.

Mom.

If only she was young again and her mother was smoothing her hair back from her face. Once upon a time Aria had loved her. Had kissed away her tears and tucked her in at night.

Mom.

What she would give to go back to those innocent days.

She forced herself back to her feet, put the ring on the counter and washed her hands and face. She couldn't go back, but she wished someone would advise her what to do next. She wanted to stay on the ranch and wanted to spend time with Jamie. The safer choice was to go on her cruise right away.

What would Aria do?

Claire smiled lopsidedly at her reflection in the mirror. Her mother never held back. Whatever she wanted, she went after full-bore.

When tears threatened to fall again, she grabbed the ring, jammed it back on her finger and fled the room.

Chapter Four

"SO, THE WEDDING'S ON LABOR DAY?" Rob asked, leaning against the stable door.

"Yep." He hoped. Jamie kept on his inspection of the horses in their stalls.

"Claire really agreed to marry you after all? She looked pretty pissed yesterday."

"Let's just say it's a work in progress. But I'll marry her in the end." He stroked Storm's head, hoping she knew how proud he was of the way she'd stolen Claire's heart. Getting Claire back on a horse was just the first step in making her fall back in love with ranch life. But it was an important step.

"Hmm. I don't know, buddy. I think Claire might be out of your league. I bet she worms her way out of it."

"Oh, yeah?" Jamie straightened, angry that Rob's words reinforced his own doubts. "You want to sweeten that bet we made?"

"Two hundred bucks?" Rob took a pace toward him.

"Five hundred." Jamie met him halfway.

"Whew—high stakes. You sure you can afford it?"

"Can you? I know your Daddy don't pay much allowance." Rob winced and Jamie knew he'd scored a point. It wasn't any secret that Rob still lived at home and received a pittance for the work he did around his father's ranch.

"I can cover it," Rob said, shaking hands, then turning on his heel. "I'll see you around."

THANK GOODNESS, a parking spot.

Claire zipped her Honda Civic close to the curb several blocks from work, grabbed her purse and her briefcase and sprinted for the front door of Ledstrom Designs. In the seven years she'd worked here, she'd never been late before now. She still couldn't believe she'd slept with Jamie during Ethan's wedding reception—or that she was still wearing his ring and keeping up this farce of an engagement. She didn't want to examine too closely why the ring still graced her finger. Instead, her mind kept filling with memories of her time with Jamie under the stars.

They hadn't even seen Ethan and Autumn leave for their honeymoon. By the time they got back to the Big House, even the guests had begun to leave. The next morning she felt like a zombie as she put Autumn's mother, sister and friend Becka back on the plane, then spent the rest of the afternoon setting everything back to rights after the wedding. Thank goodness Jamie hadn't come around to help. She'd been as jumpy as a cat waiting for him to stroll over the knoll that hid his cabin from the Big House and bunkhouse, but he hadn't and she was thankful for that. She might not have been able to resist him if he had. Or she might have dropped everything, turned tail, and run.

She wished she could run back into his arms.

A memory surfaced of a sunny day back when they were teenagers when they'd lain on the banks of Chance Creek listening to the water bubble past and talked about their plans for the future. Both of them wanted a rodeo career back then. She'd been teasing him that she'd beat him across the boards.

"Men and women don't even ride in the same events," he said, unperturbed, and she'd felt a flash of something—impatience, interest, and a tug of feeling below the belt she didn't know fully how to interpret in those days. She'd pushed away the sensation, like she always did, telling herself Jamie had nothing on Mack.

Now she realized in a burst of insight she'd picked the man who was out of reach because she wasn't ready for the man within reach. At seventeen she wanted a boyfriend the same way she wanted a fancy dress or pair of earrings—to show off to her friends and decorate herself with. Mack wouldn't touch her, but Jamie sure would have. As much as the idea of that had fascinated her, she simply wasn't ready to see it through.

She was now.

Stifling a groan, she picked up her pace. No—she wouldn't ever sleep with Jamie again, no matter how earth-shattering the experience had been. No matter how he'd made her blood sing and her nerves tingle.

No matter what he said, he didn't feel the same way.

He wasn't capable of it. So now she needed to plan a strategy to get through the next six weeks and then go back to living life without Jamie or the ranch.

She wished the prospect didn't make her feel so flat.

Focus. It would be a month at least before Autumn and Ethan were ready for paying guests and she needed to fulfill her promise to spend a week helping with trail rides. Meanwhile she'd work on the interior design for Jamie's house while she took steps to shut down Ledstrom Designs. Whenever she had the opportunity she'd take revenge on Jamie.

She had just reached the glass double door entrance to Ledstrom Designs when it opened and a man walked out.

A familiar man.

"Daniel?" A wash of dizziness overtook her, leaving her grasping for something to steady herself. Her fingers raked the faux-stone exterior of the building, scrambling for a handhold. No. It couldn't be.

"Claire." He tipped his sunglasses up to the top of his head and stared frankly down at her. "Look at you." He glanced at his watch. "Late. That's not the Claire I know."

She gaped at him. How the hell could Daniel be here? Wasn't he off on some foreign island sipping Margaritas with that idiot, Edie?

"What are you doing here?"

He grinned, and she fought the urge to slug him. "I'm the owner. Where else would I be?"

"No, you're not. You left. You…you stole my money!"

"I enjoyed the money you gave me," he corrected her. "I don't remember you asking me to pay you back."

"Of course I did!" She couldn't believe he had the gall to stand here—right here on the streets of Billings—and pretend he didn't rob her blind.

"Where's the proof? Show me the loan agreement." He shrugged. "As much as I'd like to stay and catch up on old times, I have to go—I've got a client meeting in 10 minutes. Since the police never contacted me I'm assuming you never pressed charges. You can try to now, but I wouldn't if I were you. Waiting a year to file a complaint against me makes you look like the liar, don't you think?"

He pushed past her, then turned back. "Oh, and I expect your things gone by the time I return. While the cat's away, the mice will play, I suppose, but now the cat's back. Your services are no longer necessary."

"This isn't your company anymore!"

"Really? My name's still on it."

Words failed her as she watched him walk away. Numbly, she pushed through the doors into the office and found everyone gathered around Edie, who sat at her old desk. Celia, the receptionist she'd hired soon after Daniel and Edie absconded, stood at the back of the crowd, her expression bewildered.

"I know it wasn't the best way to break things off with Ted," Edie was saying. "But Daniel's so impetuous. He couldn't wait any longer. We got married and we traveled around the world for an entire year. You wouldn't believe all the things we did."

"So why are you back here?" Claire said and cringed as everyone turned to stare at her. Was that strident sound really her voice?

Edie sat up straight and pursed her lips. The other employees eased away to their own cubicles. "Life can't all be fun and games. It's time for us to get back to work."

This couldn't be happening. Daniel couldn't just march in here and take things over. These were her clients now—it was her business.

But was it? The building's owner had been all too happy to transfer Daniel's lease to her when Daniel left, and most of the clients were thrilled to learn their projects wouldn't be disrupted. As lead designer, she'd been their contact at the company, anyway. But did that make the business—the clients—hers? She had no idea what a court would say.

Just turn around and walk out the door. You don't need the money. You were about to shut it down anyway, she told herself, but her fingers curled into fists as she scanned the office. She'd taken over Daniel's desk while he was gone, but now it was bare, her personal things piled into a box. Shit—her computer was gone. "Edie?"

"No need to shout, I'm right here."

"Where the hell is my computer?"

"You mean Daniel's computer? He took it with him. He needed it for his meeting."

His meeting. Claire realized Edie meant her meeting—with the Wilcoxes. "He's taking my meeting?"

"You're not employed here anymore." Edie lifted an eyebrow in obvious distaste. "We went on vacation, Claire—we didn't hand you our company lock, stock and barrel. Now we're back and you're not needed. Thank you for stopping by and picking up your things." She focused on a pile of paperwork on her desk, but Claire knew every other eye in the office was turned toward her. Watching her reaction. Waiting to see what she would do.

Claire's stomach gave an uneasy lurch. What the hell should she do? Daniel had stolen her money, but she couldn't prove it. Once he was gone, the office by all rights should have closed. She kept it open. Did it cross the line for her to take his clients and profit from them? She wasn't sure. All she knew was if she stayed and made a scene she might lose whatever credibility she had in this town now that she'd been fired from Ledstrom Designs. Finally, she found her voice. "Fine, I'm out of here. You can have your stupid client list and your stupid building. Wherever I set up my office, the clients will find me."

Clients? What clients? Wasn't she planning to walk away from interior design?

Not anymore.

"Whatever, sweetie. Just remember—all your current contracts are property of Ledstrom Designs."

Claire started toward the door. She had to get out of here before she did something stupid—something violent. Like heaving Edie through the front plate-glass window.

She barged out onto the street, fury propelling every step. She'd earned those contracts, every one of them. Even the projects that started back when Daniel was boss were all her work. Daniel couldn't just take them from her.

Except he had.

She came to a stop on the sidewalk outside the building, nearly colliding with a man hurrying by with a briefcase in his hand. After all her hard work, late nights, and worry over the bottom line, Daniel was going to screw her over. He was going to win.

She couldn't let him do that.

Not again.

Chapter Five

JAMIE LOOKED UP from mucking out Walter's stall late Monday morning to see Claire standing near the stable door. Dressed in her city things, she looked pale and strained, with dark smudges under her eyes. He dropped his shovel and moved toward her, but she held up a hand.

"Don't."

"What's wrong?"

"I didn't know where else to go, but so help me God, Jamie, if you touch me I'm leaving."

What the hell? Jamie leaned his shovel against the stall. Whatever had happened in the past twenty-four hours had shattered Claire and he longed to pull her into his arms and comfort her. Unfortunately, he knew too well that look in her eye. She didn't want that kind of comfort. "What happened?"

She scanned the back wall of the stable like maybe the answers were written there. "He came back. Daniel came back."

Jamie's jaw tightened. "Ledstrom?"

She seemed surprised he knew the name. She really had no idea how much energy he'd put into knowing as much about her as he possibly could. He'd seen their picture in the paper several times last year—Claire and Daniel at a charity auction in the city. Claire and Daniel at an art gallery opening. Then he'd read in the paper that her weasel-faced pretty-boy boss had suddenly left town with his ditzy secretary. Ethan had come to him then, worried about his sister, but Claire had taken over Ledstrom Designs and carried on her work without missing a beat. Jamie had breathed a sigh of relief, figuring she didn't care for Daniel, after all.

Now the bastard was back.

"What's he want?"

"My business."

"He can't take your business away from you."

"Yes, he can." Claire's eyes were huge in her face. "Because it's actually still his."

"If he walked out on his clients he doesn't have a leg to stand on."

"You don't understand. I took over all his contracts. I kept working just the same way we always had. I even kept his name on the business—I couldn't afford to make up a new sign, get a new website and all that. It was just easier to keep it. I just never thought he'd come back!"

"Why not? Because he stole another man's wife?"

She turned away. "He stole something else, too."

"What?"

She shook her head. "I don't want to tell you."

Jamie balled his fists. She didn't have to. It was as plain as day—Daniel Ledstrom had stolen her heart.

And now he was back. He had to act fast or the bastard might coerce Claire back into his bed. Now that he'd slept with her, Jamie had no intention of letting another man near her. She was going to be his wife. He planned to spend the rest of his life with her. Ledstrom wasn't going to screw that up.

"I thought you were quitting interior design. You said you were shutting down the company anyway."

"I was, but…not like this."

No, not like this, Jamie thought. Not when the bastard she'd loved but left her was coming back to steal the business from her. Her competitive spirit was rearing its head again. He knew Claire. She could walk away from a business, but she could never stand to have it taken from her. If he didn't side with her, she'd count him as an enemy. He thought hard.

"I was never his client."

"What?"

"He can't say I was on his list. I knew you way before you ever went to Billings. Design my house, and start over again. New company, new name. Clients will line up to work with you based on your merits alone." At the end of the day he didn't care if she designed interiors or organized trail rides. He just wanted her close by.

"What if no one wants to work with me anymore?"

Jamie forced himself not to take a step and pull her into his arms. He kept his voice even. "You're terrific at what you do—everyone will want to work with you.

You'll be fine."

"There aren't enough clients in Chance Creek—I need to be in a city like Billings."

"There are plenty of clients here—real clients with real houses, not fancy-schmancy condominiums." He spit out the word like it tasted bad.

Claire shot him a look. "I live in a condominium." She tapped a finger against her arm. "No, it won't work—there isn't enough money around here to keep a design business afloat."

"Then work with me on the ranch," he said desperately. Damn it, why did Ledstrom have to come back now just when he was getting somewhere with Claire?

She turned on him. "No—don't you see? That's exactly what he wants. To eliminate his competition. I can't let him do that."

Jamie ached to pound Daniel Ledstrom into pulp. Instead, he said carefully, "What are you going to do?"

She tapped her finger some more.

"The Whitfield contract."

Jamie raised an eyebrow.

"Carl Whitfield's building a huge log mansion for Lacey. He's going to need an interior designer. I planned to go after the contract before you guys bought me out. I'll go after it now." She smiled triumphantly. "I can use your house as a practice run. Go get me your blueprints. I'm going to design the best log home interior Montana's ever seen, show it to Carl, and nail that contract." She turned fever-bright eyes toward him. "And then I'm going to bury Daniel and Ledstrom Designs."

Chapter Six

CLAIRE CHECKED THE MIRROR in her ensuite bathroom to make sure she looked neat and professional. A millionaire like Carl Whitfield was used to dealing with the best of the best.

For the last two weeks she'd lived in the Big House on the ranch, spending most of her time at the huge table in the great room with Jamie's blueprints scattered about her, along with fabric swatches, sell sheets and her own handwritten notes. She'd pecked away at her laptop, creating a 3-D rendering of her designs in a CAD program. It turned out Jamie had been planning for years for the day he bought land and began to build. The minute he signed the paperwork with Ethan, he got on the phone to the contractor he wished to use. Luckily, Tom Bends had a gap in his schedule he was all too happy to fill in this slow economy, and construction started right away. Jamie already had ideas for the flooring, and in many of the rooms wanted the huge log walls to remain visible, but he had left the kitchen appointments and many other details to her. Plus he had asked her to pick out most of the major furnishings.

She'd done all this and more, and once she'd shown Jamie her results and he'd praised her to the skies, only asking for one or two minor changes, she'd polished her presentation and called Carl to ask for a meeting.

Lacey Taylor was once Ethan's fiancee. She'd left him—thank God—after she'd discovered the extent of the ranch's debts. Claire didn't think she could have stood Lacey as a sister-in-law. Lacey latched on to Carl Whitfield, a millionaire and wanna-be rancher who'd managed to piss off almost everyone in Chance Creek. Things had settled down some, and Carl and Lacey intended to get married after Lacey finished her four months in a live-in counseling program in Bozeman. Apparently she had unresolved traumas from her childhood she wanted to work on before marrying Carl. Ethan had hinted something like that before the wedding, but who would have believed Lacey Taylor had grown up enough to make such an adult decision? Carl wanted to surprise her when she returned by having his mansion built and decorated. If she could score this contract, she'd be well on her way to establishing Cruz Designs as a company worthy of notice.

She'd called every one of her old clients the day she'd left Ledstrom Designs, apprised them of the situation and told them that unfortunately she wouldn't be able to work with them on any current project they had with Daniel's company. It killed her to give up all the work she'd done, but she knew many of the clients would seek her out in the future once they found Daniel wasn't as good a designer as she was.

If she was honest, though, it was killing her to work inside while living on the ranch. She watched Jamie through the large floor-to-ceiling windows as he worked with the horses in the corrals. Ethan came and went, tending the cattle now that he and Autumn were home from their honeymoon. Autumn spent more time indoors, but even she worked in the kitchen garden.

Claire was the only one chained to a desk in the beautiful summer weather. Once or twice she'd ridden out at night with Jamie to see the building site, but she put him off whenever she could. It was so hard to turn Storm around and come back inside afterward.

Why was she torturing herself like this? Why not admit defeat and leave interior design to Daniel?

Because she refused to be defeated by a man like that. Not a second time.

She glanced at her reflection in the mirror again. Her suit was finely tailored, her hair brushed to a shine. Her makeup was understated but flattering. And Jamie's elegant ring set the whole outfit off.

It glittered there as a constant reminder of what she really wanted. For Jamie to be the kind of man she needed him to be. A man who would stick by her through thick and thin. Now that their bet had kicked in and he wasn't touching her, she was more conscious of him than ever. Every time he came near her she held her breath, wanting him to take her into his arms. But then he would lose the bet, and she didn't want him to lose, did she?

Because then the ranch and Jamie would be off limits to her for good.

She wanted him so bad. Wanted to make love to him again.

Focus, Claire.

Time to go score one of the biggest interior design contracts in Montana.

A HALF-HOUR LATER, she sat at a scarred wooden table in Linda's diner, waiting for Carl Whitfield to join her, alternately checking her laptop to make sure it was set to show him her portfolio and playing with the engagement ring.

The door opened, and Carl came in. At forty, he'd already made his millions and bought the spread next door to the Cruz ranch to live out his dreams of being a cowboy. When he'd arrived, everyone laughed at his shiny new boots and string tie, and they'd been angry at the way he bought his place for a song when he could have afforded to pay much more, but no one could turn up their noses at the way he was boosting the local economy with his building projects. And he sure seemed to love Lacey.

"Hi, Claire, how's it keeping?"

"Hi, Carl. Thanks for meeting me."

"A man's got to eat." He smiled. "Plus I never turn away the chance to spend time with a pretty woman."

Claire cringed, but kept a smile pasted on her lips. "Would you like to see what I've been planning for Jamie's house? That will give you a chance to see what I can do with a log home."

"How about we order first, then get down to business."

She took a breath and willed herself to calm down. She'd done a hundred of these meetings, so why was she acting like she was fresh out of school? "Sure, that sounds great."

Tracey Richards, the young, blonde waitress, stopped by the table and handed menus to each of them, her high pony-tail swinging. "Should I give you a few minutes?"

"I know what I want," Carl said. "A BLT, heavy on the mayo, a side of fries and a slice of apple pie."

"How about you, Claire?"

Tracey had been several classes behind Claire, but she remembered her from high school, and besides, everyone knew everyone in Chance Creek. She scanned the menu. "Tomato soup and grilled cheese for me. Plus coffee when you have a minute."

Tracey hurried away, came back a moment later with coffee for both of them and hustled off again. Linda's Diner was a standby in Chance Creek, and was always busy at lunchtime on weekdays.

"All right, show me what you've got," Carl said.

Swallowing another wave of nervousness, Claire slid the laptop over to where he could see the screen and pushed a button. "Here's a mockup of the interior of the log home Jamie's building. Of course, it's nothing compared to the size of yours...."

"I should hope not. I plan to build the biggest house in Chance Creek. Only the best for my bride."

She wished he didn't feel the need to talk quite so loudly. The last thing she wanted was a crowd to form around their table. "Of course. I'm sure yours will be twice the size of Jamie's."

"Twice? Try four times the size. Ten thousand square feet."

Ten thousand? With just him and Lacey rattling around in all that space? And the cost to heat it!

Claire composed herself. "That is a big house." Carl nodded smugly. "Think of what I'm showing you as just a hint of what I could do for you." She clicked another button. "Here's the entryway. Notice the slate floors…"

"Everyone has slate floors. I plan to import marble from Bologna—it's dark, imposing. Just the thing to let everyone know they aren't dealing with a country bumpkin."

"Oh, well that sounds nice." Marble from Bologna? She scrambled to note that down.

"What else you got?" Carl scanned the diner as if he was losing interest already. Claire hurried to show him the next image she'd mocked up.

"Well, here's the great room…"

"Great room? That looks like a closet to me. My great room's going to be bigger than Jamie's whole house. Of course he's just a hired hand."

"He's not just a hired hand," Claire blazed. "He's part-owner of the Cruz ranch now."

"Ah, yes. I heard something about that."

She bet he did. Carl had tried to buy the ranch out from under them before Jamie saved the day. She had the sudden, uncomfortable feeling that he might be here with her now as an act of revenge, rather than because he really meant to hire her.

"Anyhow, if you'll look at the furnishings." She gave herself a mental shake. So what if he didn't come expecting to become her client? Her presentation ought to speak for itself. Winning him over would be an even bigger victory than the one she'd planned.

"Yes, yes, very nice for Jamie, but you have to understand, Claire, that if you want to work for someone like me you'll need to play on an entirely different level." Carl pushed the laptop away as Tracey appeared with their lunches. She set down their plates. "This looks terrific, honey. Thank you." He took a large bite of his sandwich.

"Thanks, Tracey." Claire waited until the waitress left. "Look, Carl, I know what you're saying. I don't mean that I'd use any of the ideas I've used for Jamie on your place—I just wanted you to see that I have an eye for style and design. Of course your furnishings and materials will be on a much grander scale, but…"

"What I see is that you have an eye for the safe and pedestrian. Nothing you've shown me raises my eyebrows and makes me wonder about the man who owns that house. Nothing impresses me. You've designed an average house for an average man, and that's fine for Jamie Lassiter. But it ain't fine for me. Carl Whitfield needs a designer with vision. I agreed to this meeting out of courtesy and because I thought I might be able to throw a tip or two your way, but I've already decided who I'll be working with. Daniel Ledstrom of Ledstrom

Designs. Now there's a company with a reputation for fine work."

"Daniel?" The word came out a squeak. Claire thought fast. "Look, Carl. You're right—I wasn't thinking big enough. I knew you were building a large log home, but I had no idea just how large. If you want a spectacular design, I can give you one. I'll treat you much better than Daniel Ledstrom will."

Carl sat back. "That's all well and good, but you're the sister of my fiancee's ex-fiance. Do you get my drift? It's good policy for me to steer clear of you."

Damn it, this job was slipping away fast. "I know Lacey—I know how she thinks. Daniel Ledstrom doesn't know you two from Adam. You honestly think he can come up with a plan that will please Lacey as well as I can?" She held her breath—that was a long shot. She and Lacey had never been friends, even when the girl was dating Ethan.

Carl tapped his thick, blunt fingers on the table. "I'm heading to Dallas for the next two months," he said finally. "The foundation is due to be poured by the time I get back. Let's say you show me what you've got then. I'll send you over a set of blueprints to work from. You wow me with a plan, and maybe I'll change my mind."

It wasn't much to go on, but it was something. As they shook hands, she vowed right then and there to go him one further. Forget about mockups. Sure, she'd concoct a plan tailored to the Whitfield mansion, but first she'd transform Jamie's home into a three-dimensional showcase of her talent Carl Whitfield couldn't ignore.

"Say, you getting married?" Carl asked, lifting her hand so her ring sparkled.

"No," Claire said, yanking her hand back.

"That looked a lot like an engagement ring," he said.

"I mean…yes—yes, I'm engaged. Sorry, I'm just so taken by your plans for your house. Tell me more about this imported marble flooring. I really like the sound of it."

She sighed with relief when Carl launched into the virtues of marble, and seemed to forget all about the ring on her finger. One person in Chance Creek didn't know about her *engagement* to Jamie.

She wanted to keep it that way.

Chapter Seven

JAMIE WATCHED THE CONSTRUCTION CREW swarm over the half-finished roof of his new log home. Perched on a rise of ground overlooking the river, it stood about a mile or so northeast of the Big House, and had a view to kill for. Four bedrooms, three baths, an open plan main floor with the kitchen and dining area only separated from the living room by a flagstone hearth open to either side. South facing windows reaching all the way up to the vaulted ceiling. A home he'd be proud to share with his bride-to-be. If he could get her attention.

And convince her to marry him. A week into July, he didn't seem any closer to winning her heart.

It was time to move things forward in his plan. While Claire had pored over his blueprints with him and seemed impressed with the design he'd chosen, she'd been all business so far, and no play. They hadn't even talked about the other half of the job she was supposed to be taking on—helping him plan activities for the guests.

Today that would change. Claire was off courting her first new client—Carl Whitfield. When she returned she was bound to be full of good spirits. Carl must be planning on spending a bundle on that mansion he was building up the road, and who better than Claire to help him decorate it? He'd tell her they should kill two birds with one stone—she could talk all about her plans for Carl's house, as long as she did so on horseback, while they inspected one of the riding trails.

He wanted to cross Chance Creek Road and venture out into the rangeland northwest of the Big House, where a trail ran past the pastures to rougher territory. He glanced at his watch. She ought to be getting home soon, and everything looked fine here.

"Keep up the good work," he hollered to Tom Bends, the construction crew's foreman.

"We'll have the walls done by the end of the day. The roof should be on later this week."

It couldn't happen too soon for him, especially with Claire raring to go on the interior. He was half afraid Carl would beat him to the punch and Claire would end up spending all her time with him, rather than here where she belonged. He knew she wanted the Whitfield contract—bad—but he needed her to focus on the Cruz spread. He had to get her involved in the guest ranch business. Had to make sure she spent enough time near him for his charm to work its magic on her. He knew she wanted him. Heck, she'd jumped him the other night, hadn't she? And while she'd consumed some champagne, she wasn't drunk enough to claim it was the alcohol leading her astray.

She wanted him, but she would spook at his slightest move in her direction. Because of her mother and Mack? Maybe. But there was something else, he'd swear to it. Something about this Daniel business that didn't add up.

Why was she so intent on revenge against the man?

Sure, it was annoying—well, more than annoying— that he would come home after running off with his secretary and expect her to hand the company back over to him. But like she said, it was his company. Should he have compensated her for her work? Yes. Should he have offered her a prime place in the business? Of course. And instead he'd kicked her to the curb, so he could see why she'd be mad. Even furious.

But it wasn't like she didn't have enough money to start another company. And it wasn't like she even cared all that much about interior design.

Did she?

As much as he hated to admit it, he got the feeling she did care about it, and he'd seen she was good at it. But how could she choose interior design over horses? Was she going to lose more years of her life trying to prove Daniel was wrong when she'd already lost so much trying to prove the same thing to her mother and Mack?

Couldn't she see that in the end she was the only one that got hurt?

He wanted to shake some sense into her. It was time to move on—start enjoying her life. That's what he'd do. Forget all this interior design stuff, she should get back on horseback—maybe even get back into the rodeo. She'd say she was too old, but plenty of women competed into their thirties, forties and beyond.

He just had to keep her too busy to think until the first guests came to stay at the ranch. Autumn had said something about having a lead. He hoped it panned out and quick. The sooner he could show Claire how rewarding working on the ranch could be, the better.

When he arrived at the Big House, Claire's Civic was already in the driveway. He prepared his congratulations, but when he walked inside, he was greeted by a disaster area. The blueprints, plans and pages of notes that used to be spread all over the large dining room table now lay every which way across the floor. Claire sat at her laptop, a sketchpad beside her, alternately typing and sketching with frenetic motions.

"Hey—what's going on?"

She looked up only for a second, dashing her bangs out of her eyes. "He hated it. He said everything I'd done was boring and predictable."

"That's bullshit. It was a fantastic design. Carl Whitfield's an ass."

"Carl Whitfield's a millionaire with a mansion that's sure to end up in the pages of more than one home design magazine. I needed that contract."

"There'll be other jobs."

"Not like this one!" She reared up and pushed the laptop away. "I blew it, Jamie. I blew my one chance."

"Claire…"

"No, just shut up. You don't know anything about

interior design or what it takes to be the best. I should be the one to get this contract, but Carl wants to hire Daniel."

Shit. No wonder she was in such a state. "Look, I know you're disappointed, but you still have my contract. That's something, right?"

She turned a look on him that made his skin crawl. "It's something." Her face was pinched with anger and worry. "Small and predictable, but something. I have to start over from scratch—make a whole new plan that transforms its predictability into something breathtaking."

Jamie stiffened. "He called my place small and predictable? Hell, it's a beautiful house—you said so yourself. And I don't want you to change anything. I like what you already designed."

"It's beautiful for a little shack." She got back to work, missing his reaction to those stinging words. "Unfortunately, little shacks don't get you into Western Homes and Gardens, do they? Forget it, I can't make my name with boring interiors. I'm re-doing the whole plan. Carl's giving me a second chance. I have two months to show him that I can design something spectacular. I might be taking on the impossible trying to transform your place into something awe-inspiring, but I'm going to do my best."

A muscle jumped in his jaw. "I came here to ask you to take a ride with me, but I see you've got your work cut out for you, trying to salvage my ugly little shack. I guess I'll leave you to it."

He walked out and slammed the door.

CLAIRE KNEW SHE SHOULD GO AFTER HIM and apologize, but she didn't have time. Besides, he was still keeping up this proposal farce, so didn't have much sympathy for him.

Not that she was getting anywhere with her revenge. Instead of finding ways to torture Jamie, she'd spent every waking moment getting back at Daniel, instead. Jamie would get over her slight against his house. She'd come up with a new plan that would knock his socks off. Then when Carl came home she'd walk him through Jamie's house and wow him with what she'd done.

Her mistake had been relying too much on tradition when she chose materials and furnishings for Jamie's interior. Sure, wood and slate or river rock were the most common materials used in log homes, and furnishings tended to be solid and rustic. That didn't mean she needed to be bound by the conventional. In fact, just the opposite. She needed to start by making a list of materials and colors you wouldn't expect to find in a log home and go from there.

And forget Jamie's pitiful budget, too—she'd never impress Carl by economizing. If Jamie couldn't afford to spend more, she could. It would be investing in her own future if she spent some of her six hundred thousand dollars on the interior.

What had Carl mentioned? Imported marble flooring from Bologna? She'd go him one better…just as soon as she figured out what that was.

Chapter Eight

A WEEK AND A HALF LATER, Jamie checked once more down the line of stalls to make sure each horse he'd hand-picked for the Cruz ranch's first crop of guests was present and accounted for—as if they'd somehow slip past him out of the barn. He was more nervous than he'd have believed, but then he'd been working harder than he dreamed possible to get ready for this day, along with everyone else on the ranch.

Autumn turned out to be a whirlwind when it came to preparing the spread for its new status as guest ranch, and she also turned out to be a whiz at marketing. He'd bought into the business in early June and now here it was late July and their first guests were arriving. They'd booked their vacation at a deep discount, of course— one of Autumn's many schemes for getting customers to the table, as she put it, so they could dazzle them with the scenery, the accommodations, the quality of the horses and trail rides, and her home cooking. She would press these guests to post recommendations on all the travel sites at the end of their stay, and hope they'd tell their friends, too.

"We aren't looking to make much of a profit this year," she told Jamie one day. "We're looking to turn visitors into lifelong customers." Sounded smart to him.

With all hands on deck—well, all hands except Claire's, since she was too busy making ever more elaborate plans for the interior of his home—they'd scrubbed and polished the Big House until it shone, hauled supplies of every kind in, installed a professional grade washer and dryer in the basement to handle the new laundry load, and made a wheelchair accessible suite on the first floor.

"Why would someone who can't even ride come to a ranch for their vacation?" he asked Ethan.

His friend shrugged. "For the scenery? Fresh air? Maybe to be close to family who can? All I know is we aren't up to code unless we have one."

Autumn worked hard to update the landscaping around the house, and Jamie and Ethan tidied the barn and pens enough to look prosperous, if not clean enough to eat out of. Jamie put some thought into daily sched-ules for the guests and rode all the trails around the spread to make sure they were in good repair. Without Claire. She had moved her things to the bunkhouse now that guests were coming to stay in the Big House, and he barely saw her these days. She'd asked for his credit card and made him up the limit to an uncomfortable amount, then proceeded to order things without even getting his approval. She even had a timeline for the interior, which counted on his contractors having the home built in record time. He had no idea what would happen should something delay progress. The one time he'd balked at Claire's plans, she'd nearly decked him, and for the first time Jamie realized he was a little afraid of the woman he wanted to marry.

He wasn't making any progress on convincing her to be his wife, either. All in all, a sorry state of affairs.

But now his patience was about to pay off, because the first guests were arriving soon and Claire had to follow through on her promise to him. He planned to take full advantage of the fact they'd be sharing a tent during the campout at the end of their company's stay.

He shifted uncomfortably. Best not to think about that for too long, or he'd be unfit for company of any kind. He'd stuck to his side of the bargain—no outright flirting or touching. Not that she'd notice if he did, she was so hung up on her designs. But she was due any moment, and she'd be working with him for the next seven days. All the time in the world for him—and the horses—to work their magic. He hoped by the end of the week her eyes would lose the frantic look they always seemed to hold these days. He'd make it his business to see they did.

He looked forward to greeting the guests later this morning, too. They should pull in about an hour from now, delivered from the airport, and they would take some time to settle in their rooms and have a light brunch before their first ride. Autumn assured him that everyone in the party had prior experience on horseback.

"It's a group of friends," she explained. "Sounds like

they do this every year but the lodge they usually stay at closed, so they're looking for new stomping grounds. I'm counting on you to wow them with the scenery on your rides."

"You just feed them up good every night, and leave the rest to me," he assured her. A group of friends sounded great—a bunch of men looking to get away from their normal lives, wanting a break from girlfriends, wives and kids. He could deal with that.

He plotted a fairly vigorous week of riding and chores, banking on the fact these men probably worked jobs that bored them the rest of the year, so he should show them a little excitement. They could help herd cattle from one part of the property to the other, muck out some stalls—just enough to burn off some energy. Hell, maybe he'd let them repair a fence or two.

"Morning," Claire said behind him, her impatient tone telling him she'd prefer to be back working on his interior design.

He turned and smiled from the sheer joy of seeing her look like herself for the first time in thirteen years. She wore an old pair of jeans that hugged every curve, the same pair of boots she'd worn on Ethan's wedding day, and a plaid shirt that buttoned up the front. She even had her old cowboy hat on. The ring sparkling on her finger made his smile widen.

"Don't you look a sight," he said softly and reached for her.

"Uh uh!" she raised a hand. "Remember our agreement."

Damn. Shrewish as an old maid. Keeping away from women had turned out to be way too damn easy this past month. He was too busy helping Ethan and Autumn and worrying about Claire to even talk to one. What the hell was wrong with her that she couldn't see he only had eyes for her?

"Can't blame a man for his natural reactions when you turn up looking like that."

"What, these ol' things?" she drawled, finally smiling faintly herself. "I can't believe they still fit after all these years."

"They fit mighty well," he agreed.

"That's flirting."

"That's not flirting, that's a genuine compliment."

"Fine, I'll let it slide, but don't push it. I'm in no mood for your shit."

"All right, all right. Give me a second to get my game face on. You might want to relax yours just a bit, you'll scare the guests away." He turned around and composed himself. During the next seven days he had to work a miracle. Treat his customers well, do his job methodically, and show Claire every reason she should want to be his wife without using a drop of his manly charm.

Before he turned back, however, he heard the honk of a horn and the crunch of wheels on the gravel track that led up to the Big House.

"What the heck?"

"Crud—they're early. Autumn's going to have a fit!" Claire said, hurrying after the airport shuttle van.

Jamie strode behind her. Long before they made it

up the rise to the Big House, however, the front door opened, and Autumn stepped onto the porch with a welcoming smile. The doors to the shuttle van opened as well, and guests began to spill out, all talking excitedly.

Jamie stopped in his tracks. Female guests. One, two, three….he counted silently. Five female guests.

None of them over twenty-five.

Claire stopped, too, and turned around, the biggest smile he'd seen in years stretching across her face. "Oh, cowboy—you are in trouble."

THE LOOK ON JAMIE'S FACE was priceless when the ranch's first ever paying guests climbed out of the airport shuttle van. Claire resisted the urge to backtrack to him and lift his jaw up off the driveway. She knew the five young women had first attended a very upscale private boarding school in Maryland together and then moved on to the same university. Riding was their passion, so even now that they had scattered to various jobs and relationships, they still took a yearly trip to a western ranch to catch up on each other's lives and get the chance to spend some serious time in the saddle.

When she'd learned the makeup of the group from Autumn a week ago, and found out Jamie didn't know it yet, she persuaded Autumn not to tell him, if at all possible. Time to get a little bit of that revenge. At first, Autumn demurred, pointing out that Jamie needed to tailor his plans to the group, but when Claire promised she'd make up her own set of plans, just in case, Autumn reluctantly agreed. Last night she laughed and said it turned out to be easy. She told Jamie a group of friends was coming for the week and he just assumed they were men.

"I have to tell you, though," she said, "I don't like practical jokes."

"Even though you got married because of one of them?"

"Nope."

"Neither do I. I'm just getting back at Jamie."

"What did he do?"

"Played a joke on me, what do you think?"

Autumn rolled her eyes. "Typical. Tell me about it."

Claire found she still couldn't tell her that her engagement was fake, and was relieved when Ethan strode in, wanting his dinner. Soon enough this would all be over and she wouldn't have to lie to her friends and family anymore. She just wished thinking about her future travels gave her the kind of pleasure Autumn seemed to get from transforming the Cruz spread into a guest ranch. She looked energized by all her work—and she was pregnant and dealing with morning sickness at the same time. All Claire felt when she bent to the task of winning the Whitfield contract was cold, hard dread.

Jamie had begun to balk at the changes she was making to her design—and at the costs she was incurring when she bought the materials, so she'd stopped consulting him all together.

She knew it was wrong—knew this went against everything interior design was supposed to be. Sure, some designers dictated to their clients instead of listening to them, but that had never been her way.

Until now.

She couldn't take any chances, though. Jamie's tastes were simple—too simple. And he counted costs down to every penny for every little thing. She couldn't involve him in this. When the time came, he'd be bowled over by her improvements to her design. He'd have the most spectacular small log home in all of Montana. And if she covered all the cost overruns herself, what did it matter?

Still, she had the sneaking suspicion it would matter to Jamie. He was so careful with money and so adamant that everyone live within their means and invest wisely. Not a bad way to run a life when all was said and done. It was too bad she couldn't seem to stop spending.

How could she? She had to get back at Daniel somehow, and that meant proving she was better than him. She'd show him he'd screwed up royally when he'd abandoned her and even more royally when he stole her money, and then her business. She had to prove she was the kind of woman worth sticking around for—worth looking up to, admiring…loving.

She twisted the engagement ring around her finger.

If only Jamie's proposal was for real. If only she could stop thinking about revenge and start thinking about….love.

Love.

That was the sticking point, wasn't it? That's how she knew Jamie's proposal was fake in spite of all his elaborate pretenses to the contrary. Not once in all this time had Jamie mentioned love. If he truly wanted her to be his wife, he'd have said it dozens of times by now, right?

Jamie started walking again and she followed him slowly, envying the female guests their obvious excitement about the vacation ahead of them. She wanted to feel that excited about her future, and maybe when this was all over—when she'd designed the interior of a mansion, reveled in the publicity, and proved to the world she had what it took to succeed—she'd take some time to figure out what it was she really wanted in life.

Her gaze drifted back to Jamie and she gave herself a little shake. Besides Jamie.

Time to pull it together and do her job.

Chapter Nine

WOMEN. He was surrounded by women. Autumn greeted the guests one by one as if she'd known them for a lifetime and welcomed them to the Cruz ranch. Claire helped pull luggage out of the van and lug it up to the porch. Jamie joined her, glad for the momentary break now that he'd shaken hands all around.

Women. Five young, trim, shapely, beautiful women. And he wasn't allowed to flirt with any of them. Not even with Claire.

He caught her eye on his second trip from van to porch and shook his head at her. "I'll still win," he said under his breath as he passed.

"No, you won't," she returned cheerfully, but he narrowed his eyes. Underneath that false cheer was real strain. Why couldn't she let this Daniel stuff go? Why was it so important to design the Whitfield interior? So she might get written about in some fancy magazine. Who cared? It didn't look like she was having much fun.

Claire seemed lost. Even more adrift than she'd been for the last thirteen years since she'd left home. Maybe he was wrong. Maybe she didn't need the connection to the land and horses that he always had, but he didn't think so. He thought she'd cut herself loose from her moorings when she'd left home as a teenager, and never really found her footing again. This week outdoors would be good for her.

He hoped.

Autumn turned to them. "Thanks, I've got it from here. We'll get our guests settled and feed them. I'll have them ready to ride at 12:30, just like we planned."

"Okay," Jamie said. He turned to Claire. "Well, back to the drawing board."

"What's wrong?" she asked as they retreated to the stable.

"I was expecting five young bucks ready to throw their backs into some real work, not a gaggle of girls looking for a tea party on hooves."

"Wow. Misogynistic much?" She stepped in front of him and blocked his entry to the stable. "Show me your itinerary."

He shoved her aside with his hip. "I've got it inside." He led the way into the building, his nostrils filling once more with the comforting smell of horses. At least some things were predictable. "Here." He pointed to a lined piece of paper he'd tacked to the wall.

"Test ride," she read and nodded. "Well, that makes sense. We want to know what these women can do." Her eyes traced down his hand-written notes. After an hour long ride on trails close to the Big House to test out the guests' coordination and make sure their temperaments matched those of their mounts, he'd planned to use them to help move the main herd of Cruz cattle to fresh pasture. Ethan would join them, as well as the rest of the hands, but the guests would get to feel useful and get some practice around the herd. He planned to end the afternoon with a trip to a bend in Chance Creek where it was safe to bathe.

"I don't see the problem. This all sounds plenty do-able," Claire said.

"A bunch of women herding cattle?"

"Why not?"

"I don't know…it's men's work," he said.

"I've herded cattle with you before."

Jamie wasn't sure why he was arguing the point. It wasn't like there wouldn't be plenty of men on hand— enough men to do the job without any extra help. "One or two women are fine, but a whole passel of them….I don't know. What if they talk too much and spook the cattle?"

"For heaven's sake, Jamie, it's the twenty-first century. You sound like some ornery backwoods hick. That's not like you."

"Fine. You're right—they can help herd cattle, but the river's out, that's for sure."

She blinked. "What on earth is wrong with you? Have you got heat stroke or something?" She moved toward him as if to feel his forehead, but he stepped away.

"I don't have heat stroke. I'm just not dumb enough to suggest to a bunch of female paying customers that they strip down and swim in a creek while I watch."

Claire laughed out loud. "Actually, it sounds exactly like something you'd do if we hadn't made that bet. Just tell the women to wear their swim suits under their clothes. Problem solved. We'll tote some towels along and dry off in the sunshine before gearing up and riding home."

Jamie nodded brusquely. "All right. Sounds like a plan. So we'll stick to the itinerary for today, at least. Now, how about you? You remember how to ride one of these things? You haven't been to see Storm in weeks."

"Yes, I remember how to ride a horse."

"Prove it. We got the rest of the morning to kill and Autumn doesn't want us in for brunch her first time feeding guests, so I packed a couple of sandwiches. Let's go for a little ride."

"All right." To his surprise Claire didn't fight his suggestion. He thought she might kick up a lively fuss and come up with some chore he hadn't thought of to fill the time, so his heart rose when she strode down the center aisle of the stable until she reached Storm. He watched her approach the gray quarter horse slowly and give her time to check her out before reaching out to touch her. Soon the horse was whickering pleasantly and nuzzling Claire as if she'd known her for years. That was something he shared with Claire—the ability to communicate with horses without saying a word. Claire crooned to Storm for a moment before opening the gate and moving into the stall.

Jamie met her outside a few minutes later astride his own horse, a bay gelding named Walter after his great-granddaddy—the last Lassiter to actually own a ranch. Claire let him take the lead without a struggle, which was odd for her, but he attributed it to her absorption in reacquainting herself with the mare. He could tell she was already half in love with Storm. A few more rides and he'd bet they'd become inseparable. He thought back to her mad dash on Ethan's wedding night. Still half-wild after all this time. Who would credit it, when she acted like such a stick-in-the-mud these days?

Thinking about what else happened that night made him smile.

"Bet I can guess where we're going," she said some minutes later.

"Bet you can."

"I'm not sleeping with you again."

"No, ma'am, of course not. I'll have to be satisfied with the view." He turned his head so she couldn't see his grin and accuse him of flirting with her. When they drew rein on the rise of ground where a scant few weeks ago they'd made love under the moonlight, he didn't even look at Claire. Instead he kept his attention on the meandering river, and the hills far in the distance.

"It is lovely here," she said.

"I won't argue with that. All those years at school in Billings I just couldn't wait to get back."

"Must be nice knowing exactly what you want."

"Hmph. You seem to know what you want." That came out more bitter than he'd intended it.

She took a deep breath, then held it so long he began to worry. Finally she expelled it in a rush. "For now. I want revenge against Daniel. And against you. Then…I don't know."

"You don't need to get revenge against me. You just need to marry me."

"Don't start that again."

"Why?" He couldn't keep the anger from his voice. "Because you're still in love with Daniel?" There. He'd said it aloud.

"I hate Daniel's guts." Her eyes blazed.

"Then turn your back on him and walk away."

She pursed her lips. "I can't do that."

"Why not?"

"You don't know the whole story."

"Tell me."

For a long moment she stayed quiet and he was sure she wasn't going to tell him anything, but then she scanned the horizon and said, "He stole money from me, okay? A lot of money."

Walter sidestepped and Ethan got him back under control. "You call the police?" Once more the urge to beat Ledstrom to a bloody pulp pulsed through his veins.

"No." Claire touched her heels to Storm's flanks and moved away.

"Why not? What the hell happened?" He urged Walter forward, galloped around her and blocked her way. She wouldn't meet his eyes.

"I lent him the money, okay? Without signing anything. I thought he loved me. I thought he was going to ask me to marry him, so I just handed it over. He said he only needed it to secure a deal for a week or two until another property he owned finished up the escrow process. It was no big deal."

Finally he understood and he reeled from the realization of how Claire must have felt. Robbed by the man you wanted to marry. He forced himself to swallow. She'd wanted to marry Daniel—not him. "Then he ran off with that other lady instead and took your money. How much?"

She shook her head. "It doesn't matter."

"Sure it does. Tell me." He waited, calming his own racing mind and breathing easily, like he did when he wanted to soothe a horse. He knew his own mood could transfer to the animals. Maybe it would work on Claire, too. He had to know it all. Had to know what he was up against.

"Ninety thousand dollars."

He whistled low and long. "Damn. No wonder you're so angry."

She stroked Storm's neck, still not looking his way. "There wasn't anything I could do. We didn't sign a contract—I just gave it to him. There's no way to get it back."

"I'm sorry."

"Why should you be sorry? You're the one who made it possible for Ethan to buy me out of the ranch. Now I have six times the money I lost. You're right—I should just walk away."

"But you want to get back at him."

"It's stupid, isn't it?"

"Nah. That ninety thousand dollars is the money you made yourself, with your own hard work. Of course you want it back."

"That's why I can't let this go—I have to get Carl Whitfield's contract."

Jamie looked her over. "If you win the contract, you think you can make peace with the rest of it?"

She finally turned his way. "You mean, forget about Daniel and what he did?"

"Yeah."

She nodded slowly. "Yes. I think so. I think that would be revenge enough."

"All right then." He clicked his tongue at Walter and swung around to head on their way. "Do whatever it takes."

Chapter Ten

WHAT WAS DANIEL DOING RIGHT NOW? Claire wondered as she rode at the tail end of the line of women on their first short ride on the trails around the spread. Her thighs were sore from the unaccustomed exercise and she was sure she'd pay for jumping back into riding so suddenly after so many years away from horses. She couldn't say she regretted it, though. Storm was a sweetheart and it was all she could do not to throw her arms around the mare's neck and hug her again and again like a child who'd just received her first pony. Poor Storm; that wouldn't become her at all and nor would it become an old hand like herself. So she held back, even though it was difficult.

Was Daniel going through her contact list, sucking up to the people she'd cultivated with hard work and great design skills? Was he completing the contracts in progress and stealing more of her money? Her hands tightened on the reins.

Focus, Claire.

She turned her attention to the women and horses

strung out along the trail ahead of her. Maddy, the ring leader who'd made all the reservations and whipped everyone into shape when it was time to head out on the trail, had dark brown curls so thick that when she wrapped them into a ponytail holder they almost stood out straight. She was athletic and strong with a pep that made Claire tired just watching her, and she wasn't surprised to find out she taught physical education at a private school.

Adrienne was tall and thin, almost bony, and moved like a dancer, her blonde hair so white it was practically silver. Apparently she taught cello lessons and managed a city theater in Philadelphia.

Christine was married with a single child and Claire could tell she had some reservations about leaving her toddler behind. Evidently the year before she'd begged off the annual trip because she'd still been nursing and this year the rest of them ganged up on her and forced her to come. Of average height with short brown hair, she wasn't exactly plain, but she wasn't exactly pretty, either.

Liz worked for a publishing company and Claire just bet she looked snazzy in her business suits. Shapely, yet model thin, she wore her sleek, auburn hair up in a severe knot, but Claire had a feeling when it came down, the woman would be spectacular. She'd be the one who gave Jamie a run for his money on this trip.

Angel rounded out the group. A plush, sweet girl— Claire somehow couldn't make herself call her a woman—with wide blue eyes and honey blonde hair, she was obviously the mascot of the group, and the rest of the women seemed to automatically assume she would need extra help navigating her way through the world.

As Jamie assigned each of them a horse, they'd exchanged glances behind his back, biting their lips, widening their eyes and raising their brows to express their appreciation of his fine physique. Claire wanted to slap each of them upside the head, and was grateful she'd had the presence of mind to initiate the no flirting or touching rule. Sure, Jamie had to help the women on their horses, and more than one of them tried to take the opportunity to cop a feel of his muscled arms and broad shoulders, but he was doing his level best not to encourage them and she could feel the effort that took from here.

Would he make it through the week? She followed Christine's Appaloosa around a bend and ambled on. Maybe the question she really ought to be asking was, why did she hope so?

JAMIE WAS RELIEVED TO CONFIRM all five female guests were more than comfortable riding. Autumn had told him their background, but you never knew about a rider until you saw them in the saddle. They each had the easy grace of someone who'd grown up around horses, and Angel was the only one he'd had to switch mounts for. He'd seen right away she needed the most docile of geldings, and gave her an older bay named Sweetness.

Even the cattle herding had gone just fine. He'd positioned the women carefully and for the most part they'd stuck where they'd been told to be and did just what he asked them. Liz, the hot woman who looked like a model but did something with books, often jumped the gun instead of waiting for instructions, but her instincts were good and no harm had been done. Now he hobbled the horses while the womenfolk whooped and hollered their way into the lazy current of Chance Creek.

"Aren't you joining us, Jamie?" Maddy called. Spunky girl, that one.

"Be there in a minute," he called back. Just like the women, he'd worn bathing trunks under his jeans. Strange way to take a swim if you asked him, but then it wouldn't do to leave the family jewels on display with all these women around. Might start a riot.

When he made his way down to the river's edge their guests were all swimming in the shallow pool carved out by the bend in the creek. Claire was standing on the bank, just struggling out of her top, her jeans already in a heap by her feet. He smiled at her flushed cheeks when she reappeared. She wore a scarlet bikini with white trim that looked spectacular against her tan skin.

He bit back the flattering words that rushed to his lips. Nope—even compliments counted as flirting this week, and he wouldn't be caught.

"Last one in's a rotten egg," he said and cannon-balled into the center of the shrieking women. When he bobbed up to the surface and found himself surrounded by them, he realized he'd made a serious error. Dripping, gasping women eyed him with a mixture of attraction and playful fury and barely a second passed before Liz splashed him full in the face with a wall of water.

"Get him!"

They attacked from all sides. Splashing, shouting, laughing women in the skimpiest of skimpy bikinis vied with all their might to douse him. Jamie defended himself as best he could, smacking his powerful arms down and across the surface of the creek to send tidal waves of water back at them. He glimpsed Claire still on the bank, her hands on her hips and her head cocked, like a coach about to blow her whistle the first time she spotted an infraction.

How the hell did you have a water fight with five bikini-clad women without flirting or touching? Jamie wondered wildly. He locked eyes with Liz and saw the challenge there.

Uh oh.

Sure enough, she moved closer and he read her intentions in her face. She wanted to dunk him, and in the process she'd get her hands all over his wet, slippery body.

Nope. No can do, lady.

Jamie gulped in a breath of air and submerged himself, fought through the tangle of arms and legs of the women paddling in the water around him and came up some ten feet away. He took another breath and stroked to the farthest side of the creek.

"Okay, ladies, give our cowboy a break," Claire called from the bank as several of the women made to follow him, Liz in the lead.

"Awww."

Just like children, Jamie thought. Ravenous, man-eating children.

He stifled a laugh, knowing damn well if it wasn't for Claire's presence and the hope of being with her at the end of this week from hell, he'd still be in the midst of that water fight, taking advantage of every opportunity those women offered him.

But that was the old Jamie—the man who hadn't invested in the Cruz ranch, the man who wasn't building a life for himself here, a life he hoped included Claire.

If he was sleeping with her, he'd never give any of these women a second glance. He floated on the water, already getting cold in this lazy bend in the mountain-fed stream, and watched Claire carefully pick her way in. She was lovely, but far more cautious than she used to be. Her mother's betrayal had driven her from the ranch and while he read her love for this land in every glance she caressed it with, he also read the fear there. How angry she must have been—how hurt—to leave home, practically abandon her family, and stay away from horses—horses, for crying out loud!—the one thing she loved above all else.

He had to convince her that with Aria gone, it was safe to change her mind and stay.

THAT LIZ WAS A PUSHY ONE, Claire thought as she took a few strokes through the water. Now that their fun was over, the women were chatting and laughing, playing in the water like teenagers, but rapidly beginning to get chilled. A couple were already headed to the banks to climb out and lay on their towels in the sun to dry off. Claire kept to herself, barely rippling the surface with a smooth breast stroke. She loved this time of day, when the afternoon wound down and the comfort of a Montana summer evening loomed ahead.

Normally she'd still be hard at work designing interiors and fielding phone calls from clients who needed reassurance that yes, she'd get their projects done before the deadline. But growing up, this was the time she'd be shirking her duties in the kitchen to eke out a few more minutes with the horses before heading up to dinner.

There was no way she could get out of cleaning up the dishes and tidying the kitchen after dinner, however, so she raced through those chores, then joined her father outside on the porch to watch the sun set and the shadows gather first in the valley, then finally on the distant hills. Her father didn't talk much, but what he did have to say meant something, so she patiently waited for his words, watching him whittle away a stick to pass the time, sometimes with her own pocket knife in hand.

She used to be like Liz—pushing and pushing for what she really wanted, but that had changed the day she found her mother and Mack MacKenzie together. She'd left the ranch, left her family, left her dream of being a rodeo queen and becoming her father's partner in the business. She was still pushy, but only for surface things—only for things that didn't really matter one damn bit.

She struck out for the far side with a determined overhand crawl, suddenly needing movement to block out her confusion. She was beginning to think this week of ranch work was the worst idea she'd ever agreed to. Every familiar landmark around here dredged up old emotions best left undisturbed.

When she bumped into something hard, she splashed to a stop and came up for air gasping. Jamie stood chest deep in the water looking down at her quizzically.

"No touching!" she sputtered.

"I didn't touch a thing, you swam right into me," he said, holding his hands up.

"You could have gotten out of my way."

He stepped to the side. "Be my guest."

Claire turned her back on him and swam the other way. Time for her to join the ladies sunning themselves on the bank. Maybe if she kept herself surrounded by the women, Jamie's charms would stop insinuating themselves into her like streams of liquid fire into her veins. Even when he wasn't actively flirting he had to be the sexiest man she knew. In fact, without the shallow flirtation, he was sexier. Because underneath all that smooth charm was a man who loved horses, was as smart as a whip, and who knew what he wanted and exactly how to get it.

Up on the grassy riverbank, she spread her towel near the other women and lay down, tuning in to their conversation.

Liz sat up. "Tell us the truth, Claire—is Jamie a real cowboy or did you hire some model and train him?"

"He's the real deal," she said, instantly on alert. She

didn't like the way Liz had set her sights on Jamie like a heat seeking missile locked on its target.

"Autumn's husband is a knockout, too," Adrienne said. "Too bad he's off limits."

Murmured assents from all around.

"Any more handsome cowboys hidden on this ranch?" Liz asked.

Claire shrugged, then realized they wouldn't be able to see the gesture since she was lying down. "I guess. We employ about fifteen hands on and off. You would have seen most of them this afternoon."

"There were some cute ones," Angel spoke up in her dreamy voice. "They didn't get too close to us, though."

"Too busy working," Claire pointed out.

"I guess. Will they join us for dinner?" Liz asked.

Jeez, did the woman never let up? "You'll have to ask Autumn about that. I just do horses, not dinner." She'd let Autumn know what the women were saying, though. The hands might not mind hanging around for supper and entertaining the female customers. Although, that might open a whole new can of worms. Would they expect to get paid for their time? She pictured Ethan and Autumn building a bunkhouse for studly cowboys somewhere on the property and running a reverse bordello. Rich eastern women could fly in and pick their man for the weekend. They'd make money hand over fist.

"I wouldn't mind renting a cowboy for the week," Maddy piped up, echoing her thoughts. "Especially Jamie."

"Maddy!" Several of the women pretended to be shocked, but from the giggles all around it seemed like they all had similar feelings.

"Our hands are real people, working real hard to keep themselves and their families housed and fed. You're all adults and so are they, but we hired them to run a ranch, not to provide…entertainment…for our guests," Claire said.

"You're engaged, so you can't lust after the cow-boys," Adrienne said, pointing at her ring. "But that doesn't mean the rest of us can't."

"I'm engaged to…" She shut her mouth with a snap. Had she really been about to say she was engaged to Jamie? Sure, it would keep the ladies from hitting on him—she hoped—but that didn't make it a smart thing to do. Jamie would take that ball and run with it.

"Who are you engaged to, Claire?" Jamie drawled behind her, and Claire's cheeks burned. A glance over her shoulder told her he was standing thigh deep in the water near the riverbank. She should have known he'd listen in to their conversation.

"No one," she said.

The women looked from her to Jamie.

She felt a distinct coolness settle over the group. "Are you engaged to him?" Adrienne asked.

"No," she said at the same time Jamie said, "Yes."

"Well, which is it?" Maddy said.

"I…haven't made up my mind," Claire faltered.

Jamie climbed out of the water and stood dripping on her.

"You're wearing his ring," Adrienne pointed out coldly. "Looks to me like you've made up your mind."

Claire searched for a way to explain what had happened without sounding like a complete idiot. She was grateful when Jamie chimed in, "Better get going or we'll miss dinner!"

The women headed for the horses and Claire trailed after them. This was getting more and more out of hand.

Chapter Eleven

SEVERAL HOURS LATER, Jamie sat down in one of the folding chairs perched on the tiny front deck of the cabin he'd lived in since Mack Mackenzie cleared out six years back, and Alex Cruz hired him on full time. With a back bedroom, a tiny bathroom, and a front room that served as kitchen, dining room, living room and office, it was small but functional, and he welcomed it as a way to leave behind the father who never approved of his choices in life and the mother who understood her son but couldn't stand up to her husband.

He appreciated the peace living alone afforded him, and he appreciated his work and the lifestyle the ranch made possible. At first he saved his money because he had little to spend it on, and the habits instilled by his parents went too deep to bypass, but soon his dream of buying into the Cruz ranch coalesced in his mind.

He worried that Alex Cruz would turn him down because he wanted to pass on the ranch unencumbered to his son, but as time went by, Jamie realized something Ethan didn't seem to: Alex was worried about Aria

Cruz's expensive spending habits. More than once he caught Alex going over his books, muttering about income and expenses. From bits of conversations he overheard, he knew whenever his boss brought it up with his wife, Aria flew into a rage. Ethan remained oblivious, but Jamie went on saving every scrap of money he could drum up, convinced that someday Alex would look for a partner—if not an outright buyer—for the ranch, and he wanted to be ready for it.

When Alex and Aria died in a car accident the previous summer, Jamie braced himself for the day Ethan learned the truth about his inheritance. It had been worse than he'd imagined, and there were times he worried that Ethan would fold under the weight of his worries. Jamie had never imagined his chance to buy in the ranch would come under these circumstances and he was gripped with guilt every time he thought about stepping forward and offering the solution, afraid Ethan would see him as a vulture who'd waited for death to arrive to make his move.

So when Autumn came up with the idea of the guest ranch and convinced Ethan to sell part of their land to raise money to start the business, he was overwhelmed with gratitude. Here was his chance to step in and help—truly help—his friend without his good intentions being taken for bad.

Jamie didn't want to split up the ranch, nor did he need to wrest control of it out of Ethan's hands. All he wanted was a place to hang his hat and a chance to work with his beloved horses for the rest of his life.

And to marry Claire.

That wasn't so bad, was it?

"Got room for one more?" As if conjured out of his daydreams, Claire stood at the base of the steps. She must have walked up the path from the Big House without him noticing.

He patted the arm of the other folding chair. "I saved this one for you."

She sat down with a little groan and Jamie chuckled. "Feeling a little sore, greenhorn?"

"I can't believe it's been thirteen years since I've done any serious riding. What was I thinking?"

"I don't know—what were you thinking?" he asked easily. Her warmth made it likelier than usual she'd open up to him, but Claire was like a skittish colt. One wrong move and she'd dance away from him and he'd be back to square one.

"I was thinking I had to put the ranch behind me. Put my family behind me."

"Your mother?"

After a moment she nodded. "Yeah, Mom. I just couldn't stand being near her after I knew she was sleeping around. I couldn't stand that my dad put up with it. Their whole marriage was a lie." She shrugged. "Doesn't matter anymore, does it? They're gone."

"I think for all their troubles your parents loved each other."

Claire snorted. "Yeah. Look where that got them. If that's what love looks like, count me out."

"People aren't as simple as you'd like them to be.

You don't know what really went on in your parents' marriage."

"I know that my mother slept with Mack."

"You don't know why."

"Sure I do—because my mother needed everything to be about her. She couldn't share the limelight for a second."

"She never seemed to really belong here," Jamie said. Just like Claire, Aria kept trying to leave the ranch. Her yearly trips lasted two, three, even four months at a time. But she always came back. "I think she loved your dad no matter how she behaved."

"If my husband ever cheated on me, I'd leave him so fast it'd make his head spin. And I'd never, ever come back."

She was on her feet, down the porch steps, and striding along the path to the Big House before he could stop her. So much for a nice, friendly visit.

Jamie remained motionless in the folding chair as darkness settled over him, a new thought keeping him in place.

Is that what was going on here? Did Claire think he was the type to cheat?

He forced himself to stay calm as he thought this through. He considered himself a steady man, but did his actions match that view?

Not really. Not when it came to women. He wasn't a Casanova, but he'd had his share of casual relationships over the years. And he flirted a lot.

Flirting.

He'd be damned. No wonder she'd made that part of the bet—it was the key to the whole puzzle of the way she acted around him. Claire wanted him—he knew she did now that she'd given in to her impulses and made love to him. It wasn't a lack of desire that held her back.

It was a lack of trust.

Shame pierced Jamie like a white-hot knife. Why should she trust him? All she'd ever seen him do was flirt with every woman in reach. He'd behaved just like Mack, hadn't he? Teasing her, touching her, showing her he wanted her, and then sleeping with other women every time she turned around. He'd always told himself he was just filling the time in until she was ready to see him for the man he was and date him seriously, but what if she'd seen the type of man he was all along?

Was he a player in her eyes—the kind of guy who used women and never looked back? He tamped down the flare of anger that twisted his gut. Surely Claire knew he would never give another woman the time of day if she went out with him. But was it fair for him to wait to change his ways until after she'd said yes?

No.

It didn't work like that at all.

He had to prove to her ahead of time that he was a man she could trust. How could he have made such a mistake when he thought he had everything planned out?

Damn, damn, damn. He'd really set himself up for failure. Now all his hopes for future happiness came down to this one week. He had to prove he could ignore five horny female guests all vying for his attention.

Maybe if he succeeded she'd realize he loved only her.

CLAIRE WAS SURPRISED to find Autumn in the kitchen of the bunkhouse when she got back. She was sitting at the small table, sipping a cup of tea and fiddling with an envelope. It still seemed strange to see the renovations her brother had done to the building. The kitchen was the same as ever, but the large room that used to hold ten old-fashioned iron-framed bunk beds for the hired hands had been turned into a fair-sized living room and two medium-sized bedrooms with walk-in closets. Ethan used the closet off of his and Autumn's bedroom as an office. She'd hung up a few pairs of jeans and shirts in hers, but they barely made a dent in the empty space.

"Ethan's doing the overnight shift at the Big House," Autumn said.

Claire helped herself to tea and joined her at the table. They'd set up a cot in the small laundry room off the back entrance of the Big House and whoever took the night shift could sleep unless a guest needed them. It didn't seem right for newlyweds to sleep apart, though. Autumn took in her expression and laughed.

"I'm too tired for cuddling, anyway. It's all right. Pretty soon we'll hire someone to do the night shift. We just don't want to spend too much money until we start making some."

Claire nodded. "What's that?" She gestured to the envelope.

Autumn sighed. "I'm not sure, but something told

me not to give it to Ethan. I hope I'm not making a mistake giving it to you." She handed it over and Claire examined it.

The paper was cream colored, the handwriting bold and sharp—but still a woman's penmanship. It was addressed to Aria Cruz.

Claire's heart sank. "Ethan must have dealt with plenty of mail addressed to my parents after their deaths. Why not give him this one?"

"All of your parents' business and personal correspondence went to their post office box in town. Mail isn't delivered out here—you know that. Look at the front of the envelope again."

She did so, not understanding at first. Then she saw what Autumn meant. "There's no postmark."

"But the return address says Canada."

"I don't understand." Autumn was right, the return address was Canadian, but there was no name—only a street number and city in British Columbia.

"I don't either, but I think whoever sent the letter hand-delivered it."

"Meaning they're here in town." A shiver traced down her spine, she couldn't say why. "So why don't they know my mother is dead?"

"Maybe they just got here. Maybe they haven't talked to anyone yet. We need to let them know what's happened." Autumn rubbed her forehead. "It isn't fair of me to pass this on to you, but Ethan's had such a hard time of it so far. I couldn't force myself to give it to him."

"I know." Claire looked at the letter grimly. "You

think I should open it right now?"

Autumn shrugged. "No time like the present."

She slid a thumb under the flap and tore open the creamy envelope. When she pulled out the pages inside, the same handwriting dashed thick, solid lines across the paper. She unfolded them and turned them over. The letter was signed, *Morgan*. Turning back to the front, she read:

Dear Mom,

Where are you?

She dropped the letter on the table as if she'd been burned.

Chapter Twelve

W HEN THE BACK DOOR OPENED at five the following morning, Claire was still sitting in the kitchen, the letter in her hand. Autumn had read it, too, of course, but she'd gone to bed hours ago, casting concerned looks back over her shoulder when Claire kept her seat.

Ethan's face registered his surprise when he saw her there, but he crossed to the counter and started the coffee maker. "Morning, Sunshine."

"Morning."

"I thought you might be over at Jamie's." Ethan grabbed a frying pan, put it on the stove and got a package of bacon out of the refrigerator.

She shook her head dully. "It's not like that between us."

He grunted. "If it's not like that, then why'd you agree to marry him?" He spread the strips of bacon in the pan, then put some bread in the toaster.

That brought her out of her reverie. She still couldn't fathom why Ethan was still pretending he didn't know their engagement was a farce.

"I'm not in the mood for this."

"All right, all right. You guys have a spat or something?" When she didn't answer, he moved to the refrigerator and took out the eggs. "I think he'll make you a terrific husband. He sure surprised me when he bought a partnership in the ranch," he commented. "Who would have thought a cowboy like him saved his pennies like that."

She played with the envelope, turning it over and over in her hands. "None of us really knows anyone else."

He frowned at her bitter tone. "I wish I knew you better. You're the one who stayed away so long."

"I can't stand the ghosts here."

"Ghosts?"

"Yeah—ghosts," she said. She flicked the envelope across the table so it slid to a stop in front of his place setting. "Mom wasn't who you thought she was. Hell, she wasn't who I thought she was and I knew far more about her than you did."

"What are you talking about?"

"Mom. Her trips. Spending all that money? You know she had affairs, don't you?"

"What?" Ethan set down his spatula with a clatter on the counter and turned from the sizzling bacon and eggs. "What the hell do you mean?"

"She slept around, Ethan. She slept with Mack and who knows who else. But that's not all she did. All those trips to Europe? They were fake. Turns out she never even went there. All those months she spent away from home every year? She wasn't traveling at all. She was spending time with her other family. Her real family."

She'd never seen her younger brother at such a loss for words. No surprise there. The news was enough to flatten anyone.

"Her real family?" he finally choked out.

"Read the letter. It's from her daughter, Morgan. Her Canadian daughter. Wondering when the hell she's coming home." Claire's voice cracked and tears filled her eyes as the enormity of the letter's message finally sank in. She scraped her chair back, got to her feet and ran blindly from the room.

WHEN THE BARN DOOR OPENED, Jamie expected Claire to saunter in. Instead, it was Ethan, hatless, as pale as a ghost, clutching an envelope in his hands.

"What happened?" It had to be something awful, judging by the look on his friend's face.

Ethan leaned against the wall by the door and shook his head. Jamie didn't think he'd ever seen his friend outside without a hat on. It was like seeing him naked.

"My mother," Ethan said. He shook the letter in his hand. "Ah, Jesus, Jamie. She…"

Jamie's heart sank. Aria Cruz had already broken Ethan's heart more than once. By dying, and by drowning the family business in debt. How could she hurt Ethan more from beyond the grave?

"She had another family," Ethan said, looking bewildered. "A daughter. A man, I guess."

"Wait…hold up…another family?" That was the last thing Jamie expected.

"I have an older sister. Another older sister. Half sister. Her name's Morgan."

"How could your mother have another family?"

"Autumn just helped me look Morgan up on the internet. We found her address and her birthdate. We figured out the timing of it all. I checked my dad's notebooks, too. As much as I can piece together, Mom spent a year at the University of Victoria when she was 21. She studied anthropology, if you can believe that. I think she always wanted more excitement than Montana was going to give her. She spent that year at UVic because they have a real top-notch anthropology program—but she was already engaged to my dad at the time. They'd been dating for years. He gave her a ring when they graduated high school."

Jamie grunted. Pretty typical for these parts.

"I think she had a fling with a professor, because a guy with the same last name as Morgan still works there in the Anthropology Department. She must have gotten pregnant right away and had the baby at the end of the school year. She didn't return to Montana until fall. Dad wrote that she was doing field work over the summer. That must have been the story she fed him."

"She came home and left her kid behind?"

"That's the part I can't figure out. Why would she do that? Autumn thinks it's because she loved Dad. She still wanted to marry him."

Jamie thought this over. "This other guy—did he

take the kid?"

"Must have."

"Hell."

"All those trips. She wasn't going to Europe, Jamie."
Ethan met his gaze. "She was with them."

Jamie whistled silently. What a thing to find out
about your mother.

"That's not the worst of it, either."

It got worse?

"Her daughter—this Morgan person. She's here in
town. And she doesn't know Mom's dead."

Chapter Thirteen

CLAIRE ONLY MANAGED to snatch an hour of sleep after breaking the news of her mother's duplicity to Ethan. Now, ready or not, she had to face another day of wrangling clients with Jamie, while trying to figure out the best way to handle the latest trouble her mother had brought to the family. She decided to check in at the Big House and find out from Autumn when the guests would be ready to ride, before heading over to the stables to help Jamie prepare. When she entered the Big House's kitchen, Autumn was hard at work. She looked just as tired as Claire felt. Autumn already had way too much on her plate, being pregnant and starting a business all at the same time.

"Can I help you?" Claire said. "You should be resting more." She crossed the room and pulled out plates from a cabinet. At the very least she could set the table.

"Just keep those women entertained and out of the house long enough for me to make up all the beds this morning," Autumn said. "I couldn't sleep last night. Then Ethan got me up early. You know why."

Claire didn't feel like talking about that. "Did your guests offer to pay you to line up some dates for them with the hot local cowboys?"

"Just about," Autumn said. She sighed. "I can't blame them, though. I can't resist the local cowboys, either."

"You better be resisting all the local cowboys except my brother," Claire said lightly.

"You know it."

"You two are sickening, you know," Claire said, putting out cups and glasses. She hoped her voice sounded normal, because she sure as hell didn't feel like herself. She felt like she was walking a tightrope over a chasm so deep she couldn't see the bottom. How could she have a sister she'd never met?

"Just wait until you're married—you and Jamie'll be just like us. Now, come on, we can't ignore the elephant in the room any longer. Someone's got to go see Morgan and tell her the truth."

"She can go right back where she came from, for all I care." Claire yanked open the silverware drawer and grabbed a handful of knives and forks.

"I'm sure she will go back where she came from, once she knows," Autumn said quietly. She was slicing potatoes methodically for home fries.

"It's not my job to tell her."

"Whose job is it? Mine?" The edge to her voice surprised Claire. Usually Autumn managed to keep her calm.

"Sorry. I know I'm being a bitch," Claire said, "but

what right does that woman have to come here and make things worse than they already are? I don't need this right now." She surveyed the table. Napkins next.

"I know things have been hard for you."

"You don't know the half of it."

"You're right." Autumn put her knife down and leaned on the counter. Claire felt like a heel for being so cranky. "You hardly know me, so I don't expect you to confide in me, but I'm here if you need a friend, okay?" Claire appreciated the words, but the color of Autumn's face worried her. Although it was too early for Autumn to be showing, she'd suffered from morning sickness these last few weeks. Maybe all that energy she'd been projecting lately was entirely fake. She didn't look good this morning.

"Look, I'll handle it," Claire found herself saying. "Don't worry about a thing. I'll drive into town and see her at her hotel. I'll tell her about Mom and make sure she gets back on a plane and leaves us alone. Please tell me you'll rest this morning when breakfast is done."

"I need to do the bedrooms while you're out."

"Let me make a few calls. We need more help."

Autumn shook her head. "We can't afford more help."

"You might not be able to, but I can."

At least for now.

JAMIE SURVEYED HIS FUTURE HOME with satisfaction. Now that the roof was done, the construction crew had begun work inside. The beautiful log cabin he'd envisioned had come into being, with a wide verandah and banks of windows to let its inhabitants drink in the view. It stood as one with the property, its log walls echoing those of the Big House, but it was far enough away from the main part of the spread to make a private home for him and Claire.

He shoved his hands in his pockets and let his gaze run over the portion of the Cruz ranch that was now his. Well, it was all his in a way, since he was co-owner with Ethan, but these hundred acres were marked as his to do with as he wished. And what he wished was to marry Claire and raise a family here. Maybe others would think he was foolish to bet on a relationship that so far had gone nowhere, but one thing he'd learned during the prolonged battle with his father for control of his own life was that if he fixed his goal in his mind, things had a way of arranging themselves so he got there. His goal was to marry Claire and settle down in this house, then run the ranch with Ethan and Autumn, his kids and their kids growing up together the way he'd grown up with Ethan.

First he had to get through the rest of this week, however. And pray the news about Aria's other child didn't send his intended into cardiac arrest. He urged Walter back around and galloped down the track toward the Big House. Time to get to work.

Back at the stable, he and a very quiet Claire helped their guests saddle up for a ride over to the eastern pastures for the age-old chore of checking and repairing fences. He'd argued that no lady guest was going to want to participate in that kind of activity, but Claire overrode him, saying, "They wanted a ranch experience, they're getting a ranch experience." He had a feeling that the women's attempts at flirtation, combined with this latest development, were getting on her nerves and she wanted to punish them. That was all right by him; her jealousy told him she had some kind of feelings for him, even if she wasn't ready to admit them.

The ride out to the pastures was calm enough. Even Liz seemed somewhat tired from the previous day's activities, but as the sun climbed higher in the sky and temperatures rose, Jamie sensed dissension in the ranks.

"This isn't nearly as pretty as yesterday's ride," Adrienne said, flipping her white-blonde hair over her shoulder.

"It isn't a joy ride. We're doing a job, right, Jamie?" Maddy said. "This is a working ranch, remember? We all agreed it's what we wanted to do."

"We're just riding in a line," Adrienne said.

"We're riding in a line along fences," Maddy said. "We're making sure nothing's broken. That's an important job."

"She's right," Jamie said. "Nothing cuts down a ranch's profits like losing a few hundred head of cattle. One rotten post or broken wire can cost a rancher a bundle of cash."

"And he can make it back by charging his guests a bundle of cash," Adrienne said, just loudly enough he knew he was meant to hear the snide remark.

"Ma'am, if you're feeling poorly, I can take you back

to the Big House," Claire chimed in from further down the line, her tone barely respectful. Jamie tensed, knowing she was already at the end of her tether and liable to snap at a problematic guest.

"I'm not feeling poorly," Adrienne said. "I'm feeling bored."

Jamie bit back the urge tell her exactly how he was feeling. "Well, you're lucky, then, because here's our first stop." He dismounted Walter and gestured at a post that was bent so far over it would have scraped the short range grass if the wires attached to it weren't holding it up. After a quick rundown of the correct way to repair such a problem, he let the women take turns using the tools and together they reset the fence post properly. All of the women seemed to enjoy the chance to get their hands dirty, so to speak, except Adrienne, who remained surly throughout the process. Jamie shot Claire a pleading look when they all re-mounted and breathed a sigh of relief when she managed to get Adrienne aside. Maybe the woman was having female troubles.

Or maybe she was just a spoiled bitch. Either way, he wouldn't be hard pressed to keep from flirting with her. He couldn't abide a whiner.

"Who wants to ride beside me and help spot the next problem?" he called and wasn't surprised at all when Liz pushed forward.

"Bet I'm good at it," she said. "I can spot a mistake a mile away."

"I'm sure you'll do fine," he said gallantly, and glanced back at Claire again. She and Adrienne were talking heatedly now, the blonde gesturing widely.

"I'm sorry this morning's chore isn't to your liking," he heard Claire say. "I've already offered to escort you back to the lodge. I don't know what else I can do."

"Jamie! Claire! Good to see you."

Jamie swiveled in his saddle to see Rob and Cab riding up.

"Hi, Rob. Cab. Good to see you again!" Claire rode forward, probably happy to shelve her conversation with Adrienne for the time being. "Ladies, let me introduce you to more of Chance Creek's most eligible bachelors, Rob Matheson and Cab Johnson. Rob's family owns the spread next door to the Cruz ranch and Cab is the county sheriff. Rob, Cab, meet our very first guests. This is Maddy, Adrienne, Christine, Liz and Angel. The ladies are helping us ride fences this morning, but I'm just about to ride back to the house with Adrienne. She's not too keen on fences."

"I'm fine with fences, Claire," Adrienne spoke up swiftly, her gaze running up and down Rob's body with open appreciation. "I told you, I was feeling a little poorly for a minute there, but I'm much better now."

Claire's expression spoke volumes as Adrienne nudged her horse forward through the crowd to where she could shake hands with Rob and Cab.

"What's your spread like, Rob?" Christine asked brightly. "Is it as nice as this one?"

"Much nicer," Rob said and seemed gratified to get a chuckle from his feminine audience. "And about twice the size. We know how to run things right on the

Double Bar K."

"Is that so?" Jamie said. "Rumor has it you know how to run a video camera, anyway."

"Keep your mouth shut, Lassiter," Rob growled and Jamie nodded, but smiled. Rob was still trying to live down the bad reputation he'd gained as a result of Ethan's last practical joke on him—the joke that had spurred Rob to place the video Wife Wanted ad on the internet for Ethan, and which had resulted in Autumn coming to Chance Creek and falling in love with him.

Ethan, knowing Rob was a ladies' man, had waited until he was out at the local bar one night and sneaked into Rob's house to set up a video camera, back drop, and lights in his bedroom, so that when he brought his date home later that evening it looked like he'd planned ahead to make a sex video. The poor young lady took one look and made a run for it, but not before spreading the gossip far and wide about what a sleaze Rob was. He'd been hard put to get a date ever since.

Jamie figured Rob thought this new crop of women were ignorant of his sordid past. No wonder he managed to show up in the east pasture out of the blue. Adrienne seemed more than willing to bite, and as far as Jamie was concerned, Rob could have her. Heck, he could have the whole damn lot of them. Although it served him right if he never got laid for the rest of his life. After all, it was Rob's fault Claire still didn't believe he really wanted to marry her.

It's your own damn fault, too, for being such a flirt.

Well, he was doing everything he could to remedy

that.

"We've got some time to kill," Rob said. "Mind if we tag along?"

"Not at all," Liz said.

"I'd sure like to hear what it's like to be a sheriff," Maddy said, taking a place next to Cab.

Jamie smiled. Cab wasn't often the center of attention when it came to women, and he deserved his fair share. Maddy had just raised her position in his books, but then she seemed much more down to earth than her friends.

"Cab's got lots of good stories. Just keep pressing him until he tells you one or two," Jamie called to her, then waited for Christine and Angel to move after the others before joining Claire in the rear.

"Just in time," she said, nodding at Cab and Rob. "Adrienne was about to flip her lid. She wanted us to reroute the whole morning's ride somewhere to a 'scenic vista' as she put it. Can you believe her?"

"Maybe we should start telling the women our plans the night before so they can opt in or out," Jamie said.

"What if they opt out? Then Autumn will be stuck with them all morning while she's trying to clean up."

"I guess we'd better discuss that with Autumn and Ethan. At least we should be good for now. You all right?"

"I'm fine," Claire said and urged her horse past him.

And they were. In fact, they managed to cover more of the fencing than Jamie had even hoped for, with Rob and Cab moving the group along swiftly from post to post. Rob flirted openly with Adrienne, Liz, and even Christine. Cab regaled Maddy and Angel with stories of various Chance Creek criminals' exploits, and everyone helped out when they found a downed post.

Afterwards, Rob and Cab rode all the way back to the Big House with them and seemed more than happy to join the crowd for lunch when Autumn asked them to.

"You have enough food?" Jamie asked her when everyone went in to wash up. "I can always feed Claire back at my place."

"I've got plenty," she assured him. "Ethan warned me they were coming. They stopped by to talk to him before riding out to find you guys."

"Got it."

Inside, Jamie was surprised to see Tracey Richards behind the half wall that divided the kitchen from the rest of the great room. She was dishing salad into bowls and arranging them on a tray to bring to the guests. He nodded at her and took a seat next to Claire at the Cruz's huge dining room table. The great room was two stories high, with floor to ceiling windows that framed the most spectacular view he'd ever seen from inside a building. He hoped to reproduce the effect in his own house when it was done, but he had to hand it to Ethan and Claire's parents—they really built a beautiful home.

As the table filled up, the roar of conversation filled the room and mouth-watering aromas wafted from Autumn's kitchen.

"I'm starved," he said to Claire.

"Me, too."

"Hey, lovebirds," Rob bellowed from the far end of the table. Everyone hushed and glanced his way. "Where are you going for your honeymoon?"

CLAIRE SLAMMED THE DOOR on her Civic, reversed, swung the car around and headed down the lane to the highway as fast as she dared. Somehow she'd clung to her temper as Rob tormented her and Jamie throughout lunch.

Now she was driving to town to confront her mother's other daughter, the one she didn't even want to admit existed. Morgan. What kind of a name was that?

What kind of a woman was her mother?

It didn't matter, did it? She'd done without Aria for a long, long time—ever since she'd found her with Mack in the stable. She'd always envisioned her mother having a string of foreign lovers when she traveled to Europe on her months-long jaunts. So why was it worse to know she'd only gone back to one man, time and time again? Or at least, she'd gone back to her daughter.

Maybe her mother's affair with that daughter's father was short-lived.

Maybe it wasn't.

She couldn't be sure of anything at this point.

As she pulled into the small parking lot at the Big Sky Motel, on Fourth Avenue, she ran her gaze over the nondescript two story building. It was clean, but that was about all you could say about it. A family run operation, like so many businesses in town, it had no pretensions to rating five stars.

She bypassed the front office and took a set of concrete stairs up to the second level, walking down a long exterior hallway to room number 29. She took a deep breath and knocked.

A second later the door flung open. "Mom!" A woman with blue eyes and hair the same shade as Claire's but long and wavy, looked out, and her excited smile turned to a puzzled frown. "Oh, I'm sorry. I was expecting someone else.

"I know," Claire said. "You were expecting my mother."

Chapter Fourteen

JAMIE SAT ON THE WOODEN RAILINGS of a corral with their five female guests watching Rob demonstrate barrel riding. Rob should've been one of the foremost contenders on the circuit, but he lacked the drive to really go for it. Or maybe the confidence. As the youngest of four boys in a very wealthy family, Jamie thought Rob was never pushed hard enough in anything. Holt Matheson, Rob's father, still kept his finger in every pie on that ranch, and Jake, Ned and Luke were all capable men in their own right. There wasn't much left over for Rob to take charge of.

Like his brothers, Rob had his own cabin on the property, but in Jamie's opinion that wasn't separation enough from his parents to truly allow him to grow up. Rob wasn't completely spoiled, but he wasn't on track to make anything of himself, either. He was bored. Anyone could see that. And bored men made trouble wherever they went. Rob sure did.

Maybe he should talk to Ethan about hiring Rob on if Claire didn't stick to the job. He was a natural entertainer. He loved to talk and show off and be the center of attention. They weren't making enough money to pay for his services, but in the future…

Or he could take the son-of-a-bitch out behind the barn and give him a whupping for screwing up his chances with Claire.

Angel leaned in from his left. "I could watch this all day. You should have a rodeo school—teach people how to do all of this." She waved a hand vaguely at the corral and Rob on his horse.

"You want to learn to barrel ride?" Maddy asked, bending forward to look down the row at Angel.

"No—I'd just watch."

The others exchanged a glance over Angel's head, something Jamie had seen them do several times so far on the trip. He understood why, too. Angel was the kind of woman who wafted through life with no idea how much work everyone else did to make things easy for her. Pretty, in a soft and floaty way, she seemed perfectly content to let her friends make all the decisions and plans.

"You're watching right now," Liz pointed out.

Angel shrugged. "Yep."

Liz sighed. "She's actually right, you know. You should open a riding school here. It would complement your guest ranch business."

"We've talked about it," Jamie said. They'd talked about a lot of things, but agreed they needed to take everything one step at a time. He'd enjoy giving riding lessons, but aside from keeping the guests busy, he still had a lot of work to do on the ranch, plus he was building a house and wanted to start breeding horses.

His mind wandered to Claire. How was she getting on? He hadn't liked letting her drive into town alone—how the hell did you break it to your long-lost sister that your mother was dead?—but they couldn't both abandon Ethan and Autumn, not with guests present.

"Can we go to that swimming hole again?" Adrienne asked in a lazy drawl. "I'm all sweaty from being in the sun for so long."

The other women chimed in and Jamie found himself agreeing although he didn't think it was a good idea. Without Claire to shield him from their attention, he might get into trouble.

Well, if he did, at least Claire wouldn't be there to see.

Rob rode up and the ladies applauded and cheered. "Are you coming with us to the creek for a swim?" Adrienne called to him.

"Hell, yeah—sounds like a great idea!"

In the general confusion of climbing down from the corral fence and heading back to the Big House to change, Jamie found himself surrounded by the women. As they surged past, all talking and laughing excitedly, someone grabbed his ass and squeezed, hard.

Jamie jumped and looked around.

But the women surged on, not a one of them giving him a second glance. He turned around. Rob was at the far side of the corral, leading his horse through the gate. Who the heck had pinched him? He didn't have a clue.

What if whoever it was did it again when Claire was watching?

He could lose her for good.

CLAIRE SAT AT THE SMALL, square table in the corner of Morgan's motel room, gazing out the window at the cars and trucks in the parking lot below.

Morgan finally sat down across from her. Her face was red and mottled, her hair damp around the edges from the water she'd splashed on it to wash away her tears. "I knew something was wrong. Really wrong. But my dad said to leave her be. He said she'd come back around when she was ready. I can't believe she's gone." Her voice was ragged and strained.

Telling Morgan about their mother's death was one of the hardest, ugliest things Claire had ever had to do. The other woman's obvious heartbreak made it impossible to hold onto her own rage and now all she felt was tired and empty.

"She never told you anything about me, did she?" Morgan went on.

"Nope. Nothing." But if she'd had any reservations about whether Morgan was really Aria's daughter, they went out the window the moment she saw her. Morgan looked like Aria. They both did. No one would be surprised to find out they were sisters.

"I knew all about you."

Claire looked up in surprise.

Morgan went on. "They had to tell me—the situation was too complicated."

"In what way?"

"My father has a wife, Amy. They were already married when he had the affair with Mom and he didn't want to leave her when Aria got pregnant with me. He has other children, you know—two of them. They're both in Vancouver now. Mom decided she still loved your dad and wanted to go back to him—back to Montana—but she was afraid he would ditch her if she came home with a child. So my dad's parents raised me. He saw me on weekends once or twice a month and Mom would come for several months at a time when she could. Gramma and Gramps were my mainstays."

"I can't believe she lied to us all those years." Claire couldn't believe any of this. She wanted to stare at Morgan—to force herself to see that she was real—that this was the daughter her Mom really wanted to be with, the one she left her for so many times.

"She made a mistake, and then she did the best she could, I guess." Morgan swiped at another tear that leaked from her eye.

"This is the best she could? Sneaking around, lying, cheating on my Dad?"

"She was young, Claire. Haven't you ever made a mistake? I know I have."

Sure, she'd made plenty of mistakes. Trusting Daniel. Sleeping with Jamie. But nothing compared to the colossal mess her mother had made of all their lives.

"She let you grow up alone and she nearly bankrupted my family."

Morgan looked up. "Bankrupted you? How?"

"The trips. All that money she spent on you!"

Morgan shook her head. "I'm sure the plane tickets cost a bit and she bought me things now and then, but her visits shouldn't have been that expensive. She lived with my grandparents and me when she came. Once I was grown up and on my own, she stayed at my apartment."

"I'll bet she paid for that apartment."

"No, she didn't," Morgan said firmly. "And she didn't pay for my grandparents' expenses either. I talked about it all with them. They disapproved of Mom and wouldn't take her money. They did their duty as they saw it—allowed her to visit and gave her a room when she was there—but they weren't chummy with her. I think they felt that if she paid for everything she could take me away whenever she wanted to." She sighed. "They meant well. They just thought she wasn't a very good mother."

"She must have bought you things, though—meals, clothes, bicycles, cars?" Claire challenged.

"Meals and clothes, sure, sometimes. She never bought me a car. Maybe if you guys didn't have much money to begin with I could see it putting a strain on your budget, but she always talked about the ranch like it was doing quite well."

"However she spent it, she spent it," Claire said. "Believe me, we're still recovering from it." Or, at least, Ethan and Autumn were. She was just fine, although her recent expenditures had nibbled away at her six hundred thousand dollars.

"Mom was pretty frugal," Morgan persisted. "I

mean, she worked when she was in Victoria."

"What?" It was Claire's turn to look up in shock. Aria Cruz hadn't worked a day in her life, if you didn't count weeding the kitchen garden.

"At the University. She was a research assistant in the Anthropology Department. Dad was such a big shot, he made it happen for her. Otherwise there's no way they'd put up with her erratic comings and goings."

Claire folded her hands in her lap and stared out the window again.

She didn't know her mother at all.

BY THE TIME JAMIE and the women arrived at the watering hole, Rob was there and he'd brought his brothers along. Jamie breathed a sigh of relief. Four extra cowboys ought to dilute the attention from him a bit. He'd been on edge since the butt pinch, constantly looking over his shoulder to catch one of the ladies sneaking up on him again.

It wasn't right, women coming on to men so boldly. He was as big a flirt as they came, ordinarily, but he liked to get the ball rolling, not be bulldozed by a woman's advances. He still didn't know who the culprit was, either. Liz, most likely. Maybe Adrienne, although she seemed to be making a play for Rob. Plucky Maddy was a possibility, but not Christine—she was married. And certainly not Angel who even now was floating lazily in the water like some kind of nymph.

Rob and his oldest brother, Jake, stood waist deep in the water tossing a foam football around with Maddy and Liz. Adrienne sat on the bank of the creek with her legs in the current, deep in discussion with Ned—Rob's second oldest brother. Christine, still on dry ground, was slathering sunscreen on every inch of exposed skin. Luke, the last of the Mathesons, had a bucket full of water and was creeping up behind Rob. Jamie waited for the inevitable result and wasn't disappointed. As soon as the cold water splashed down over Rob's head, he spun around and tackled Luke. Both went underwater and came back up shouting and sputtering.

Happy that the women's attention was directed away from him, Jamie took his time stripping down to his swim trunks and moved a few yards away before slipping into the cool water. He forgot to worry about who had pinched his butt earlier and instead focused on Claire. How was her interview with Morgan going? How had the woman reacted? What did this long-lost daughter of Aria Cruz look like?

Claire and Ethan had a sister. How weird was that?

"Jamie! Jamie, come on!"

He opened his eyes to find that all-out war had broken out in Chance Creek. The three older Mathesons had ganged up on Rob. The ladies were rallying around him, splashing his brothers with everything they had. The whole creek roiled with their thrashing arms and kicking feet.

Which side should he join? A grin split his face.

A few quick strokes brought him in line with Jake, Ned and Luke.

"Traitor!" Rob gasped as a well-time splash from

Ned filled his mouth with water. The women squealed and shrieked and for just a minute he forgot all of his troubles as he sent wave after wave cascading toward them.

"Take that!" Maddy called, slapping her hands on the surface of the creek. He retaliated with a wall of water that broke over the crown of her head. Laughing, she surged forward, drumming her arms into the water and slamming into him. He caught her around the waist, but lost his footing and they both submerged. Underwater, bubbles streamed from her mouth as she continued to laugh. When they managed to stand up, she leaned against his chest, breathing hard. "I guess you win," she said, her sunny smile undeterred.

"Now you have to join our side," he said, all too aware of Maddy's shapely, bikini-clad breasts pressed against his skin. Shit, he was touching her. Good thing Claire wasn't here to see. He carefully detached himself and sighed in relief when she didn't cling to him. Instead, she pushed off and went after Christine.

Jake stumbled over to him, under assault by Adrienne. "This is what you do for a living, Jamie? Hell, I wouldn't mind your job."

"You couldn't handle my job," Jamie said.

Adrienne sent a sheet of water his way. "Get back on our side where you belong. You're supposed to be taking care of us."

He shouldered Jake aside and went after Adrienne himself. For a skinny woman she sure kicked up a heck of a lot of water. When another of her assaults caught him square in the face, he dove forward and dunked her, hard.

Unlike Maddy, Adrienne didn't find this funny. She surged to her feet before he could even get his bearings and jumped on top of him, forcing him back under the water just as he came up for air. She caught at his hair, wrapped her fingers around it and pushed him down again.

Flailing around, Jamie managed to get an arm behind him and take hold of her waist. Using his superior weight as a lever, he pulled her down and pushed himself up at the same time, exchanging their positions. She let go of his hair and scrabbled at his chest. When he finally let her go and they both surfaced, she hit him. "What the hell are you doing?"

"Making sure you don't drown me. What the hell are you doing?"

"Playing." She was breathing hard, her chest rising and falling—her breasts rising and falling. Heck, why couldn't these women be ugly?

"If you're going to play you better be sure you can take as well as you give," he said. He had no patience with crybabies. Claire had always kept up with the boys. Heck, she'd often led them.

"Oh, I can take as well as I can give, cowboy. You can be sure of that," she said, and brushed past him, her fingertips skimming down his arm. She squeezed his hand meaningfully, then let go, splashing her way back to the others.

Lord have mercy. Claire had better stay in town for

the rest of the week or he was going to lose this bet before sundown.

He shouldn't have participated in the waterfight at all, now that he thought about it. Claire was right—he was nothing but a flirt.

Time to mend his ways.

"So YOU'LL BE GOING BACK TO VICTORIA, now, right?" Claire asked. She stood by the door, itching to be on the other side of it, back in her car and on her way home. This visit had upset her even more than she'd imagined. All those years she'd longed to have her mother's undivided attention, and now she knew what had kept her on her months' long trips abroad. Somehow knowing she'd been spending time with another daughter was worse than thinking she was shacking up with another man. If she strayed from her marriage it was her husband's fault. If she felt the need to spend time with another daughter, had it been from some failing of Claire's?

No. Of course not. What a childish thought.

She felt like a child right now. She longed to see her mother again—to confront her. To have Aria tell her that she was the only daughter she really loved. To have her say that she loved her at all. Her mother had loved her, hadn't she? A familiar ache filled her chest at the knowledge she'd never see her again to ask.

Morgan was blinking back tears, too. "I can't believe she's gone," she said. "I can't believe she's been dead for months and I didn't even know. I always came second with her. She always put you and Ethan first. She loved you two so much."

Claire stiffened, anger quickly replacing her sorrow. "Are you kidding? She took off to see you all the time. She was never here when I needed her! Don't pretend you're the injured party in this."

Morgan's eyes went wide. "You think you have it worse than me? You have your brother still. You have the ranch. You belong somewhere. I have nothing!"

"You have your father and your grandparents."

Morgan shook her head. "My grandparents are dead and I share my dad with two other half-siblings who hate my guts. Do you know how hard that's been?"

"Do you know how hard it's been to have your mother leave for months at a time and not even know where she is?" Claire stood her ground. Morgan wasn't going to steal her right to mourn all that she'd lost.

Morgan pressed the heels of her hands to her eyes. "This is insane. We've both lost our mother. We're both heartbroken. We don't have to be enemies, you know. We could help each other."

"How?" Claire took a step closer to the door. She didn't want to have this conversation. She just wanted to go home and forget all about her brand new half-sister.

"We could start by piecing the whole story together—filling each other in on the details. There are a lot of things I'd like to know—about Mom, and about you and Ethan."

Claire stared at her. "You think we're going to be one big happy family now, don't you—now that my father's dead? You think we're going to hold our arms open and welcome you to the fold?"

Morgan looked stricken. "I just thought we could talk."

"No." Claire grabbed the door handle. "You thought a lot more than that. You thought you'd weasel your way in and become part of the family. One of us. A Cruz. Well, forget it. You might be Aria's daughter, but you'll never be my sister. Leave us alone."

She whipped through the door and slammed it behind her, running down the exterior hallway and concrete stairs to the parking lot. Propelled by the fear that Morgan would come after her, she picked up speed as she hit the pavement. She had almost made it to her car when a man intercepted her, stepping out from behind a pickup truck.

"Claire. I thought that was you."

She wanted to groan. Daniel. What was he doing here?

"Get out of my way," she said and tried to push past him. He caught hold of her elbow.

"Not so fast. I heard you're sniffing around my contract with Carl Whitfield. Do I really have to remind you what will happen if you poach any more of my clients?"

Had he followed her? "He isn't your client yet. He has the right to choose anyone he pleases. I was already on my own when I approached him." She tried to pull away from his grip, but he tightened it.

"Keep away from him."

"Keep away from me!" She shoved him with both

palms. He overbalanced and fell back against a Chevy Malibu, but was on his feet and in her face before she could move. He clutched the fabric of her shirt at her throat and pushed her backward until she was pressed against a panel van.

"You don't scare me, Claire Cruz. You're a bitch and a know-it-all and the biggest shrew in Billings, but you're weak and pathetic and a washup as an interior designer. You have no style. How could you? You've never been anywhere except Montana. Your mother should have taken you with her on a few of those trips of hers. Oh, I forgot. She didn't want your sorry ass along for the ride. Too busy screwing other guys, right? Wasn't that your sob story? So freaking pathetic." He loomed over her, forcing Claire to crane her neck just to look him in the eye. She wanted to say something back—something just as biting and cruel, but words failed her. She'd never seen Daniel like this. Sure, he could be mean; he yelled like a sonofabitch when he didn't get his way. One time he'd even punched a hole in her kitchen wall. But he'd never pushed her around.

She tried to shove him away, and when that didn't work she kicked him in the shin, but she barely grazed him, he was standing so close. Daniel just laughed. He bent down and whispered in her ear, "I always wondered what it would be like to get a little rough with you. You're such a fighter. I bet you'd like it. What do you say? We could get a room."

"Bastard!"

"Leave her alone. Get off of her!"

Morgan appeared around the side of the van brandishing a baseball bat. When Daniel didn't move, she wound up and swung it at him, landing a solid thump on his back.

"You bitch!" Daniel dropped Claire and spun on his heel, grabbing for the bat. Morgan pulled it out of his reach, wound up again and swung. "Damn it!"

"Go. Away." Morgan hit him again. "I'll pound you into the pavement, asshole!"

Daniel warded off her blows with raised arms. "Keep away from Carl, Claire," he shouted as he darted toward his BMW. "You talk to him again and I'll be back." The sportscar's engine roared to life and he peeled out of the parking lot. Claire watched him go, stunned.

"Are you okay?" Morgan asked, rushing up to her and putting a hand on her arm.

"Yeah, I'm fine." She shrugged her off. "I'm totally fine. I could have handled that myself."

Morgan blinked. "You looked like you needed a little help." She leaned on the bat.

"Well, I didn't."

"Look, Claire. I know you're upset. I'm upset, too…"

"You don't know anything," Claire blazed, realizing as she said the words she was being entirely unfair. She didn't care. When had life been fair to her? "Just leave me alone, would you?"

This time she made it to her car and when she left the parking lot, Morgan stood back and watched her go.

Chapter Fifteen

"W E'D BETTER HEAD BACK to the Big House," Jamie said to the women sunning themselves on the riverbank. "Autumn will have dinner ready for us soon. We wouldn't want to keep her waiting."

Maddy sat up and began to gather her things, but the other women moved more slowly. He'd wager half of them had fallen asleep where they lay in the sunshine. The Mathesons were long gone back to their own ranch, after Jake and Ned made pointed comments about how hard he was working.

Let them envy his job. It wasn't turning out to be nearly as easy as he thought it would be, and he missed Claire today. Not that she was a whole lot of fun lately. He wished they could go back to their teenage days, just for a little while. Back then, Claire knew how to enjoy life. She'd pursued everything with a fearlessness that left him speechless with admiration. Unfortunately she'd pursued Mack just as fearlessly and he'd been more than a match for her.

Had Aria really slept with him? Was she so wanton?

She'd always seemed so distant, so severe—such a force unto herself. She didn't mix with the ranch work. Just decorated her home, cooked up a storm when she was around, and spent a lot of time in her garden. He hadn't thought much about her when they were young and even less as he'd grown up. Ethan and Claire had always been closer to their dad than to Aria. But they'd loved her, both of them.

He hurried to help the women back on their mounts, eager to be back at the Big House, hearing about Claire's day. She was already wound up so tight. He hoped this new wrinkle wouldn't cause her any more pain.

NEARLY AN HOUR LATER, he'd finally gotten all the horses tended and the guests back up to the Big House. Ducking into his own cabin, he showered and changed, then headed up the path to join the rest of them for dinner.

"No way! I don't want to see her ever again!"

Jamie stopped in his tracks. That was Claire's voice, coming from the open back door of the bunkhouse. Who was she yelling at?

"I don't want to see her, either, but I think we have to."

Ethan.

He hesitated. It wasn't really his place to interfere, but his feet made up his mind for him and soon he was peering in through the screen door into the bunkhouse kitchen. "Everything all right?"

"No, it isn't." Claire crossed the room and let him in.

"Morgan's an interloper. She wants something from us, I know it."

"You said she wants to talk about Mom."

"I already told her what happened. What more does she need to know?"

"I don't know. Maybe we should find out."

Their voices were rising again. Jamie held out a hand. "Hold up. Claire, tell me what happened."

She crossed her arms over her chest and leaned against the kitchen counter. "I went to Morgan's hotel room and told her that Mom had died. She cried. She knew all about Ethan and me. Turns out Mom got pregnant in college with a professor at the University of Victoria when she studied abroad. She had the baby there and left her with her fuck-buddy's parents to raise. All those trips she took to Europe were lies; she was visiting her. Him, too, probably. That man she slept with—Edward Tate. Morgan claims Mom didn't spend much money on her. She actually claims Mom worked while she was there—at the university with Edward—doing anthropology research, whatever that means. It doesn't make any sense. Of course that's where all the money went. She probably paid for his parents to raise her brat and never told Morgan."

Jamie had never seen Claire so furious, and he was pretty sure it wasn't about the money. He'd watched her chase after her mother for far too long not to know it killed her that Aria was off raising another daughter whenever she left home.

"Let's just have her over and talk to her. Get to the

bottom of this," Ethan said.

"No."

"It sounds wise to me," Jamie said.

Claire rounded on him. "Who the hell cares what you think? You're not even part of this family."

Ethan looked shocked. "He'll be part of this family pretty soon," he said.

"The hell he will! You can buy your way into part-ownership of this ranch, but you can't buy your way into my family, Jamie Lassiter."

"I'm not buying anything. I'm going to marry you."

"Oh, for God's sake." She strode out the back door and let it slam behind her. Jamie met Ethan's gaze.

"Sorry, buddy. You know I'm on your side," Ethan said.

"Too bad I'm not trying to marry you."

"USUALLY, I just tear lettuce up into bite-sized chunks," Rose said the following morning.

Claire looked down and realized she'd shredded the leaves beyond recognition. She was helping prepare a picnic lunch while Rose handled breakfast. Autumn had taken her up on her offer and hired Rose and Tracey Richards to take turns helping her with the cooking and cleaning, and somehow both the younger women knew more about preparing food than she seemed to.

She pushed the salad bowl away with a scowl. "Why the hell am I even here? I should be working on the design for Jamie's house—Carl will be back soon." After another sleepless night, the last thing she felt like doing was spending the day in the company of a bunch of catty women. Still, she said she'd do it, and she wasn't one to go back on her word. She got up early and showered, taking care not to look at the bruises Daniel's hand had left on her arm. Although the day was warm, she wore a long-sleeved shirt to cover them. As she walked the few hundred yards to the Big House, she found herself looking over her shoulder. She would never admit to anyone else that Daniel had her spooked, but he hadn't been playing around in the parking lot. She'd scuffled with enough boys in fun when she was a kid to know what that felt like. Daniel had been angry. Truly angry. He'd wanted to hurt her.

He must need more money—why else would he and Edie come back to boring old Montana after a year abroad? They must have really lived the high life if he'd blown his own savings, the business' earnings, plus the money he took from her.

What would he do to her when he realized she was going after Carl with everything she had?

What would he have done yesterday if Morgan hadn't come after him with her baseball bat?

He would have hurt you, that's what. She shivered, grateful that she hadn't married him.

"How's the design coming?" Rose asked. "I heard about you doing the interior of Jamie's house. Have you been by there lately? The exterior is pretty much done! They'll be ready for you in no time."

Claire bit her lip. She had so many materials and so much furniture on order now that her head was spinning with it all. She kept changing her mind. Just when she thought she'd come up with a fresh and innovative design, Carl's words rang through her head again: *small and predictable*. And each time she went back to the drawing board.

Trouble was, sometimes she'd already placed an order, and lots of things had already arrived. Since she was staying at the bunkhouse these days, and she wanted to look over the materials before showing them to Jamie, she'd decided to have them shipped to her condo in Billings. It had only taken her a day to find a young acquaintance willing to stay for free in her condo for a few weeks and let the delivery men in. She just hoped Carrie didn't have too many parties and piss off her neighbors. The plan had the additional benefit of hiding all her purchases from Jamie. She was afraid he'd freak out when he saw everything that was coming in. As soon as their guests left and she had a chance to look at it all, she'd send back what she didn't need. Hopefully, most of the money would get refunded.

She'd stopped showing the invoices to Jamie long ago, once she began to order two or three or four different sets of materials for each element. He wouldn't understand how hard it had become for her to make up her mind. It wasn't like her—she'd always been decisive when it came to her designs. Her clients loved that about her. When they couldn't make up their own minds she steered them in the right direction—and it always was the right direction.

Until now.

Now she doubted her every move. She needed to place her last few orders, STAT, or Jamie's house wouldn't be done in time to impress Carl when he came home. She had a schedule made for the entire process and it depended on getting started the day after the guests left the ranch.

If she was late, all of it would be for nothing. She hadn't checked her bank account in over a week. It wasn't like she was going to run through six hundred thousand dollars any time soon, but the bills for the materials were adding up fast. She really needed to balance her checkbook.

Soon.

"Claire?" Rose poked her gently. "You still in there? I asked you how the design for Jamie's house is coming."

"Oh. It's fine."

"Don't you love the ring he bought you? Congratulations, by the way. I didn't get a chance to say that at Ethan and Autumn's wedding."

That's right—why hadn't she realized Jamie would have bought the ring from the store Rose worked at? It was the only jewelry store in town. She hesitated just a moment too long. "Thanks."

Rose looked at her. "Is everything all right?"

"Yeah, of course."

"Well, let me see how it looks." She crossed the kitchen and took Claire's hand. "I love it—it's perfect for you." She gave it a tug. "A little tight, maybe, but we can fix that." She studied Claire's face. "Are you sure there's nothing wrong?"

Claire pulled her hand away. "Why? Your sixth sense telling you my marriage is doomed to fail? You're supposed to be able to tell, right? Not that I believe in that mumbo-jumbo crap."

Rose turned away and got back to work at the other counter. Claire could tell from the set of her shoulders that she'd hurt her feelings, but it was true—she didn't believe in any kind of clairvoyance. Rose had a reputation of getting hunches about whether couples would make it or not. Seeing as how her day job was selling wedding rings, Claire thought it was a good racket.

Still.

"Sorry," she said finally. "I didn't mean to be so blunt about it."

"I don't like it, you know," Rose said. "Everybody assumes it's a game and I get to feel special or something. No one ever thinks what it feels like to me when I sell a ring to a couple and don't get a good feeling about them. I should never have told Rob about it in the first place—I talked about it in confidence once and he's blabbed it all over town. People come right up and ask me now, Claire. It sucks!"

"So you actually get a hunch?" Claire found herself asking.

"Only about couples who really belong together. I'm sure there are plenty of people whose marriages will last that I don't get the hunch about because they're still learning to love each other. Maybe there's something in their past that's holding them back, or maybe there's still some obstacle to overcome. I don't know. It's just some people have this feeling when you see them together. They've found their life partner, you know? Their energy is connected."

Rose was almost pleading with her to understand, and Claire nodded her head. That didn't seem so outlandish. Maybe Rose was good at reading people's intentions. Some couples took their marriage vows so seriously they would simply make their marriage work—come what may. All Rose had to be was a good judge of character.

"So what about me and Jamie?" The words slipped out before she thought them through. "I mean, he's a total player, so we're bound to fail, right?" She forced a laugh. Hell, they weren't even getting married, so who cared what Rose said?

"Jamie's a player? Who has he cheated on?" Rose turned all the way around to face her, the orange she was peeling still in her hand.

"I just mean…all those women he's been with. He's a total flirt."

"Being a flirt is different than cheating," Rose pointed out.

"Whatever. Well—what about us?"

Rose sized her up, then turned away and busied herself cutting up fruit. "What do you mean?"

"What do you think I mean? Are we one of those couples? Are we going to be together forever?" She couldn't believe she was even asking the question.

For a long moment, Rose didn't say anything. Finally she shook her head. Glancing back over her shoulder, she said, "I'm sorry, Claire. I want to say yes, but I can't. When I look at the two of you I see all the energy on Jamie's side. He's there, one hundred percent—just waiting for you. But you're not even close to that. All your energy is..." she trailed off.

"What?" Claire forced herself to ask.

"It's..." Rose's cheeks pinked. "Well...it's all swirling back on itself."

"What the hell does that mean?"

"Oh, I shouldn't have said anything. I don't know you very well, and I'm no counselor..."

"Spit it out. You might as well at this point," Claire blazed.

"Well...I think it means that you're so busy thinking about yourself you have no love to give."

Claire gripped the edge of the counter with shaking hands. "You know what, Rose? You're right. You shouldn't have said a god-damned thing."

Chapter Sixteen

WHAT THE HELL was he going to do about Claire? Jamie lathered up for his morning shave. Was he chasing a lost cause, or would she come around in time? He had hoped once she got involved with decorating his house and riding with their guests, she'd realize how much fun they could have together, but so far it had been a bust. He couldn't shirk his duties with his guests, but he needed to step up his game, think of something that would remind Claire that he was a man and she was a woman and they belonged together.

He thought back to the night they'd made love under the moon. Only a month ago, but it felt like ancient history. God, she'd been a sight, silver and sleek in the unearthly light. Writhing in his arms, calling out his name...

Best not to dwell on it.

He made short work of the rest of his morning routine and opened the door to head on over to the Big House for breakfast. No one had exactly planned that everyone would eat together—the guests, Ethan and

Autumn, Claire and him—it just worked out that way, and it worked well. They were able to talk about the day's plans in an informal setting and the guests got to hear more about the running of the ranch. Today was the last day they'd stay close to home. Tomorrow he and Claire would take the ladies on an overnight ride and camp out on the range.

Ought to be cozy.

Smiling, he stopped in his tracks when he saw the vase on his front porch holding a single red rose. Claire's apology, no doubt. Maybe she felt the time was right for romance, too. His grin widened and he picked it up, finding a note tucked underneath.

Jamie—

Been thinking about you. I want to see you tonight. Meet me at the stable at midnight.

He frowned. Was that Claire's handwriting? It wasn't like he'd ever studied it. He thought back to the notes she'd written on her first set of interior design plans. It was blocky and bold, like hers, but it wasn't a match.

So who had left him a rose? Who wanted to meet him in the stable?

Liz?

Adrienne?

When he was a younger man, he'd have been there with bells on, no matter who it was. Not anymore. Now Claire was within his sights, he wouldn't come within a mile of the barn tonight.

But if he left a client waiting for him at midnight all

alone in the stables, would they make some kind of a fuss? Maybe bad mouth the ranch on the internet? He needed this business to succeed.

He tapped his foot until inspiration struck.

He needed a stand in.

Rob. About time the man started making up for the trouble he'd caused.

"IF YOU KEEP SHOWING UP HERE, we're going to have to put you on the payroll," Claire said to Rob as they saddled up. This morning's ride was a long climb into the hills north of their property to a site with a vista their guests hadn't seen before. The sloping ground and curving track would provide more of a challenge than their previous rides and the longer time spent in the saddle would be a good preparation for their two day trip starting tomorrow.

"Well, Jamie says you're not as keen as he thought you'd be for the job, so maybe I'll be your replacement."

She was still raw from Rose's earlier words and now she felt a stab of wounded pride mixed with regret. Jamie was giving up on her already? She still thought his proposal was a joke—she couldn't believe she'd asked Rose about their chances as a couple—but it hurt her to think that he was already looking for her replacement as a business partner. Couldn't he give her a little time? Once she'd finished his house and secured Carl Whitfield's contract she'd be able to clear her head and make decisions more rationally. With Morgan's arrival, Daniel's attack and packages arriving at her Billings condo on a daily basis, she didn't have time to choose her path for the rest of her life right now. Maybe once she'd showed Daniel she'd always beat him at interior design she'd be ready to try something else.

Like staying on the ranch and raising horses. Helping with the guests. She needed time to figure it out.

Jamie ought to know that. He ought to back off and be helpful, not yank this job away from her before she'd even given it a fair shake.

She paused while tightening a strap around Storm. Not that she was giving it a fair shake; not really. She'd been so wrapped up in her other problems she'd barely thought about the trail rides. If Jamie had given up on her, it served her right—she'd shown so little attention to what she was doing. Maybe Rose was right—maybe she was too busy thinking about her own problems to worry about anyone else.

Maybe Jamie would be better off without her. Ethan and Autumn, too.

She had the strangest feeling, just for a moment—as if the ground tilted and was sliding away—all her happiness sliding away with it. Her knees felt weak and she wondered if anyone would notice if she just sat down and put her head in her hands. She held onto Storm's saddle for balance until the dizziness passed, shaking her head to clear her thoughts.

Did she even want to be an interior designer? Did she really need to beat Daniel before she moved on?

What about that trip she was supposed to take? What about seeing the world?

Another wave of dizziness passed over her. Damn, was she getting sick?

No, this was stress, plain and simple. Everything was going wrong at once. In the past, she'd put her head down and run for the hills every time things like this happened. She wasn't going to do that now.

She needed to concentrate. She needed to take things one step at a time. First she would show Daniel he hadn't crushed her when he took her money and ran. That meant finishing Jamie's house, showing it to Carl and landing the Whitfield contract. Next, she needed to sort out Morgan and send her back to Canada. No matter what Ethan said, she wasn't becoming part of her family.

Last, she needed to make a decision about the rest of her life. When she had time to think it through—away from Jamie and everyone else.

Jamie.

She stroked Storm's neck as she considered the man at the center of all the chaos in her life. Why couldn't he be the man she needed him to be? Why couldn't he be faithful?

Rose said she thought he was ready to be part of a lasting relationship. That he was one hundred percent committed.

Could his proposal possibly be serious?

No, that didn't make sense—it was all part of that practical joke—the face goo, the stupid note, and his proposal in front of all his friends. Even if by some crazy chance he had been serious, it didn't matter.

Jamie didn't have staying power, no matter what Rose said. She had no doubt a wedding with him would be wonderful and the honeymoon spectacular. But the marriage… How long before another woman caught his eye and led him astray? She wouldn't live through that kind of betrayal.

Let everyone think she didn't care enough about Jamie to marry him. She knew the truth.

She cared far too much.

Chapter Seventeen

"WHO'S THAT?" Autumn said. Jamie turned and held his hand up to shade his eyes from the strong morning sunshine. He was collecting the picnic Autumn and Rose had packed them to take along on today's ride. He'd distribute the food and drinks among everyone's saddlebags and warn them not to get into it until noon.

Rob had been more than willing to ride along and spend the evening with them, too, when Jamie asked. He promised he'd hang out at his cabin until midnight, then go to intercept Jamie's would-be lover.

"I'm more than happy to take one for the team," was the way he'd put it when Jamie warned him that the guest who met him there might expect him to put out. Jamie just bet he was, after his long drought.

An unfamiliar car pulled into the drive and parked near the Big House. A woman in her early thirties got out. There was something familiar about her dark hair and strong jaw, but it wasn't until she turned to face them straight on that Jamie realized who it had to be.

"Morgan," Autumn said, echoing his thoughts.

"Yep." He scanned the surroundings, hoping Claire was still in the stable.

Autumn walked down the front porch's steps. "Can I help you?"

"I'm looking for Ethan Cruz." Morgan came to meet them. Dressed in jeans, a t-shirt and cowboy boots, she could have been a local, but Jamie detected a slight accent in her voice. Nothing he could put his finger on, exactly, but enough to set her apart as different.

"I'll go get him." Autumn shot Jamie a look, and went back inside.

"Why don't you have a seat," Jamie said.

"I'm not sure I'm staying long enough for that to be practical," she said and smiled. "Hi, I'm Morgan. I don't know if you've heard of me."

He nodded. "I sure have. Claire gave me an earful last night after she got home."

"Did she tell you what happened? With that guy, Daniel?"

Daniel. Jamie frowned. "No. What happened?"

The anger in his tone must have made her wary. She looked him up and down. "Who are you, again?"

He stuck his hand out. "I'm Jamie Lassiter. An old friend of the Cruz's and now part-owner of the ranch."

"And you like Claire."

Taken aback, he let his hand drop. "She tell you that?"

Morgan smiled again. "It's plain all over your face, cowboy."

"So what happened with Daniel?"

She moved over to one of the rattan chairs that dotted the wide verandah and sat down. "I'd better not say if she didn't tell you herself. But he's a mean sonofabitch. I think she needs to watch out for him."

Jamie narrowed his eyes, but before he could press her further, the door opened and Autumn came back out onto the porch, followed by Ethan.

Morgan stood up. "Ethan. I'm Morgan. I'm...your sister."

"NO. ABSOLUTELY NOT," Claire hissed when Ethan cornered her in the stable and told her that Morgan was joining her and Jamie and their guests for the trail ride and picnic today.

"I already told her she could come. Don't make a scene in front of our guests; we've already kept them waiting too long this morning."

"Whose fault is that?"

"Mine. I take full responsibility. But now it's time to get going."

"Why does she have to come with me? Why can't she go with you?"

"Because I'm going with you, too. Now shut up and help me saddle Charlie."

Claire counted to ten before leading Storm out of the stable and leaving her brother behind. Let him saddle his own damn horse, and as far as she was concerned he could entertain their unwelcome half-sister, too. She sure as hell wasn't going to talk to her.

But when she joined the rest of the group milling around on horseback at the front of the Big House, she realized she didn't need to. Jamie was already deep in conversation with the interloper. As she watched, he threw back his head and roared with laughter at something Morgan said.

Rob pulled up Monty beside her and leaned over. "Damn, Claire, seeing your sister is uncanny. She's like you, only pretty." He chuckled and moved away into the center of their female guests. Claire fought the urge to hurl something at his retreating back and wheeled around, waiting for Ethan to appear. She couldn't wait until this farce was over.

Things only got worse from there, however. She found herself stuck at the end of the line while Ethan and Jamie vied for Morgan's attention. Ethan was acting like Morgan was their long lost...well...sister or something, while from the way Jamie couldn't stop talking to her, she figured she didn't have to worry about his unwelcome advances anymore.

Somehow that left her feeling lonelier than ever.

Rob flirted with each and every one of the guests, making his way up and down the line with the ease of many years spent in the saddle. He should take on her job when the week was done. He'd be far more successful at it than she was. No one wanted to talk to her.

Why would they when all she'd done all week was mope? As she rode along, the distance from her troubles was giving her clarity. She had a condo filled with tiles, floor coverings, cabinets and more—far more than she could use for ten log houses. She needed to make some decisions and send the rest back. She needed to get her finances in order.

She needed to figure out what she wanted to do with her life.

Her gaze strayed ahead of her to Jamie where he rode easily, chatting and laughing with Morgan, Ethan and Christine, who'd come up behind them. His laughter and good spirits had been a part of her life as she'd grown up on the ranch. His constant presence and his unerring desire to get her attention—and keep it—made it all too easy to discount him as anything special.

But he was special, much as she hated to admit it. Who else could pick out the perfect horse for her when she hadn't ridden in over a decade? Who else worked beside her so easily—never trying to boss her around or second-guess her decisions? Who else put up with her temper and moods?

Jamie had seen the worst of her. She closed her eyes as her cheeks heated. The best of her, too. He knew her in a way no other man did. Should she give him a chance?

No—she'd been ready to give him a chance the night she came to tell him she'd been a fool for years. She'd been on fire that night to get everything out in the open, to tell Jamie she'd finally seen him for the man he was. And he'd been getting it on with Hannah O'Dell.

He was a flirt and cheat. Always would be.

Right?

Rose's words crossed Claire's mind, and this time she

considered them more seriously. How had Rose put it? Being a flirt was different than being a cheat.

Was Jamie a cheat?

He hadn't cheated on her when he was with Hannah. She'd given him the cold shoulder for years at that point. Did she really think he'd stay celibate all that time when she certainly hadn't? She'd never given him the barest encouragement—not the slightest hint that she was interested. What right did she have to be angry when he wasn't sitting home alone, waiting for her?

That night, staring in his window while he undressed Hannah, she'd felt just as hurt as when she'd caught her mother and Mack together. But Jamie wasn't married. He was a single man who'd found someone else to be with when she refused him over and over again.

Had Jamie ever cheated? She thought back to the various women he'd dated over the years. All strong, independent types who were just as capable of playing Jamie as of being played by him. Women who wanted a boyfriend to squire them around, but weren't interested in settling down. She couldn't remember anyone shedding any tears over him.

Jamie liked women, no doubt about that. Was he a flirt?

Yes, definitely.

Was he a two-timer?

Maybe not.

Did Jamie truly want to be with her? Was he husband material?

She narrowed her eyes as Morgan reached over and

put her hand on Jamie's arm. Talking as if no one else was around. What the hell did those two find to connect over? Why couldn't he take his gaze off of her?

She decided she needed to find out.

As the trail narrowed, Jamie let Ethan move ahead of him.

"Claire's coming," Ethan said in a low voice as he passed.

Jamie turned to look over his shoulder. Yep, here she came. Probably ready to blast him for fraternizing with the enemy.

"Hi, Claire," Morgan called out.

He hoped Claire would at least nod at her half-sister, but she didn't. She didn't say a word.

"What's up?" Jamie asked her as Morgan fell behind them.

"Just decided to check in. Getting a little sick of eating dust."

"Want me to take the rear for a while?"

"You in a big hurry to get away from me?"

He looked up at her sharp tone. Heck, was Claire a little jealous of the attention he'd been giving to her sister? Morgan was nice, and pretty, but she wasn't Claire—not by a long shot. "Nah, I can stand you for a little while."

He just caught her distress as she turned away. Shit. Usually she could take anything he had to dish out and give it back twice as bad. "Hey, I'm joking. You know I'd spend every minute with you if I could. You're the one keeping us apart, honey."

"I just got dirt in my eye." She straightened her shoulders as if bracing herself to perform an unpleasant duty. "Sorry for yelling last night. I was upset."

"I can see why."

"You don't seem to have any problem talking to her."

He glanced over his shoulder to make sure Morgan couldn't hear them. "Why should I? She's not my kin."

"What did she have to say?"

"That she took a week off of her job to come see what happened to her mother. That she still can't believe she's gone, but she'd known something awful must have happened since she never came back. That really she's been mourning her for months."

"She seems pretty cheerful for someone who's in mourning."

He stifled the urge to call Claire on the cattiness of that remark. "I'd say *seems* about covers it. I think she's pretty shaken up. She's trying not to spoil everyone else's day."

Like you are, he left unspoken.

Claire pressed her lips together in a thin line. "I don't want to hear how broken up she is."

"Then we'll talk about something else," Jamie said easily. "Did you know that she works at a winery in Victoria? She helps manage it—oversees the grapes growing and the distillery. She wants a vineyard of her own someday."

"Hmmm."

"If you weren't so busy trying to hate her, I think you'd like her," he said. "Maybe you should ask her to stay at the ranch for another week. Get to know her better. Didn't you ever wish for a sister?" A glance over his shoulder told him Rob was flirting with Morgan now. Claire probably wouldn't like that.

"As far as I'm concerned, the sooner she leaves, the better."

Jamie cocked his head. "You want to tell me what happened with Daniel yesterday?"

"Nope." She clicked her tongue at Storm and left him behind.

"WE SHOULD HAVE LEFT CLAIRE back at the ranch. She's being damn rude," Ethan said thirty minutes later as they hobbled the horses and checked them over. Jamie looked up and scanned the hillside where they'd stopped to eat lunch. Morgan sat in the midst of the female guests chattering away. Claire was busy taking the food out of the saddle bags, slamming the containers and plastic silverware around, making it all too clear she was unhappy with the situation.

"She's upset that Morgan came along for the ride."

"I guess I can understand that. I thought I'd be angry, when I heard that Mom…well, you know," Ethan said. "I was for a little while, but not anymore. Now I'm curious. Morgan's grandparents and Mom and Dad are all gone." He shrugged. "Seems like those of us that are left should be able to work things out."

Jamie considered this. "Claire took it harder than

you—all your Mom's comings and goings."

Ethan frowned. "She never said anything."

"She didn't have to—what she did said everything she needed to say."

Pausing with one hand on Storm's withers, Ethan nodded slowly. "All those fights? The running wild? Yeah. I guess so. But that's water under the bridge now."

"I don't think it is for Claire. Morgan being here is like salt in her wounds. Think about it this way—when your Mom went away it was to be with Morgan. Every time she left, it was Morgan's fault."

"Like she was cheating on Claire with another daughter," Ethan said and laughed shortly. "Okay, I see it now. Claire's really mad at Mom, but Mom's gone, so…"

"So she's taking it out on the only other target left."

"So we kick Morgan to the curb?"

Jamie patted the gentle mare that Adrienne was riding today. "That's the easy solution, but I don't think it's the best one. We've got to throw those two together, let them go at it and hope they fight their way through the problem to the other side."

Ethan looked skeptical. "That sounds messy."

"Life is messy."

When Ethan took a long moment to answer, Jamie figured he was thinking of his own recent history. "Yeah. You got that right."

Jamie's thoughts returned to the spark of jealousy Claire'd shown when he spent too much time around Morgan on the ride. So far he'd done a crap job of seducing her. He'd hoped that by interesting her in the projects that interested him—his house and the guest ranch business—he'd convince her she wanted to spend more time with him. Since that hadn't worked, it was time to step things up a notch. Claire avoided him as much as she could. He'd always taken that for disinterest. What if he was wrong? What if that signaled an abundance of interest?

Time to test that theory out.

CLAIRE WATCHED IN DISMAY as Jamie stuck to Morgan like burrs on a mule for the remainder of their lunch break. He sat next to her at lunch, his leg almost pressed against hers as they shared a log for a seat. From across the way, she heard them discuss the food, the ride, the guests, and the prospects for buying breeding stock this year, in a general, disinterested way. She couldn't accuse him of flirting, but damn it, that was exactly what he was doing.

Morgan was eating up his attention and why shouldn't she? A good looking, capable man like Jamie was hard to find, especially one with a head for business and a desire to settle down and raise a family.

With a lurch of her heart, Claire realized she was jealous of Morgan. Jealous because she wanted a good looking, capable man. A man with a head for business she could settle down and raise a family with. She was sick of holding back, sick of being alone, sick to death of focusing on revenge instead of on her future. Now that she knew what kind of man Daniel really was, getting back at him seemed less important. Let Edie have him and good riddance.

As long as Jamie was available she'd felt like she'd had all the time in the world to get around to him, and little inclination to do so. Seeing Morgan cozy up to him brought that illusion crashing down. If she kept guarding her heart so carefully, she would never find out what Jamie's intentions really were, and she risked someone else—someone like Morgan—coming along and snatching him away from her.

She couldn't be sure if Jamie really cared for her, or if he was just playing an increasingly elaborate practical joke, but the thing she was coming to realize was that she had to find out—whether or not that meant getting hurt.

She wanted Jamie. She wanted to stop playing games and say yes to his proposal. She wanted to look him in the eye and learn the truth.

Should she admit that to him?

No. In spite of her realizations, she wasn't ready to lose their bet. In fact—she straightened as a new idea hit her—tempting him to lose it sounded like so much more fun.

When they saddled up for the return ride, she let Ethan lead the pack and fell back to ride alongside of Jamie.

And she stuck by him for the rest of the day.

Jamie didn't acknowledge this new arrangement, but he didn't fight it either. She figured he was waiting to see what she did next. Fine. She'd keep him guessing.

She saw Adrienne and Liz exchange a glance at one

point, but with Ethan and Rob along, none of the ladies seemed too put out by Jamie's abandonment of them.

Claire kept alert for any overt sign he was flirting with her, but although Jamie was warm and interested in everything she had to say, he didn't touch her once—even though they were certainly close enough on this narrow track.

She should know—she made a point to touch him often. Each time she did, her ring sparkled in the sunshine.

Her engagement ring.

Could she tantalize him so much he'd ask her to marry him and really mean it?

As the afternoon stretched on, she made a game of it. Never allowing her fingertips to land on the same square of his skin twice. His arm. His thigh. His shoulder. Each time they connected, his warmth left her tingling. She could almost imagine him touching her back. Placing a hand on her knee, stroking her, moving upwards until...

Suddenly hot, she turned her face aside, hoping he didn't notice the blush she was sure was creeping up her cheeks.

Still, she couldn't stop her thoughts from leaping to a much more sensual scenario—Jamie poised above her, like he'd been that night a month ago, out on the range. Ready to plunge into her. Ready to make love to her until she cried aloud.

"Claire?"

She darted a glance his way, then ducked her head

again, willing her thoughts to safer ground. "What?"

"I asked what Autumn was making for dinner."

"I…I don't know." Dinner? Who could think about dinner? All she could think about was Jamie—naked. Hard. Ready for her. Hell, she was ready for him—right now.

"Something on your mind?"

She stifled an urge to hit him. Yes, something was on her mind. Him. Sex. "Yeah."

"What?" It wasn't flirtation, exactly. But his voice was inviting. Husky.

"Nothing." But another glance told her she'd given herself away. She didn't know how he knew what had been on her mind, but he knew all right. She wanted to rub that self-satisfied look right off his face. Damn men. How did they do that? Sit so easy in their bodies? Let a tilt of their jaw or the way they sat in the saddle let you know that they felt supremely confident they could have you crying out in passion when the time was right. Jamie was just as insufferable as the rest of them.

"I've missed you all these years you've lived in Billings," he said and jolted her right out of her angry train of thought. That wasn't self-satisfied or insufferable. That was…real. She opened her mouth to speak, then closed it again when nothing coherent formed in her mind to say. He went on. "When we were growing up I loved everything about this place, and I came here for a bunch of reasons. To hang out with Ethan, with your Dad, with the horses. But I also came because of you."

"You had a crush on me," she managed to say.

"Yeah, I did. Still do. But that's not the half of it." He looked away, checking up and down the line. "You were so on fire for life. So brave, so clear about everything. You knew what you wanted and you took it, or at least you tried."

"That was a long time ago." She didn't trust her voice suddenly.

"I enjoyed being around you," he went on. "It wasn't just about lust. It still isn't. Life's better when you're near me." He smiled. "And that's as close to flirting as I'm going to get. The way you've been spending my money, I won't have any left to buy your cruise ticket if I lose this bet." He sat back and looked at her straight on. "I'm here, Claire—whenever you're ready. Just give me a sign."

She thought he'd ride off then and leave her to mull over his parting words, but after a few minutes she realized he meant what he said.

He wasn't going anywhere.

The thought turned her on more than she wanted to admit.

Chapter Eighteen

JAMIE HAD JUST CONGRATULATED HIMSELF on getting under Claire's skin when she said something that jolted every nerve in his body awake.

"I've been ready for years." She caught his gaze squarely. "I spend every night dreaming about you touching me."

His mouth suddenly dry, Jamie just caught himself before he reached out for her.

Wait. Was this a trick? A sneaky way to win the bet?

He wasn't allowed to touch her or flirt with her or she won automatically, and he would never be able to propose to her again.

Did she really want him? Or did she want him to reach for her so she could win once and for all? Damn it, he couldn't tell from the crafty smile that played at the corners of her mouth.

"You admitting you want to marry me?" His voice came out like a rusty violin.

"You mean am I confessing that you've won the bet? Not by a long shot, cowboy." She grinned. "All I'm saying is I love the feel of your hands on my breasts."

Damn it, that wasn't fair at all. Well, if she wanted to play this game, he could give as well as he could take. "You could always show them to me."

"That's flirting!" she crowed.

"No, it ain't," he said calmly. "I'm stating a fact."

She considered this. "Okay, you're right," she said finally. "I could do that. How about now?"

He nodded toward the other riders ahead of them. "This doesn't quite seem like the place." Cruel woman. She was playing with him—something fierce.

She pulled Storm to a halt. "Rob!"

"Yeah?" Rob reined in and looked back over his shoulder.

"Go on ahead. Me and Jamie'll catch up in a minute."

"Sure thing."

Was she for real? Jamie fought against the desire flaring up in his body. No matter what she did, he was not going to rise to her bait. He would be damned if he lost over a trick.

A few minutes later the rest of the group were out of sight.

"You really going to do this?"

"Why not? It's not like you're going to touch me, right?" She draped Storm's reins over her saddle, unbuttoned her shirt and slid it off her shoulders to hang over her arms. She unclasped the front hook of her bra and peeled it back.

Hell.

Jamie scraped his chin with the back of his hand. "You do have lovely breasts, Claire."

"Flirting?"

"Just an observation." He was dying to do a hell of a lot more than observe.

"They feel pretty nice, too." She edged Storm closer to Walter and leaned forward to take his wrist. She lifted his hand to cup her left breast. "See?" She gave his hand a squeeze.

Oh, hell.

"Very nice," he ground out.

She transferred his hand to her other breast. "This one, too."

"Yes."

"I think the horses are getting in the way," she said. In a practiced move, she dismounted Storm and came to stand near Walter. "Come down."

"Yes, Ma'am." He did what he was told, although he knew he was a fool for it. Taking his wrist, she led him off the trail toward a small grove of pine trees. Stopping beneath one, she took both of his hands and lifted them once more. This time she made sure his fingertips brushed her nipples, which hardened under his touch.

"Now you can really get the idea," she said.

"Much better," he agreed. Surely this was hell. Standing so close to Claire, touching her, and yet not being allowed to pull her close.

"There's a lot more to me, you know," she said after a moment. "You probably should check the rest of it out."

"As delightful as this is, you can't trick me into flirting or touching. I'm not going to lose this bet."

"Oh, I know I don't interest you in the slightest," Claire said. "I know you'd rather be fishing or something."

Jamie choked back a snort. Fishing? "Just so we're clear. I'm in this for the long haul. I want a wife, not a one night stand."

"That's what you keep saying," she said, kicking off her boots and unzipping her pants. She skimmed them off and left them in a heap by her shirt and bra. She slipped off her panties, too. Now she stood before him, naked except his ring on her finger.

Radiant.

His Claire.

It took every ounce of strength he had not to move. Laughing at him, she stepped closer, took hold of his wrists, wrapped his arms around her body and helped him cup her ass. His breathing hitched and for one awful moment he thought his fingers might move of their own accord. Another part of his anatomy certainly was.

"You can't win this way," he said. His voice was strangled.

"Oh, I bet I can." She tugged him down to the ground and began to undress him. The next few minutes were some of the most agonizing of Jamie's life. He couldn't help her in the slightest with her attempts to get his clothes off without losing the bet…and she was so slow. He would have laughed at her struggles to free his pants from his torso if every inch of his body hadn't been on fire. Finally, when he lay there as naked as she was, she began a new conquest of torture.

She started at his mouth, kissing his lips, his cheeks, his jaw, and then under his chin. She trailed down to his chest, his stomach and after lavishing her attention there, descended even lower. While she touched and ministered to every inch of him, he clung to bent and broken stalks of bracken, willing himself not to go over the edge. Finally, she straddled him and lowered herself, inch by agonizing inch onto the length of him.

From the look on her face she was almost as undone by the whole affair as he was.

"You feel good," she said. "So good." Her teasing tone was gone.

He bit his lip. He wanted to tell her what she was doing to him, how much he loved her, how he wanted to spend his life with her. He could only nod.

She began to ride him, lifting up and sliding down again, over and over, slowly at first, and then much faster. Her breasts swayed in rhythm with her hips, her head tilted back and her lips parted. She was a glorious sight and he loved her, wanted her, needed her...

With a wild cry she bucked against him and Jamie came, too, caught up in her abandon. He swallowed his groans but he couldn't stop his orgasm. It rocked through him from toe to tip, leaving him shaken, shuddering, and longing to do it all again.

Claire slumped forward against him and it killed him he couldn't embrace her and whisper all his thoughts into her ear. When she sat up again and disengaged from him, he smiled weakly.

"That was nice."

Chapter Nineteen

THE MOMENT THEY REACHED THE STABLE, Jamie knew something was wrong. Autumn was waiting for them, a worried frown creasing her face. Rob and Ethan were already seeing to the other horses. The guests were trailing up to the front porch. He and Claire had ridden the rest of the way home silently, but quickly, twin silly smiles on their faces. Jamie had no idea what had happened back there. Was Claire only trying to win the bet? Or had her sensual attack meant something more? He'd hoped she would tell him before they got back to work, but from the look of things, any discussion would have to wait.

"Claire? Can I talk to you?" Autumn said.

Claire turned to him. "Can you take care of the horses?"

"Sure—go on." But as he watched her walk away, he wanted to stay by her side. Autumn hadn't brought good news—that was obvious—and he didn't want Claire to face whatever it was alone.

Jamie got to work. The horses needed to be unsaddled, rubbed down and checked to make sure their hooves hadn't picked up any stones during the ride. As he pulled the saddle off of Storm and went to put it in its place, he was surprised to see Adrienne leaning against the stable door, waiting for him.

"Can I help you?"

"We didn't get a chance to talk today. Claire was monopolizing you."

Jamie shrugged. "We had some things to discuss."

"But I'm the one who's paying for your time. How about you give me a little attention." She touched his arm, running her hand over his muscles.

"That's not exactly what you're paying for, is it?" he said, pulling away with a quick look over his shoulder. He didn't want Ethan to see what she was doing. "And if I don't see to these horses, they're going to suffer for it."

She pouted. "I'm not so hard to look at, am I? That's all I'm asking for—a little of your attention."

He stopped and met her gaze. "Really? That's all you're asking for?" He refused to look away until she was the one that broke the staring contest.

"Fine. You got me. I am asking for a little more. This is my vacation—my chance to get away and blow off steam."

Jamie returned to the horses and began to undo Storm's saddle. "I bet you usually don't have any problem finding someone to help you with that." When he looked her way, she was smiling.

"No. Not usually. You're proving a harder nut to crack, though."

"Maybe you ought to be trying to crack another nut."

Adrienne laughed. "Maybe. But I like a challenge. I think I'll keep trying to crack you." She intercepted him as he crossed the stable again. "Come on. No one has to know."

"Look, Adrienne. You're a pretty woman. You know that—you don't need me to come on to you so you can feel good."

"You're right, I don't. But I do need you to fuck me so I can feel good." She put both her hands on his chest and rose up on tiptoes to kiss the underside of his chin. "I bet you can make me feel real good."

Wow. He had to put a stop to this, fast. Obviously, she wasn't the one who'd left him the note—she wasn't patient enough to wait for midnight. All he needed now was for Claire to walk in on them.

He caught both of her hands and pushed her aside. "I don't want to be rude, Ma'am, but you haven't given me a choice. I've got a woman already, and I'm not looking for any more company."

"Who—Claire? What's a man like you want with a cold fish like her? She's not going to keep you warm at night."

"You'd be surprised." He hauled the saddle off of Walter and put it in its place. "I've got work to do, Adrienne. I'll see you up at the Big House."

"Fine. Be a wet rag. There's plenty more where you came from." She stalked out of the stable and Jamie heaved a sigh of relief. He hoped that was the end of it—at least with Adrienne. He needed to keep Rob closer to hand for emergencies like this one. At least he'd fend off his midnight caller's advances. Maybe it was time to hire all the Matheson brothers on for the rest of the week. That'd be four guests kept busy. And Angel wasn't going to bother anyone.

"WHAT IS IT? What happened?" Claire asked, her heart beating hard. She was still shaken from her interlude with Jamie—shaken in a good way. She'd never made love to a man like that—taking all control. It had been one of the most sensual experiences of her life. Maybe someday they could turn the tables—what would it be like to be entirely under Jamie's mastery? The thought left her a little breathless.

"There's a police officer on the phone for you. From Billings," Autumn said and led the way indoors, handing her the house phone when they got to the kitchen.

"Hello?" Claire said.

"Claire Cruz? I'm officer Bradley with the Billings PD. We got a call from your subletter—Carrie Ellis. There's been a break-in at your condominium. We tried your cell, but couldn't get through. I'm glad we got a hold of you."

"Oh, my God. When? What'd they take?"

"This morning, we think. And we hoped you'd be able to help us figure out what's missing. Carrie mentioned you had a lot of boxes in the main living area? How many of them were there?"

"They took the boxes?" Claire said, her heart sinking. "Oh, my God. Oh, no."

"What is it? What was in them?" Autumn said.

Claire shook her head. "What about the garage?" All those materials. All those pieces of furniture. Thousands of dollars' worth of supplies.

"The garage was empty, too. Ms. Ellis said you had things stored in there. Is that true?"

She thought she was going to faint. How much money was tied up in those purchases? She'd meant to send most of them back just as soon as she'd made up her mind which ones not to use. They couldn't be gone. They just couldn't be.

"I'll be there as soon as I can."

"Just hold on a minute, ma'am. I have a few questions."

"They can wait." She clicked the phone off, slammed it down on the counter and headed for the front door.

"Claire," Autumn called after her. "When will you be back?"

"I don't know."

AT NINE O'CLOCK Claire still hadn't come home and she wasn't answering his phone calls, either. Jamie paced the small living room in his cabin and tried to decide whether or not to go after her. She could very well be on her way back already, so if he drove off to Billings he could start a wild goose chase that would go on for hours.

"She was really upset. Give her time to figure out what to do," Autumn had advised him earlier. The Mathesons were playing cards in the Big House with the female guests and he'd decided he could slip out early to the quiet of his own home. No telling how late that party would last.

Rob promised to stop by his cabin on his way to meet the mystery woman at the stable. While he was curious as to who it would be—his money was on Liz or Maddy—he cared far more for how Claire was getting on in Billings.

No wonder she was upset. Nothing was worse than getting robbed.

Maybe she'll move back to the ranch for good.

He sure wanted her to, but not under these circumstances. And what was with the boxes? Autumn said she was upset because she'd had things stored in her house and now they were gone. What was she storing?

Something expensive? He hoped she had insurance.

He checked his phone again. Where the hell was she?

Nine oh one.

That was it. He was going after her. He headed for the door, but when he pushed it open, it smacked into someone on the other side.

"Ow!"

A definitely feminine someone.

"Christine? Is that you?" He peered through the gloom to make out the small woman who teetered on his front porch in jeans, a strappy t-shirt and high heeled shoes. How the hell had she made it all the way from the Big House in those?

"Jamie. I need you." Unlike Adrienne, she didn't wait for foreplay. She lunged at him, slid her hand down the waist of his jeans and searched his crotch like she was fishing car keys from the bottom of a purse.

"Whoa! Hold on there." He unceremoniously yanked her hand free and shoved her away. "What the hell do you think you're doing?"

"No one loves me," Christine wailed. Heck, she was drunker than a cow in a poppy field. "My husband doesn't love me."

He did not need this right now. Not when he needed to go after Claire. "I'm sure your husband adores you. You should go back to your room and call him."

"He asked me for a divorce," she wailed.

Shit. "Do your friends know?"

"No! Of course not. I can't tell them my marriage is tanking. How could I face them?"

"They're your friends." He turned her in a circle and pointed her toward the steps down to the path. "They're supposed to support you when times are tough."

She snorted. "Not bloody likely. They'll say all the right things to my face, then talk about me behind my back."

"Then they're not your friends." He began to frog-march her back toward the Big House. As she wobbled along he considered carrying her. It would sure be faster.

"I don't have any friends," she wailed.

How he got through the next fifteen minutes he couldn't say. Thank goodness Claire wasn't there to see Christine alternately paw him and push him away. He deposited her on the front porch and got Autumn. "She's a mess. I'm sorry to dump her on you but I've got to find out what's happened to Claire."

"Morgan went after her," Autumn said.

"I'm still going."

"I'm not going to stop you." Autumn patted Christine's head and smiled. "Somehow I thought running a guest ranch would be more fun."

"Me, too."

"Ready to quit?"

"Not quite." He ran a hand over his face. "How about you—you doing okay?"

"Yeah. I'm hanging in there. Go on, find Claire. I hope everything's all right."

"So do I."

"IT'S GOT TO BE DANIEL," Claire said when the police finally left. She stood with Morgan in the stark square living room of her Billings condo. The police had questioned her for what seemed like hours when all she wanted to do was throw herself on the ground and cry. Carrie had been all tears and apologies. She'd been at her boyfriend's house when the thieves struck. Claire didn't blame her. She hadn't stipulated Carrie needed to remain on site at all times. When she couldn't take the girl's tears anymore, she sent her home.

Finally she'd had the place to herself, but moments later another knock sounded on the door. She'd thought it was the police returning to ask even more pointless questions, and she'd been ready to give them a piece of her mind. But when she opened the door, there stood Morgan, and to her surprise she found she was glad for the company. Morgan was practical, and she had a temper to match her own. She wouldn't stand around asking stupid questions. She'd be ready to act.

"Did the police say they'd talk to him?"

"Yeah, but when I asked if they'd search all his properties they said no. They thought it was just a regular robbery. They kept telling me to watch eBay or Craigslist to see if my stuff turned up there. How the hell would I tell if it was mine? It isn't antiques that got stolen—it's building materials, brand new in their boxes."

"How much do you think you lost?"

Claire bit her lip. She didn't want to tell anyone, let alone Morgan, but all her secrecy had gotten her nowhere so far. A favorite saying of her father's flashed through her mind: when all else fails, you've got your family. Funny, she'd never thought to follow that advice.

"Thirty thousand dollars' worth. Maybe more. I'm not sure." She hesitated. "Maybe fifty thousand."

Morgan cocked her head. "Are you always this vague about money?"

"No. This isn't like me at all." She waited for Morgan to react with shock or disgust, but she didn't. She surveyed the room again, her expression focused.

"Fill me in—on all of it. Start at the beginning. Seriously," she added when Claire began to protest. "Don't frill it out with a million details—just give me the bare bones. It'll go faster than you think. Once I know the history of you and Daniel, I can help make a plan."

Hesitantly, Claire began, but as she told Morgan about her fights with her mother, her desperate bids for attention, catching her with Mack and then leaving home to move to Billings, going to work at Ledstroms and falling for Daniel, she warmed to the story. Morgan listened avidly, asking one or two questions, but otherwise keeping silent. Claire went on to describe working with Daniel, becoming his lover, how his betrayal hurt her, but she saved the company and continued to run it under the same name. How he came back and took it away from her. His threats.

"And you saw how he was in the parking lot," she added.

"Yeah, high as a kite."

"Really? You think he was high?"

Morgan shook her head at her. "You know, on the one hand you're tough and practical. On the other hand, you're kind of sheltered, aren't you?"

Claire bristled. "Victoria isn't exactly Compton Heights from what I've heard. I bet you're pretty sheltered, too."

"I've seen a thing or two," Morgan said. "I know when someone's on something, and he was definitely on something. Cocaine, maybe."

Claire thought back to her time with Daniel, thoroughly taken aback. She'd never seen him do drugs. Sure, he'd been erratic, but most creative people were. He'd kept her separate from his other friends, but she'd taken that as a compliment at the time—that he hadn't wanted to share her with them. Had he actually not wanted her to know what they were doing?

He was secretive. Sometimes he'd gotten phone calls and left the room to take them. Other times he went out and wouldn't tell her where. She hadn't liked it, but he was her boss as well as her boyfriend and had one hell of a temper. He'd definitely had all the power in their relationship. Afterward, she'd assumed those phone calls and meetings involved Edie.

Maybe not all of them.

"I'm still not sure I believe that," she said finally.

"Suit yourself. I'll bet a bundle I'm right. I bet he's into other trouble, as well."

"So what do we do?"

"You tell me. If Daniel was going to hide a whole bunch of boxes, where would he store them?"

"Not at the office—he knows I'd tell the police to look there." She tapped her foot. "At his Mom's house. It's out on Old Hardin Road—outside Billings. Her health is failing, and she moved into a care facility last year, but he hadn't sold it when he ran off."

"Let's go check it out."

Chapter Twenty

J AMIE WAS JUST ABOUT TO PULL OUT of the driveway
when Jake Matheson jogged up beside him and
called through the open window, "Want some company?"

"I thought you were entertaining the ladies."

"Autumn told me what you were up to. I thought I'd
come along, just in case."

"In case of what?"

"In case of trouble," Ethan said, coming up beside
Jake. "Morgan told me Daniel was hassling Autumn
yesterday. I don't like the sound of it. Now her house
has been broken into. Too much of a coincidence to me.
I'm coming, too. So's Rob."

"Rob?"

"Don't worry, I've got Ned covering for me with
your mystery midnight caller," Rob said, catching up to
them.

"I'm surprised Luke isn't along for the ride, too,"
Jamie drawled, tapping his fingers impatiently as they
climbed into his truck.

"He's helping Autumn," Jake said.

While Jamie had always been closest to Rob, the rest of the Mathesons hung around a lot when he was growing up, so he knew Jake well. They rode to Billings in a comfortable silence, although as the minutes ticked away, he worried more and more about what they'd find when they got there.

"Have you talked to her?" Jake asked when they were more than an hour into the drive.

"No. She's not picking up her cell."

"I've got Morgan's number. She programmed it into my phone today," Ethan said, perking up. He pulled out his phone and punched a button. Jamie kept his eyes on the road. He knew Ethan never used the thing, hated gadgets and technology. But couldn't he have thought of it just this once? Would have been helpful to have that bit of information long before this. "Hey. It's Ethan. Are you at Claire's?" He listened a moment. "You're what? Bad idea, Morgan. We're on our way—we'll be there in half an hour. Just sit tight, okay?" He was silent again. "I don't care how close you are, I don't want you going any farther until we get there." A short pause. "I say so. I'm your brother, that's who. Sit tight. Fuck—she hung up on me."

"Sounds like she takes after Claire," Jake said.

"Both of them are insane. They're going after this Daniel guy—just the two of them. Claire thinks she knows where Daniel put her stuff."

"Where?"

"His mom's house. She said something about Old

Hardin Road. Near Noblewood."

"That's not much to go on; there's got to be a hundred houses near there," Jamie said.

"Give me that," Jake said and took the phone from Ethan. "I'm surprised you know how to work this thing."

"I don't," Ethan grumbled. "Morgan showed me which button to push to reach her."

"That's a top of the line model," Rob said, leaning in to look at what Jake was doing.

"Claire bought it. She wanted another way to boss me around."

They all laughed, but the atmosphere in the truck remained tense in spite of it. They didn't know anything was wrong, Jamie thought. Not in any concrete sense. Daniel might not have had a thing to do with the break in. But that didn't matter, because every man present had the gut feeling trouble was brewing, and if all four of them felt it, they were probably right.

"Here. I've got it. Ethel Ledstrom, 6500 Old Hardin Rd. I'll give you directions when we get closer."

Jamie pushed the accelerator down. "Call Cab. Tell him what's going down."

"I WISH YOU HAD TWO OF THOSE," Claire said, nodding at the baseball bat Morgan gripped in her right hand. "Did you find it in your rental car or did you bring it with you on the plane?"

"It was in the closet of my motel. From now on I'm packing one in my carry-on bag, though. I had no idea how handy they are. Are you ready?"

"I guess."

"I could call Ethan back."

"Forget it, we don't need brawn, we need stealth."

They'd stopped in a home and garden store on their way out of Billings and purchased a crowbar and pair of long-handled snips. "We should just grab a couple of ski masks while we're at it," Morgan had said, but the cashier didn't look at them twice when they checked out. As they exited the car, Claire hefted them and realized she was now the better armed of the two.

She hoped it didn't come to violence.

Although she'd like to punch Daniel right between the eyes.

"Do you think anyone's home?" Morgan said as she came around the car and joined Claire where she stood surveying the small house. There was a low light burning inside but nothing was visible through the thick curtains. No vehicles were parked in the driveway, but several cars and trucks were parked on the road nearby.

"Maybe. We'd better be quiet. We'll check around and see what we can see. If we spot my stuff we'll call the police and sit tight until they get here."

"I don't know. Maybe we should wait for Rob and Ethan to arrive."

"They'd want to call the police first, and then the police would say they needed a search warrant. If we can tell them we've seen the boxes, maybe they'll actually come and look."

"It might be dangerous."

"Fine. Stay here. I'm going."

Claire crossed the road and after a moment, Morgan followed her. They kept close to the side of the property, hugging the bushy hedge that ran between the house and its neighbor. The shadows were thick here, and nothing moved in the yard except for them. Claire held her breath as they passed the small, old-fashioned house. Moving into the back yard, she let it out in relief. Back here no one could see them except from the house itself and while the windows in the rear of the building were uncovered, the rooms beyond them were dim and most likely empty.

"Should we peek in?" Morgan asked.

Claire shook her head. "He'll put it in the garage." She pointed to a large structure at the end of the drive-way near the back of the property. "He could drive right up to it and unload everything without anyone noticing."

Once more Claire led the way. The garage was shab-bier than the house, a shingled wide building with two sliding doors whose rows of square window panes were blacked out with paint. Claire looked it over and her stomach sank. Could they break a window without waking up the entire neighborhood? She didn't see how they could get in this way.

"Let's go around—there might be another door in back. A regular door," Morgan said.

"Okay."

They crept along the edge of the building, fumbling their way along as the shadows grew deeper.

"Here it is," Morgan whispered.

Claire peered in the glass in the upper half of an old-fashioned door. The interior of the garage was very dark but it was filled with something that looked like boxes.

"Let's check it out," Claire said.

Morgan nodded.

Claire turned the handle of the knob. It didn't open. She tried again with the same result. Anger surged through her. Anger at Daniel, at her own stupidity—at how nothing ever seemed to go her way. She lifted the crowbar and jabbed one end sharply through the glass.

"Claire!"

She dropped the crowbar, stuck a hand through and turned the knob from the inside. "No one's around. I have to see if it's my stuff." She tip-toed through the open door and peered inside, not willing to turn on the light despite her bold words. She took several steps forward before bumping into something. She ran her fingers over it. A box—definitely a box. Reaching out, she felt another one. And another. They were piled high. She used the snips to cut through the packing tape on the first one, set them down and felt inside. Tiles. She was sure of it.

"We were right—these are mine," she hissed as Morgan came up beside her.

"They were yours," a deep voice corrected. The lights snapped on and Claire whirled to see Daniel in the doorway, backed by two other men she didn't know. Two other large men—one in a blue windbreaker, the other sporting a leather jacket. They nudged each other and giggled, an incongruous sound that made her insides tighten with dread. There was something off about all three of them. Something that told her they were drunk…or high.

Definitely high, she thought. Daniel looked furious, which set her heart thumping, but the two behind him terrified her. One had begun to smile, a feral expression like a pit bull spotting its prey.

"They're still mine," she said loudly, desperately hoping that if she acted tough she could bluff her way out of this. Beside her, Morgan pulled out her phone and lifted it to her ear.

"Ethan," she managed to say before Daniel lurched forward, ripped it out of her hand and threw it across the garage. Morgan retaliated with a swing of her bat, but she only held it in one hand and the blow bounced uselessly off Daniel's shoulder. Claire scrabbled for the crow bar, realized it was outside and grabbed for the snips, instead. She held them in front of her like a shield. Daniel just laughed.

"Kyle, take care of that one." He pointed to Morgan.

One of the goons in the doorway lunged at her and she walloped him hard with the bat. He grunted, grabbed it and yanked it away from her, tossing it to Daniel, who caught it easily.

"Take her up to the house," Daniel said. He ran a hand down the bat's length and grinned. "Have your fun, but make sure she doesn't make any noise." Before Claire could react, Morgan scrambled onto the pile of boxes, but Kyle grabbed her ankle, jerked her back, and tossed her to the floor, pinning her wrists behind her back.

"Morgan!" Claire cried, trying to push the man off of her. She shoved against his nylon-covered shoulders, but he elbowed her, knocking her to the ground as he stood up, tossed Morgan over his shoulder like a saddlebag and hauled her outside. The other one followed, shutting the door behind them.

Claire surged to her feet, desperate to go after her, but Daniel stepped into her path, the bat held high as if he were about to swing. "Don't worry about her," he said as the men's ugly laughter and Morgan's muffled shrieks died away in the distance. "Worry about yourself. Ron and Kyle like to have their fun, but who knows? Maybe she'll like their games." Her stomach curled as she watched him warily. If he was saying what she thought he was saying, she would tear him to pieces with her bare hands. He took a step forward. "I don't play games, though. I've had enough of your interference."

Morgan was right, she thought wildly as he advanced. Daniel was definitely on something. His eyes had a gleam she didn't recognize, and his wiry body was taut with energy. He tightened his grip on the bat and raised it.

She held up the snips, their long handles giving her some bargaining room, at least. His first swing nearly ripped them out of her fingers, but she managed to block him, barely. Her palms stung from the force of the collision and she retreated a step, backing up against the pile of boxes behind her. Daniel wound up again.

"I'm going to enjoy watching you die."

Feeling behind her, hoping against hope she could

scramble on top of the boxes and get away from Daniel, one of the flaps came free, and she realized it was the box she'd opened earlier. What was in it? She felt around frantically. Tiles. Grasping the top one, she pulled it out—one of the Bologna marble tiles Carl had gone on about.

Daniel began to swing and she did the only thing she could—threw the heavy square with all her might. It caught him flush in the face, splitting his cheek until it blossomed with blood.

"Damn it!" Daniel dropped the bat and clapped his hands to his face. Claire scooped it up and ran for the door, pulling it open and slamming it shut behind her, wishing she could lock him in.

Somehow she had to get Morgan away from those two monsters and both of them to her car. As she dashed across the lawn she felt her pocket. Thank goodness—she still had her keys. She raced up the back steps, opened the door carefully and peered inside, the bat held ready. The room she entered was only dimly lit, but she heard a cry and a thump from behind a door down the hall. She bit her lip to keep from calling out to Morgan. The only shot she had was to catch her captors by surprise.

When she opened the door, however, all thoughts of stealth went out of her mind. Morgan lay on the bed, her blouse ripped open and one of the men—Kyle—straddling her. The other man sat in an easy chair as if ready to watch a television show.

She only hesitated a second before she launched herself across the room.

"Get off her! Get off my sister!"

A LIGHT WAS ON at 6500 Old Hardin Way when Jamie pulled up in front.

"That's Claire's car," Ethan said, pointing to where it sat across the street. He opened his door and in moments all of them were out of the truck.

"Hold up, let's check things from the outside first," Jake said.

They all froze as a woman's voice called out, muffled but definitely in distress.

"Claire!" Jamie took off like a shot, raced across the lawn and pounded up the three concrete steps to the front door. Footsteps echoed behind him. The door was locked and he scanned the house for another way in.

"Window," Rob said. He jumped off the stoop, picked up an empty terra cotta flower pot and hurled it at the plate glass front window. It shattered and Rob ducked, then knocked a few shards off the lower edge and began to climb in. Jamie waited his turn impatiently. Claire was in there. She needed help.

Once inside they tore through the house until they came to a back bedroom whose door was wide open.

Jamie barreled inside, the others close on his heels, to find Morgan, her shirt torn nearly in half, beating a man over the head with a table lamp. Claire was tussling with a second man, who was trying to wrench a baseball bat out of her hands.

Rob pushed past him and tackled the man with Morgan on the bed. As he heard the smack of fist against skin, Jamie went for the other one, the goon trying to wrest the bat away from Claire. Wrapping an arm around his throat, he wrestled him to the floor. Claire delivered a blow with the bat across his knees that set the man bellowing. When Ethan and Jake joined in, together they subdued the two men in a matter of seconds.

"Daniel," Claire gasped, bent over and breathing hard like she'd just run a race.

"What about him?" Jamie growled.

"He's…"

"I'm right here," a new voice said from the door. "Miss me already, Claire?"

Jamie heard the unmistakable sound of a pistol being cocked. The itch between his shoulder blades told him the gun was pointed straight at him.

"Fuck off, Daniel," Claire said, her eyes blazing.

"No, I don't think I will," Daniel said. "But I do think I'll kill you. After I kill this asshole."

Jamie felt the gun's barrel against the back of his head.

"No!" Claire cried.

"Drop it!"

Jamie would know that voice anywhere. Cab. He closed his eyes and expelled a gust of air when the pressure of the barrel disappeared and Claire surged forward and wrapped her arms around him. "Jamie!"

A glance over his shoulder told him what he needed to know. Cab and several other men in sheriff's uniforms swarmed into the room, quickly taking Daniel and the other two men into custody. Glancing from one shocked face to another, he saw that Ethan and Jake had thought he was a goner.

Rob was too busy comforting a crying Morgan to notice anything else. Claire gripped him like she would never let go.

He never wanted her to let go.

As he went to hug her back just as tightly, he remembered he had promised not to touch her. Claire looked up at him, her eyes brimming with tears. "To hell with the bet."

He bent down and lifted her into his arms, carrying her out of the house and onto the front stoop. He sat down as gently as possible, and perched her on his lap. "Are you okay?"

She nodded, still clinging to him. "He wanted to kill me."

He hugged her tighter. "I've got you. No one's ever going to hurt you."

She burrowed into his embrace. "Jamie." Her voice cracked and his anger soared again. How dare anyone terrify Claire—his Claire? He turned to look for Daniel again, only to see him hauled out of the house in handcuffs, barely able to stand as two officers dragged him off. A deep breath restored a little calm. Justice would be done. Claire was safe now.

Safe in his arms.

HOURS LATER they were back in the Big House, gathered in the living room while Autumn served tea and coffee cake. None of them would be good for anything in the morning, Claire thought, but who could sleep?

She sat next to Jamie, who'd kept an arm around her every moment since back at Daniel's mother's house.

Although the night was warm, she was wrapped in a blanket. She couldn't stop shaking, a fine tremor that even made drinking tea difficult.

She felt sick. All of this was because of her greed. Her need to prove to everyone she was worth something. Thank God all the supplies Daniel stole were unharmed. She would arrange to return every last one of them first thing tomorrow. But going after him like that—without help? Morgan had almost been raped. They both could have been killed.

She took a ragged breath. The others were scattered around the room, talking in low voices. Rob stuck as close to Morgan as Jamie was sticking to her.

"Were all those boxes things for my house?" Jamie asked softly.

Pain flooded through her as she forced herself to nod.

"Seems like a lot."

He was being as gentle as possible, she knew. Time to fess up. All she could do was hope he wouldn't hate her guts. "I kept changing my mind. I kept buying more. I just couldn't get the design right."

"I liked your first design, you know." He stroked her hair.

"I know. I kind of went crazy. I wanted the Whitfield contract so bad." She took a shuddering breath, trying with all her might to stop her hands from shaking.

His arm tightened around her. "I wish you cared as much about my home as you do about his."

"Jamie." Tears stung her lids again as she put a hand on his thigh and turned to face him. "I do care about your home. I care about it a lot." *I care about you a lot,* she wanted to add, but she couldn't—not when she'd messed up so badly. He had to hate her for what she'd done—trying to make his perfect log home into a stupid showplace just to impress Carl. And for what? To get back at Daniel, a man she should have left behind months ago?

Jamie was right. All this time she'd kept her focus on Daniel instead of paying attention to him. Worse—she'd judged him and found him wanting based on nothing except for her own jealousy. She didn't deserve his compassion now. She deserved his disgust.

"It's no mansion."

"I don't care about mansions," she said, wishing she'd never heard of Carl Whitfield or his stupid contract.

He kissed her on the cheek and Claire blinked back tears. Why was he being so nice to her?

"It's predictable." His kiss trailed down her throat to the base of her neck.

She drew in a quick breath, hardly daring to move. "I love predictable," she whispered.

He titled her chin up until their gaze met. "I hope you love unpredictable, too."

Her lips trembled and she knew she was one breath away from breaking down. But Jamie didn't look angry, or disgusted, or even put out.

"I'm so sorry," she said, and the tears did fall, sliding down her face as fast as she could wipe them away. "I…"

"Shh." Jamie pulled her close. "I don't care about the house, or how much money you spent or anything but the fact that you're safe and here with me. I love you.

You know that, right? Tell me you know that, Claire."

She sobbed and buried her face in his chest.

"Claire." He bent over her, stroking her back.

"That's the first time you said it." Her voice was high and thin.

"Said what, honey?"

"That you love me."

He stilled and she could tell he was thinking. "I guess I thought you always knew. I've loved you about as long as I've known you. I've wanted to marry you practically all my life."

She pushed away from him, straightening up until they were eye to eye. "Your proposal was real?"

"Of course it was real. I've been telling you that for weeks."

All the fight went out of her at once. Jamie loved her. He really loved her. "You win," she said shakily. "I don't want to travel around the world. I just want to come home."

"Claire, I don't want to keep you from having adventures, or doing the work you love or any of it—understand? If you'll be my wife I'll help make all of your dreams come true. Just let me be by your side."

"Okay." Her voice was barely a whisper.

Jamie searched her face, as if looking for the truth. "You mean that? You'll stay with me? You'll marry me?"

She nodded and hid her face in his neck as he pulled her close again.

"Claire Cruz, you've just made me the happiest man alive."

Chapter Twenty-One

SEVERAL HOURS LATER, after Claire had cried her heart out in his arms, and he'd nearly shed a tear or two himself, they'd come to a more peaceful place where they could talk about life together; their hopes and dreams. They even managed to talk about the house, about returning to Claire's initial design. They day-dreamed about living in it together, and working together, traveling someday, and as they designed a life together, Claire's fear passed away and a smile returned to her face.

The rest of the party turned in for the night, including Morgan, who would stay in one of the empty rooms in the Big House, and Rob who insisted on camping out on one of the living room sofas, just in case she needed him. Jamie offered to escort Claire back to the bunk-house.

"I want to stay with you," she said and his heart expanded until he didn't know how it could still fit in his chest. Walking with her up the trail to his cabin, he only meant to hold her hand, but they hadn't got a third of the way there before she was in his arms. They kissed long and hard, swaying against each other, before he tore himself away and hurried her along the path. Another few hundred yards and they stopped again, kisses leading to heavy petting. Jamie unbuttoned Claire's shirt as she devoured his mouth. She helped him unhook her bra and then her breasts were free, warm and full under his hands.

When she went to work on his shirt, he tore it off himself, relishing the feel of skin on skin as he drew her back into his embrace. He couldn't kiss enough of her, couldn't touch enough of her, and he was beginning to think if they didn't reach the cabin soon, he'd have to make love to her right here on the path.

He lifted her up and carried her the rest of the way, nearly tripping once or twice in the dark, but managing to keep his feet. Up to the front porch, fumbling with the door, and then inside. When he deposited her on the bed, he collapsed beside her.

"Am I that heavy?" she asked, laughing.

"You're perfect," he growled, and pounced on her.

He soon peeled off every stitch of clothing she wore and flung it to the floor. He wanted her naked. He wanted to touch every inch of her, kiss every inch of her, and then do it all over again. As far as he was concerned the rest of the world could go to hell. He had everything he wanted here in his arms.

She lay back and held still, even when he kissed her. Jamie slowed down, afraid he'd scared her off—afraid she wasn't actually ready for this, especially after the night's events. "You okay?" he whispered.

"Yes." But she ducked her head and wouldn't meet his eye.

"What is it?"

Her voice was muffled. "Remember on the trail? What I did?"

Hell, he'd never forget that as long as he lived. "Yeah. You want to do it again?"

"Kind of. I want...you to be the one who...."

An electric jolt coursed through his body. Oh yeah. He was up for that. "You got it," he said, and tilted her chin up to kiss her. "You just lie back and let me work my magic."

Claire did just that, reaching up over her head to grasp the headboard. With her arms raised, her breasts were irresistible, and he didn't hold back. As he showered them with kisses, tugging first one nipple, then the other into his mouth, squeezing them and laving them with his tongue, her breathing quickened and she closed her eyes. He kneed her legs apart and she gasped, opening them again.

He knew what she wanted and she was going to get it, but now he wanted to take his time. He kissed a trail down her stomach to her mound and then lower still. Claire groaned and bit her lip.

"Is this good?" he asked, as if he didn't know the answer.

She looked at him with shining eyes. "It's nice," she said, but she couldn't fool him.

He dipped his head again. She was so sensual, so responsive. For once, all of her attention focused solely on him. He dipped lower, tasting her, teasing her, browsing her secret folds and places until she was fighting to keep from crying aloud. As he brought her to the peak of sensation, he pulled away, all of a sudden desperate to be within her—to be joined with her. A longer session would have to wait.

He moved over her, groaning himself when he positioned himself near her core. "Claire?" he whispered.

"I'm ready." Her fingers clutching the headboard were white.

She gazed at him with loving eyes and he was overcome by the strength of her trust in him. Unable to hold back any longer, he pushed inside her with a strong stroke and was rewarded with her passionate groan.

Jamie pulled out and thrust into her again, spurred on by her response. Sliding out and in again, slowly and deliberately, he moved within her until he could barely retain control. Then he sped up, the sensation building to crescendo inside him. When Claire cried out, he went over the edge with her, grunting his own release as wave after wave of feeling overpowered him.

He loved Claire, loved this woman he cradled in his arms. If she wasn't already wearing his ring, he'd have put it on her finger tonight. They would spend their lives together, and he would make love to her every night.

He kissed her soundly and rolled off of her, snuggling her into the crook of his arm. Claire was finally his—forever.

Chapter Twenty-Two

SINCE NO ONE HAD GOTTEN a good night's sleep, Ethan and Jamie decided to postpone the campout until the following day, and Rose and Tracey volunteered to take the ladies to Billings to go shopping. Claire helped Autumn do up the rooms and give the Big House a thorough cleaning. By the time the women returned, happily laden down with packages, Autumn had a gourmet dinner on that pleased everyone.

The following morning, everyone met early at the stables to saddle up for their overnight trip out onto the range. The party had swelled to nearly twice its intended size with Morgan and all the Matheson men joining in. Autumn had shaken her head, sighed, and packed more provisions into the saddle bags. She wouldn't be coming along. Instead, Rose was taking her place as cook on the campout.

As happy as she could ever remember being, Claire helped Jamie get their guests' horses ready for the long trek.

"I'm a little saddle sore and I haven't even been in

the saddle," he said, sneaking close for a kiss before tending to the little gray mare that Angel had ridden all week.

"You think you're saddle sore." Claire smiled at the memory of their previous night's lovemaking. Slow and tender and unforgettable. "Tomorrow will be worse, you know."

"Because of the ride?"

"Because of the way I'm going to ride you tonight." She blushed a little at her own boldness. Jamie's look told her much more of that and he'd shuck off her clothes right here and now and to hell with the horses and guests.

She sobered at the thought and turned away. No illicit sex in the stable—she wasn't her mother. A pang of unease swept through her. She was taking a hell of a chance, hitching her heart to a man like Jamie. Women adored him. How long before he got bored of her and strayed from her side?

She tried to shake off the thought. Jamie wasn't Mack. And she wasn't her mother. Surely the two of them could make a go of this.

Ned came into the stable and said something in low tones to Jamie. Frowning, Claire let her fingers tighten the strap she was working on. What were they talking about?

"You don't say. Maddy? I thought she'd be more straightforward."

"She was pretty straightforward when we got down to it," Ned laughed.

"She didn't mind the substitution?"

"She called it an upgrade." Ned slapped Jamie on the back. "Thanks, man."

"Thank you." Jamie glanced in her direction and stiffened when he caught her watching them. Ned left the stable, whistling.

"What was all that?" Claire asked the next time Jamie passed her.

He looked sheepish. "One of the guests tried to organize a little…one-on-one time with me the other night. I let Ned handle it."

"You passed up a chance for a roll in the hay? Was that before or after you found out what Morgan and I were up to?"

"Meaning would I have slept with someone else if I hadn't known you were in danger?" There was an edge to his voice. "No, Claire. I wouldn't have slept with her. I already arranged things with Rob. He passed it off to Ned when he heard about you and Morgan."

She dropped her gaze. "Sorry." She hated to admit to herself how much the thought of Jamie with another woman burned her through and through.

"Not sorry enough. Get it through your head. You're the only woman for me."

She busied herself with the horses, not daring to answer that. When they exited the barn, she caught Rose's eye. Rose was already mounted on her horse and as her gaze swept Claire and Jamie, she started in surprise, then a smile spread over her face.

Claire raised an eyebrow. What had Rose seen? Remembering their conversation in Autumn's kitchen, she looked Jamie over, then stared down at herself. Had her energy…changed?

God, she hoped so.

ALL IN ALL, the ride went smoothly enough and there were plenty of hands to make setting up the camp at the end of the day quick work. Rose might not have been the gourmet chef that Autumn was turning out to be, but the evening meal was incredibly tasty after a day out in the fresh air, and as dusk deepened into night the group sat around a campfire telling stories and jokes, even singing a song or two.

Autumn packed plenty of beer, and the evening definitely took on a mellow feel as it progressed. Maddy, who hadn't made eye contact with Jamie all day, sat close to Ned. Jake and Luke made a point of squiring Liz and Adrienne around. Ethan and Christine were engaged in a conversation about the best time to wean infants. Angel had already gone to bed.

Ethan headed off to his tent. Christine went to hers. Several of the other couples slipped off into the night and Jamie grimaced as he thought the Cruz Guest Ranch might get a reputation it wasn't entirely after. Still, he couldn't blame anyone. He sure planned to make the most of his time with Claire.

She was busy helping Rose pack things away for the night. Rob was looking after the horses, checking them one last time before turning in. Jamie wanted to clean up a bit before his night with Claire. He joined her where she was packing the food into a bag near a rope dangling over an overhead tree branch. Once she was done, she'd haul it up high away from marauding animals.

"Want help with that?"

"I've got it."

"Meet you back at the tent?"

"You in a rush?" She smiled.

"I've got a thing or two to do before you get there. See you soon."

He'd set up their tent a little ways apart from the others in a stand of pine trees. Claire was a ranch girl and she wasn't squeamish, but a day on the trail had him as stinky as a skunk in heat. There wasn't a lot he could do to fix that, but he'd at least give it a try.

He hadn't been in the tent for two minutes, however, when footsteps approached and someone cleared her throat outside. "Jamie?"

It wasn't Claire. He swore softly. He'd been rummaging in a bag by flashlight, trying to find some soap and a wash rag. The tent was hard to move around in, with bedding and bags piled up to one side.

"Yeah."

"It's Morgan. Can I come in?"

He relaxed. Not one of his oversexed guests, then. "Sure thing." He unzipped the door and she stepped in, the flashlight sending odd shadows to her face. She moved stiffly and he wondered if the ride had been more than she was used to.

"I didn't want to tell Claire, because she's already so freaked out about putting me in danger," she began.

"She should be," Jamie interrupted. "That was a damn fool trick."

"I went along with it," she said shortly. "Anyway, I'm really sore."

"From the ride?"

"No. Those guys…they were pretty rough the other night. They knocked me around a bit. Something really hurts between my shoulder blades."

Jamie sucked in a breath, a haze of anger surging upwards in him again. He didn't know how much time would have to pass before he could think of the previous night's events without being overcome by the desire to pound Ledstrom to a bloody pulp.

"I can't see it," Morgan went on. "Like I said, I didn't want to ask Claire to look. She feels so bad already. I can't ask Rob, either. I'm having a hard enough time fending him off. If I start undoing my shirt he'll be all over me."

Jamie suppressed a smile. "I thought you liked him."

"I do. Sort of. But my life isn't here—it's back in Canada. Why start something I can't finish? Anyway," she sighed. "I know this is weird but would you just look at my back. I swear I won't jump you."

"Sure. Better do it quick, though, if you don't want Claire to see, too. She'll be here in a minute."

Morgan turned her back to him, undid a few buttons of her shirt and dropped it down over her shoulders so it hung near her waist. "See anything?"

Jamie held up the flashlight. "Shit." A dark blue-black bruise spread over most of her back. "Morgan, I've never seen anything like that."

CLAIRE FROZE AS SHE APPROACHED the tent where it lay
secluded in a stand of wiry pine trees. A flashlight inside
lit the canvas structure and highlighted two silhouettes
against a backdrop of white.

A man and a woman.

Jamie and Morgan.

Their shadows juddered and dodged, but they stood
close together, Morgan's head turned to Jamie, his hands
stretched out to touch her.

"Morgan," Jamie said, his voice low and husky. "I've
never seen anything like that."

Like what? What was she showing him?

Morgan moved and her shadow clarified. Something
bunched around her waist—her shirt?—her breasts
sharply delineated against the nylon. Half undressed, she
moved closer to Jamie.

"Hold still," he said. "I want a closer look."

Rage surged inside her. This could not be happening
again—not again. First her mother and Mack, then
Daniel and Edie. Now Jamie? Her fiance?

He couldn't even wait until after the wedding to
cheat on her?

No.

She couldn't stand it.

With a cry of pain, she darted forward, unzipped the
tent and pushed inside. "You bitch!" She leaped forward
to shove her half-sister to the ground. "I knew it! I knew
you weren't what you were pretending to be!"

"Claire!" Jamie caught Morgan before she hit the floor. Claire fell on top of her and all three of them crashed to the ground.

"Ouch!" The pile of bedding beside them moved, jerked, and a blonde head popped out, followed by a naked set of shoulders.

"Angel? What the hell are you doing here?" Claire said. Morgan tried to scramble to her knees, but Claire shoved her down again.

"I was waiting for Jamie," Angel said in her dreamy voice. "I must have fallen asleep. You took so long," she whined at him.

Claire's rage turned to outright fury. "Two women? Two of them? What were you planning, an orgy?"

"Jesus, Claire, calm down." Jamie lifted Morgan off his lap and slid out from under her. "I was just..."

"I don't want to hear it. I don't want to have anything to do with you. Screw your house and screw you, Jamie Lassiter!" She tugged the engagement ring she'd worn for over a month off and threw it in his face. Fumbling her way out of the tent, the pain of understanding that it was over—absolutely over between them—took her breath away.

"Claire, stop! Where are you going?"

"Back to Billings. I'm done with all of you."

IT TOOK FOREVER to restore a sobbing Morgan back to Rob and escort Angel to her tent with firm instructions not to leave it again for the duration of the night. By that time, Claire and Storm were gone.

It was madness for her to set off in the dark over open rangeland. There was no path to follow—no way for her to get home without careful attention to landmarks and directions. How the hell she planned to do that in the dark, he didn't know.

"What's going on?" Ethan asked, materializing by his side as he saddled his horse.

"Claire caught me with Morgan and Angel. I wasn't doing anything," he snapped as Ethan's eyebrow's rose. "I want your sister, not your…half-sister, for god's sake."

"Yeah, I know. Where is Claire?"

"Gone."

Ethan sighed. "Not again."

"I can handle this one alone."

After a moment's hesitation Ethan nodded. "Go get her."

"That's exactly what I plan to do."

CLAIRE WANTED TO URGE STORM on to a canter, or even a full out gallop, but while she might risk it on known territory, she wouldn't do that to a horse here. She couldn't believe she'd been tricked again. Couldn't believe she'd fallen for the one man she knew beyond a shadow of a doubt was incapable of fidelity. So much for the difference between flirting and cheating. If one led to the other, who cared about definitions?

Face it, she wasn't special enough to keep a man's attention. She wasn't even good enough to keep her own mother's attention.

She swiped a tear with the back of her hand and scanned the ground in front of her as best she could. Was she even heading in the right direction? One part of her didn't care—wanted to get lost in these rolling hills. The other part, the rational part who'd grown up here in the wide-open spaces of Montana, knew that she had little water and no food and wouldn't last long if she got lost. She'd better slow down and get her bearings.

As she reined Storm in to a halt, however, she heard hoofbeats behind her and Jamie rode up before she could urge her horse forward again.

"For God's sake, Claire, would you listen to me for once? Really listen?" he said without preamble.

"There's nothing more for you to say."

"Yes, there is. There's plenty. You walked in on me back there in a situation that looked like something it wasn't. You need to let me explain."

"I don't need to let you do anything. There's one thing I'm perfectly clear about—I'm not going to be the little woman who sits at home while you flirt and sleep with everything in a skirt. I'm not going to do it. I'm worth more than that!"

Her voice hitched and more tears slipped from her eyes. Damn it, she wasn't going to cry—she was angry, not sad.

"Claire." Jamie came up beside her and reached out. She slapped his hand away.

"Don't." Storm sidestepped beneath her and she patted her flank to try to calm the mare. "I can't do this. I can't be afraid every minute about how you'll betray me next."

"I've never betrayed you," Jamie said angrily. "I've never betrayed anyone. Morgan was hurt and she didn't want you to know. She said you blamed yourself enough already and she didn't want to add to your worry. She's got an awful bruise on her back—she shouldn't even be on this ride—and she asked me to check it out so that neither you nor Rob would flip your lids."

"What about Angel?"

"What about her? She's a lunatic. I didn't even know she was there."

"What about the others—I've seen the way they look at you."

"Have you seen me return any of their attention? At all? I've kept up my side of the bargain. I haven't flirted with anyone. I haven't given them the time of day."

"You sure gave the time of day to Hannah O'Dell. You couldn't keep your hands off of her!"

Jamie stared at her as if she'd lost her mind. "Hannah O'Dell? What the heck are you talking about?"

"I saw you with her—two years ago in your cabin. All over her."

For a minute Jamie couldn't seem to catch up. Finally, he said, "Let me get this straight—you spied on me and Hannah O'Dell? Why the hell would you do that?"

She swung Storm away from him, clicking her teeth, but Jamie headed her off. "Tell me—why would you be at my cabin in the middle of the night?"

"I came...I wanted..." Damn it, she could barely talk for the ache in her throat.

"Jesus, Claire did you come to see me? Two years ago?" Jamie swung down off his horse, ducked around it and reached up for her. Before she could pull away, he'd tugged her down off of Storm. "I was breaking up with her, did you realize that? I was breaking up with her because I hoped you finally wanted to be with me. Then...you never came back. You fell for Ledstrom instead."

The anguish was all too clear in his voice.

"Funny way to break up with her," she finally made herself say, weighed down with the knowledge that she'd been guilty of break-up sex once or twice herself. "It doesn't matter. None of this matters. We can't get married because if we do you'll be sick of me in a matter of days."

"How can you say that?" Jamie gripped her tighter. "I could look at you all day long, every day, and not get tired of you. I have looked at you, listened to you, worked with you all day long and all it's ever done is leave me hungry for more. Nothing matters to me except being with you."

"You say that now, but everyone leaves me—my mother, Daniel..."

She tried to pull back but he wrapped his arms around her and bent closer.

"I will never leave you. Everything I've done in my life, I've done for you. Every damn last thing. Working like a dog, saving my money, buying into the ranch...all of it."

This time, the sob that welled up in her throat

wouldn't be pushed down. Tears spilled over her cheeks and she couldn't stop them. She shook her head.

"How can you not know that I love you?" he growled. "All I do is try to show you."

"I know you love me. Now. But it won't last, it never does, and I can't bear the thought of you leaving me," she said through her tears. "I can't bear it, Jamie."

"It won't happen. I promise." He held her even tighter.

Her chest hurt so bad she could barely breathe. "You can't promise that." She thought of the day her parents died. Ethan's phone call. The knowledge sinking into her heart that she'd never see them again.

Somehow Jamie knew where her thoughts had gone. "Your mother didn't want to leave you. Neither did your father," he said softly.

His quiet words burst the dam that held all the pain she'd been holding back. "I miss her, I miss both of them," she cried. "Oh, God, Jamie, I didn't get to say good-bye!"

"I know, honey." He brushed his lips over the top of her head.

"She thought I hated her. I was so angry…"

"She knew you loved her. She knows it now."

"Why didn't she just tell us what had happened? So we knew why she had to leave all the time? Why didn't she tell us the truth?" Her words came out in broken phrases.

"She was afraid," Jamie said softly. "Fear makes us do strange things."

Claire laughed, a painful, torn sound. "It made me keep buying materials for your house until I had four times as much as I could possibly use."

"It made me jump the gun and propose before we'd ever gone out on a date."

She took a deep, shuddering breath and wiped her face with the back of her hand. "It's kept me from loving you."

"I know." He tightened his embrace. "Please stop being afraid. I want to make a life with you."

Claire lowered her head onto his chest and listened to the beat of his heart. She could change history right now, she knew. She could stop the cycle of fear and pain if she only had the courage to do it.

"What if I screw this up, too? What if I get scared again and can't do it?"

"I'll wait for you," Jamie said. "You're worth waiting for, Claire."

IN THE END they slept out on the open range, making love once more under a crescent moon while the horses stood nearby. This time their lovemaking was slow and sensual, a thorough exploration of each by the other. When Claire fell asleep in his arms, exhausted by the long day and heavy emotions, Jamie watched the moonlight trace shadows over the contours of her face.

This woman he knew so well held enough mysteries to keep his attention riveted for a lifetime, and he had no doubt they would dream up plenty of schemes to keep themselves busy throughout it, too. It had seemed important to him that Claire give up her interior design work and return to the ranch business when she was his wife, and he saw now that was based on fear, too.

It didn't matter if they worked together, or if they spent their days apart; he and Claire would last—he would bet on that.

In the morning, when he woke up, she was gazing at him.

"Hey, how're you feeling?" he asked, coming up on one elbow.

"Good. Peaceful." She rolled onto her back. The sight of her brought lustful thoughts swirling into his brain, but he kept them in check. He wanted to hear what she had to say.

"The open country helps me sort my thoughts, you know what I mean?"

He nodded. "Yep. Same for me."

"Mom tried to have it all—she tried to be everything to everyone without admitting she'd made mistakes and she ended up hurting us all. But what she did isn't who she is. Was." Jamie braced himself, ready for more tears, but Claire remained dry-eyed. "She loved all of us. Every last one. Me, Ethan, Dad, Morgan. She did her best."

"She did."

"I like Morgan."

Jamie laughed. "As much as you don't want to?"

She rolled to face him again, nodding ruefully. "I really wanted to hate her, but I can't. She's pretty cool."

"Crazy, too. Going with you after Daniel."

"You should see her swing a bat." She sobered. "You

said she's hurt? We should get her to a doctor."

"It's just a really big bruise. Really, really big. We'll get her checked out but she'll be okay."

"I should never have gotten her involved."

"You should have gotten me involved. I'd do anything to help you, you know that, right?"

She was silent a minute. "I guess I do now."

"Claire," he sat up and drew her up, too. "Will you marry me?"

"I already said yes."

"I need to hear you say it again."

"Yes."

"Forever?"

"Yes."

"For always?

"Yes!" She lunged forward, wrapped her arms around his neck and kissed him until he fell over. "Yes, yes, yes, yes, yes!"

"I'd put a ring on your finger, but it's already there," he said, holding it up.

"And it's never coming off again."

Chapter Twenty-Three

A MORE RAGGED AND WOEBEGONE GROUP OF RIDERS had probably never straggled their way onto the Cruz ranch, Claire thought as she followed the rest of them up to the stable yard. Half the participants were nursing a horrendous hangover. The other half had barely slept. The long ride and bright sunshine tired everyone out.

"I hope Autumn's got a hell of a dinner planned," Ethan mumbled as he helped them begin to unsaddle the horses. The guests made their way slowly up to the Big House. The Mathesons stayed to unpack gear, then went home to clean up. They would return for dinner since it was their guests' last big meal, but she had a feeling it would be an early night. The women would board a plane back to Pennsylvania in the morning. Morgan's flight would leave soon after.

"I wonder what kind of reviews they're going to write. I hope this was all worth it," Claire said as she and Jamie staggered back to his cabin. She'd already picked up a change of clothes.

Jamie shook his head. "I can only imagine."

"I call the shower first."

"Me, too."

She sagged into him, laughing, and he put an arm around her waist.

This is good, she thought, relishing the feel of him. *I can get used to this.*

"I'LL SEE YOU IN SEPTEMBER," Morgan said.

"That's a long time." Rob looked awfully serious, Jamie thought as he and Claire hung back to give the other two some privacy before Morgan got on her plane.

"You've got my email."

"That's not the same."

Morgan cocked her head. "So, come visit."

"Canada? Hell, I've hardly been out of Montana."

"The change will do you good."

Amen to that, Jamie thought. Rob was a good friend, but the man's interests were limited. He could stand to broaden his experience.

"You could come back here sooner," Rob said.

"I have a job."

Rob sighed. Claire laughed out loud at his hang-dog expression. "They're boarding your flight, Morgan."

"I know." She touched Rob's hand. "You know where to find me, cowboy." Turning to Claire and Ethan she added, "I'll miss you guys so much."

"We'll miss you, too," Claire said. "We have so much more to find out about each other."

"I'm looking forward to finding it all out. 'Bye. Love

you!" With shining eyes, she hurried away to join the line of passengers waiting for their turn to show their tickets to the flight attendant.

Claire looked wistful, but judging by Rob's expression, he was going to miss Morgan more than she was, Jamie thought. Normally, Rob was a love-'em-and-leave-'em kind of guy, but he sensed this ran deeper. Maybe his friend had finally met his match. Judging by the quick, furtive kiss he and Morgan exchanged when Claire wasn't looking, she returned his interest, at least a little.

She had promised to come back on Labor Day to be in their wedding. Claire asked her to stand up with her and Morgan had accepted with a shout of happiness that had them all covering their ears.

"Who's your best man going to be?" Rob had asked him.

"Maybe it should be Ethan, since he asked me to be his," Jamie said, grinning at Rob's reaction.

"Ethan? Come on, what about me? We've always been friends."

"Or maybe Cab. He's someone I can depend on."

"To hell with Cab! You know I'm the one who always bails you out."

It was too much fun tormenting Rob to let him know he'd already decided to ask him to be his best man. Let him sweat a few more days, at least.

"You should have asked her to stay," Rob said to Claire.

"On the ranch?"

"Why not?"

"You heard her—she has a job. Her life's in Victoria."

"Some life. Working for other people. Living alone. She belongs here." Rob shoved his hands in his pockets and glanced at Jamie. "Don't see what you're smiling about."

"Someone owes me some money," he said. His grin widened when Rob's shoulders slumped.

"I'll get it to you as soon as I can." He wandered off toward the window overlooking the tarmac.

Claire took Jamie's hand. "What was that all about?"

"Just getting a little revenge."

SEVERAL WEEKS LATER, Claire held Jamie's hand again while they watched the sun set in a blaze of reds and pinks. They stood on the front steps of Jamie's log house, sharing a bottle of beer. Most of the interior work was finished, but they hadn't moved the furniture in yet. They'd carried an air mattress and sleeping bags over from the cabin and planned to camp out here tonight, to get the feel for the space, as she'd put it to him earlier.

"I'm glad you'll be able to get your money back for most of that extra stuff you bought," Jamie said.

"Yeah. Most of it. The rest I'll save for future projects. We'll use it or sell it one way or another." She'd already packed up most of her belongings and moved them to Jamie's cabin until the log house was finished. Carrie and her boyfriend planned to take over the lease on her condo.

They both turned around as a truck pulled up the dirt

driveway to the house.

"Who the hell is that?" Jamie said, getting to his feet.

This was a strange time for visitors, Claire agreed. Then she recognized the top-of-the-line luxury truck. "It's Carl."

Jamie sighed and moved forward to meet him. Carl climbed down from the cab, looking awkward in his cowboy boots. Claire felt a pang of sympathy for the man. He really was a fish out of water in these parts, no matter how hard he tried to fit in.

"Claire—I've been looking for you everywhere," he said as he met them in the drive. "Took a devil of a lot of asking to get Autumn to tell me where you'd gotten to."

"Where's the fire?" Jamie asked.

"Just got back in town and I want to hire you for my decorating project before your schedule gets full up," Carl said. "That Daniel Ledstrom turned out to be some piece of work. Did you know he's an addict?"

"Yeah," Claire said. "We had an idea."

"Can't have a criminal decorating my house. That's not good enough for Lacey."

"Are you saying I am?" Claire asked him, holding his gaze.

His cheeks reddened. "I might have been a little caustic with you before and I apologize for that. Business is like that. You've got to push to get the best out of people sometimes."

"Things are different around here," Jamie said. "Here we get to know one another. We take character into account. Reward good work and loyalty."

"I'm learning that," Carl said. He turned back to Claire. "I looked over your original designs again and they're good. You made solid choices and you worked to keep the bottom line under control. I appreciate that. I might want some upgrades—I've got money to spend—but I think you can handle the job just fine. Will you take it?"

She glanced at Jamie. "I don't think so. I'm going into a whole new line of work."

Carl's face fell, and she felt a pinch of disappointment herself. A project as large as Carl's didn't come along every day.

Jamie squeezed her hand. "You don't have to give up your passions for me," he said.

"I want to work with you. I like being around the horses."

"Why not do both?"

A thrill of excitement coursed through her. "You think I could?"

"I don't see why not. When you feel like decorating a mansion, decorate a mansion. When the horses call you, come on a ride. Just carve out a night for me now and then, okay?"

Pure happiness warmed her from within. "Every night."

Carl cleared his throat. "I'll leave you two to your romantic evening. Come by tomorrow and we'll set up a contract, Claire."

"Sure will," she said.

When he was gone, she leaned into Jamie. "Thank

you."

"For what?"

"For seeing all of me, and…"

"Loving you?" He pulled her into an embrace. "I do love you, Claire. I always will."

"I've been thinking about our bet," she added, snuggling closer to him, "and I realized you lost, after all. You touched me before I agreed to marry you."

"Are you kidding? I won, definitely." The contentment in his voice made her smile.

"Actually," she said, feeling pretty content herself. "I think we both did."

The **Cowboys of Chance Creek** series continues with
The Cowboy Imports a Bride.

Be the first to know about Cora Seton's new releases!
Sign up for her newsletter here!

Other books in the Cowboys of Chance Creek Series:

The Cowboy Inherits a Bride (Volume 0)
The Cowboy's E-Mail Order Bride (Volume 1)
The Cowboy Imports a Bride (Volume 3)
The Cowgirl Ropes a Billionaire (Volume 4)
The Sheriff Catches a Bride (Volume 5)
The Cowboy Lassos a Bride (Volume 6)
The Cowboy Rescues a Bride (Volume 7)
The Cowboy Earns a Bride (Volume 8)
The Cowboy's Christmas Bride (Volume 9)

Sign up for my newsletter HERE.
www.coraseton.com/sign-up-for-my-newsletter

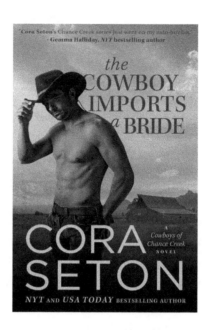

Read on for an excerpt of
The Cowboy Imports a Bride.

"I'M GOING TO MAKE THIS SHORT AND SWEET." Holt Matheson stalked into the dining room and hung his cowboy hat on the back of the nearest chair. He braced his hands against the walnut dining room table and looked from one to the other of his grown children, who sat two per side in varying degrees of boredom and irritation. All of them were dusty from the day's work. Usually Holt convened these meetings right after dinner. Today it was barely two in the afternoon—and they'd been summoned inside smack in the middle of their ranching chores.

"I have four sons ranging in age from 28 to 33. Four sons," he repeated, slapping his hand on the polished surface of the table. "And not one single daughter-in-law or grandchild in sight. What the hell is wrong with all of you?"

Rob Matheson, the youngest of the four, tilted his chair back on two legs and laced his hands behind his neck, exchanging a puzzled glance with his oldest brother, Jake. Normally Holt stuck to tried and true subjects: get up before the sun and don't stop working until it's dark; don't turn your back on an unbroken horse; just because you elect a government doesn't mean it isn't out to get you; and his perennial favorite—take your darn boots off before you enter the house.

Marriage was a new topic at the Matheson table.

"You saying you want us to go knock someone up?" Ned drawled. Rob coughed to cover his laugh. Second eldest, Ned always could get away with baiting their father. If he'd said that, he'd more than likely be flat on the floor by now. As the afternoon sun slanted through the windows, a fly droned somewhere out of sight. It was August, hotter than hell, and as usual his father refused to turn on the air-conditioning.

"I'm saying I'm starting to wonder if you all are batting for the wrong team," Holt said, straightening up. His rectangular belt buckle, emblazoned with a bald eagle, glinted in the sunlight.

"Holt," Lisa chided from the opposite end of the table. "Set a good example for the children."

Rob bit back another laugh. After thirty-four years of

marriage to his father, his mother was still trying to civilize him. He rubbed a hand across his forehead and added his voice to the discussion. "What's wrong, Dad—you need some more cheap labor?"

Ned snorted. "More like free labor."

Luke, only a year older than Rob, grinned, flashing white teeth against his tanned skin. All four Matheson boys were blond and blue-eyed. They got their height and broad shoulders from their father, but their mother's Viking heritage won out as far as hair was concerned. When they were together, they attracted a lot of female attention. Rob didn't mind that one bit—as long as most of it was directed his way.

"Show some respect!" Holt boomed. "You get paid plenty." The room fell silent. It was true their father paid them—if you counted a roof over their heads, three meals a day and housekeeping service as payment. They each received a small spending allowance as well, but nothing to write home about. Holt kept them in line by keeping them cash-poor. "Now I've heard plenty about your exploits down at the Dancing Boot, and I've seen more than one pretty filly creeping out of here on a Sunday morning who didn't look like she was heading to church, so I'll assume that it's possible I'll one day have a grandchild, but I'm getting mighty impatient waiting for that day to come. By the time I was Rob's age I had four sons!"

Holt caught each of their gazes in turn and let his point sink home. "I can't force you to marry, but I can lay out a few enticements in your path. So here's how it's going to be. The first one of you who brings home a bride will get 200 acres near the river to do with exactly as you see fit."

Jake sat up straight, and Rob understood why: 200 acres was nothing to sneeze at. A man could do a lot with 200 acres. "No meddling?" he asked.

Holt's eyebrows lowered. "When do I ever meddle?"

"When do you not meddle, you old coot?" Lisa said. "You run our children's lives like they were still in diapers." Holt shot her a hard look but she didn't back down.

"No meddling," Holt confirmed after a long moment. "200 acres to the first one who gets a girl to the altar and marries her. Now get back to work."

He strode from the room. Lisa pushed her chair back from the table, stood up and followed him. Rob wondered if the rest of his brothers felt as blindsided as he did. 200 acres. All his own. What could he do with 200 acres if his father kept his nose out of it?

He wasn't sure. But he wanted like hell to find out.

"I WON'T BE ABLE to make it on Saturday after all."

Morgan Tate closed her eyes at her father's words. Clutching the cell phone to her ear, she checked to make sure her office door was shut. Barely bigger than a broom closet, it was still a mark of how far she'd risen at Cassidy Wineries. Assistant Manager of the distillery—a far cry from the grunt work she used to do when she joined the company ten years ago. In three days the company was unveiling the first vintage produced entirely under her supervision. She'd hoped her father would come to the tasting room for the celebration being hosted in its honor.

"Why not?" She tried to keep the anger out of her voice. When did he ever come to anything she invited him to? She shouldn't be surprised he'd back out now.

"It's Linda—she's pregnant." Pride rang out clearly in his voice. "Everyone's coming to celebrate!"

Linda. His other daughter. His *real* daughter. The one he'd had under the sanction of marriage—not the one he'd fathered during an illicit affair with a student. As always, Morgan felt the sting of shame of her birth. She was used to being kept in the shadows, though—the child no one had wanted. The daughter her father wished would disappear. He might never say as much, and he still did his duty by her when it suited him, but more than once he'd hinted that he wouldn't take it amiss if she moved to Toronto, or even to the United States—anywhere far from Victoria.

She forced herself to take a deep, steadying breath, twirling a strand of her thick, long dark hair around one finger. "Congratulations, Dad. I know you'll be a terrific grandfather."

Of course Linda would beat her to motherhood, too. Linda seemed to make it her life's work to be the perfect daughter—the daughter Edward Tate could be proud of. She'd beat Morgan in grades, looks, scholarships, jobs, marriage and now this. Not that they ever talked—of course not—but her father made sure to keep her up-to-the-minute on his true children's exploits. She was sure he didn't go trumpeting her successes to them.

"Yes, well." Edward cleared his throat, obviously impatient to end the call. He'd managed to weasel out of another occasion, so now he'd head back to his ivory tower to work on his precious research. Studying other cultures was far more interesting than learning about your own daughter. He spent more time with his graduate students than he ever spent with her.

"Okay. See you soon," she said.

The phone clicked before she even finished the sentence.

Damn, damn, damn. Why did she always do this? Seek approval from the one man determined never to give it to her? It'd been worse in the weeks since she'd learned her mother died. Aria Cruz had always been out of reach, too, living with her husband and children in Chance Creek, Montana, but at least Morgan knew that when she did come to Victoria to visit—one month out of every year—she'd focus her complete attention on her. Aria had loved her. Not enough to risk ruining her marriage to Alex Cruz, of course. She'd only been twenty the year she'd spent in Victoria, studying anthropology at UVic. Swept away by a much older, distinguished professor, she'd gotten pregnant that fall, had the baby in the spring, and left her infant with Edward's parents to raise when she returned in September to Montana and married Alex.

Morgan had always known the truth of her parentage. She'd always known she came last—after the legitimate children of her mother and father's marriages.

She'd learned to be a realist—to depend only on herself. But she couldn't help hoping that one day—just once—she'd come first with her father.

With any man.

If she was smart, she thought as she tucked her cell phone back in her pocket, she'd turn her back on men all together. Stay single.

Join a nunnery, even.

But her biological clock was ticking with a vengeance these days. Now that she'd reached this milestone in her career, it suddenly became obvious how much the rest of her life was lagging behind. Maybe it was meeting her half-brother and sister in Montana for the first time last month when she went to find out why her mother missed her yearly visit.

Maybe it was her mother's death.

She stared out the window that overlooked the Cassidy vineyards. She'd half-known that something bad had happened before she arrived in Montana. Her mother had never let her down like that before. Then her worst fears were confirmed when Aria's daughter, Claire, told her their mother was dead. She hadn't been prepared for the grief that had come and gone in waves ever since. Aria was far from a perfect mother—but she was Morgan's mother, nonetheless. Now she was gone, and more than ever Morgan found herself alone in the world.

At least she'd come to know Claire and Ethan during that trip—the children Aria had never allowed her to meet during her lifetime. They'd known nothing about her, of course, or of her father, Edward. They'd been angry at first, but soon absolved her of their mother's sins and welcomed her to the family.

Her last few days in Montana had been some of the happiest she'd known—shot through with grief over Aria's death. Ethan and his wife, Autumn, and Claire and her intended, Jamie Lassiter, lived on the Cruz ranch and were working together to build a guest ranch business. She'd also met Cab Johnson, county sheriff, and Rose Bellingham and Tracey Richards, who helped Autumn out with the inside chores.

Most importantly, she'd met Rob Matheson, the handsomest cowboy in all Montana. The man who took her breath away. He'd grown up on the ranch next door to the Cruzes, and was fast friends with Ethan, Cab and Jamie.

She wanted to go back to Chance Creek. She wanted a life like Ethan and Autumn's—or Claire and Jamie's. She wanted a husband, children on the way. She wanted her own business, too—a winery she controlled from top to bottom.

Everyone else was getting exactly what they wanted.

Why couldn't she?

"ROB, SHE'S HERE—she'll be landing at the airport in a couple of minutes!" Claire Cruz called out of the window of her Honda Civic.

She'd driven the long lane up to the Matheson house so fast she'd raised a trail of dust that must be visible for miles, Rob thought, startled out of his nap in the shade of the verandah. Unlike his brothers who'd leapt up from their father's bizarre challenge raring to get to the next block of ranch chores, he'd decided to put his feet up for a while and think things through. The nap just kind of snuck up on him.

Now he sat up straight, as alert as an eagle looking for prey. "Who's here? What are you talking about?" Claire lived on the ranch next door and they'd grown up side-by-side like brother and sister. He'd never seen her this excited about anything. Her sleek, dark bob swung against her jaw as she leaned out the window and beckoned to him.

"Morgan! She just arrived. She came early to surprise everyone. Hop in, you can ride with me!"

Rob was off the porch in a flash. He hadn't seen Morgan Tate in weeks, not since she'd flown back to Canada.

"Why the hell didn't she call me?" he demanded as he climbed into Claire's teeny-tiny car, already wishing for the leg room of his Chevy truck. You'd think now that Claire was settling down with Jamie on the Cruz ranch she'd get herself a decent set of wheels.

"Like I said, it's supposed to be a surprise. I didn't know how to lure you out to the airport without telling you, though. Hurry up. She's waiting!"

Excitement and desire tightened Rob's gut. Morgan. Here in Chance Creek. More than two whole weeks early for Claire and Jamie's wedding.

"Last time I talked to her, she told me there was no way she could take any time off work. She said she could only come here for the weekend of the wedding," he said, gazing out the window as Claire made a tight u-turn and headed back out the lane. Luckily it was only fifteen minutes to the airport. Ten, the way Claire was driving.

"I think she was leading you on so she could surprise you better," Claire said. She seemed thrilled at the prospect of seeing her half-sister. Which made sense. After Claire got over her initial shock and anger at finding her mother had a daughter she'd never told anyone about, Claire had embraced her sister, only to have her leave again. He wondered if the happiness on her face was mirrored on his own.

"She's going to help me with all the last minute details about the wedding," she added.

"You don't get to hog her the whole time, though," Rob said, comfortably. Two years older than him, Claire used to boss him around as much as she did Ethan when they were kids. Once he got bigger than her, however, he'd had his revenge through multiple practical jokes over the years. He never got tired of giving her a hard time.

Still, he was happy for her and Jamie, and looked forward to their wedding, not the least because it meant that Morgan would be in town again.

Except she was already here.

Rob ran a hand through his hair and looked down at the jeans and t-shirt he wore. He'd worked all morning and he suddenly became aware how ripe he was. Hell, if he'd known Morgan was coming he'd have spiffed up a bit. Put on a fresh shirt at least.

"She won't mind your stink," Claire said.

"She won't notice my stink under your stink," Rob said, elbowing her. The car's path wobbled.

"Hey, watch it." Claire got the Civic back under control and soon they were pulling into the airport parking lot. The Chance Creek Regional Airport had been refurbished a few years back and it sported a modern glass and granite façade.

Inside, though, it still was the same pokey little terminal it had always been. She tugged him down the single long corridor to the point beyond which airport security blocked their way.

"That's her flight," Claire called out, pointing to a line of people spilling into the building from an airplane boarding ramp. "We made it just in time."

Rob realized he hadn't told anyone back at the ranch he was leaving. His father had asked him to sort out the equipment stored in the south stable this afternoon. Luckily it wasn't an important job. If Holt was in some kind of all-fired hurry, he would have to find someone else to do it. With three brothers, there was always someone to fill in for him.

He craned his neck as each passenger came through the entrance. Each time he was disappointed. Morgan must be sitting near the rear of the plane.

The number of passengers slowed to a trickle and then stopped.

"Where is she?" Rob demanded, turning on Claire. He caught her wide smile and his stomach sank.

Damn it.

"Got you! You should have seen your face when I

said she was here," Claire crowed. "Ooooh, Rob's in love!"

"Stow it," Rob said, jamming his fists in his pockets and trying to restrain himself from picking Claire up, shoving her into a suitcase and sending her to Timbuktu.

"Come on—you play jokes on other people all the time. What's wrong? You can dish it out, but you can't take it?" Claire danced around him, enjoying her triumph all too much.

"If you don't shut your trap, I'm going to dish something out," Rob said, turning on his heel back the way they'd come. Claire's laughter followed him. She was right, though; he had put many people in the same spot he was now. He was sure some day this would seem funny to him, too.

But not now. He was aching for Morgan, and she was a thousand miles away.

He stopped in his tracks when Ethan, Autumn, Claire, Jamie, Cab—hell, even Ned, Jake and Luke—appeared before him, all laughing fit to burst.

What the hell?

"Got it all on camera!" Ethan hollered, holding up the cell phone Rob knew Claire had bought him a couple of months back. Someone must have finally showed Ethan how to use it.

"Very funny." Okay, he could see why Ethan would want to film his humiliation—he'd made a movie of Ethan's drunken rant about the qualities necessary for a ranch wife last spring, and posted it on the Internet as a wife-wanted ad. The movie had gone viral, and Autumn had been one of the women to answer the ad. She'd been all set to write a scathing article for the magazine she worked for about cowboys and their arrogance when she arrived in Montana. Instead, she and Ethan fell in love.

He'd expected gratitude. Not retaliation.

"Should we send it to Morgan? Show her how much you looooove her?" Jamie asked, knocking back his cowboy hat, the better see Rob. His dark hair was falling into his eyes as usual. A bit shorter than Rob and Ethan, Jamie's model-good looks still caught the eye of every woman who walked by.

Rob supposed he deserved that, too. After all, he had screwed up Jamie's proposal to Claire with a well-timed practical joke, as well.

"No—don't get her hopes up," Claire chimed in. "Morgan deserves a real man. One who isn't afraid of commitment."

"You mean a guy who can date a woman more than two weeks running?" Rose said, laughing like she knew all about it. Well, she did, didn't she?

Everyone did.

"Has he ever dated anyone for two weeks running?" Cab said. The sheriff had way too much time on his hands if he could show up at the airport for this. Usually the large man held his peace, but this time he seemed all too happy to throw his lot in with the rest of these jokers.

Everyone else laughed.

Ethan looked the sheriff up and down. "Hey, I've

got an idea, Cab. Why don't *you* date Morgan? Get her to move to Montana for good. If Rob here keeps going after her, she'll end up running away to Alaska or something."

Rob stiffened. *Cab? Dating Morgan?* "Hey!"

They all ignored him. "Cab's perfect," Claire said, turning an appraising eye on the big man. "You'd be part of the family, then. You know, after the two of you got married."

Married? Cab and Morgan? Rob fought to keep his hands from clenching into fists.

Cab appeared to consider this. "She's awfully pretty," he agreed. "Got a good head on her shoulders, too."

"Lay off!" Rob couldn't keep his voice from rising.

"Why—you getting serious about her?" Cab goaded him.

"Serious? Rob?" Claire said. "That'll be the day."

Feeling like an unbroken horse caught in a corral, Rob glared at all of them. "I can be serious."

Everybody laughed like he'd uttered a terrific joke. Damn it, wasn't anyone going to back him up?

He saw Autumn lingering behind Ethan. Despite her months on the Cruz ranch, she still stood out from the rest. Her long, brown hair and elfin face always made her look a little other-worldly. He knew from experience she didn't like practical jokes—didn't like it when people got laughed at—and now he understood why. It sucked being on the receiving end, didn't it? Why had he ever become such a prankster?

Well, he knew exactly why, didn't he? To keep three

older brothers off of his back. To keep everyone else from teasing him. He'd been different, once—too sensitive, too much of a dreamer—but that was a long time ago—a hell of a long time ago. No one messed with him now.

Not usually.

"I'm out of here," he said, and stalked off down the hall toward the exit. He realized he didn't even have his own truck to ride home in. Well, he'd be damned if he took a ride from one of his so-called friends. He hoped there'd be a cab out front when he reached the door.

There was, thank God, and he climbed in and told the driver to take him to the Dancing Boot before anyone else reached the pavement.

To hell with all of them. He could be serious. He could date a woman for more than two weeks.

He just hadn't tried it yet.

MORGAN CLICKED THROUGH HER TEXT MESSAGES to find the one she'd received from the caterer that morning. Jillian Hodgeson was probably sick of her by now, but she was determined that the event scheduled for her vintage's debut would go off without a hitch. Check and recheck every detail—that was her motto when she ran these affairs. So far it had paid off. Taking on this extra role at the winery was one of the things which brought her to the owner's attention. Elliot Cassidy was a crusty old man whom she didn't particularly like, but respected because of his position. His son, Duncan, was another matter. He was an ass.

She paused when she spotted the text Claire had sent her earlier in the day. Asking her again what she knew about the way their mother had spent her money. Morgan pressed her lips together. She knew what Claire was after. Aria had blown through large amounts of the Cruz ranch's profits, and when she and Alex died in a car accident the preceding August, Ethan and Claire had been left with a business seriously in debt. Only by taking on Jamie as a partner and turning the spread into a guest ranch had Ethan been able to refinance it and buy out Claire's share. Claire was rich now, but she couldn't let the mystery go: how had Aria spent all that money? Claire seemed sure her mother had blown it on Morgan.

Morgan had already told her a hundred times that while Aria had taken her to restaurants and bought her clothes now and then when she came to visit, she had not underwritten her day-to-day upkeep—as a child or an adult.

It must be galling to her siblings that Aria had siphoned so much money from the ranch, but it hurt her that Claire still blamed her for the loss of the cash—even if her texts were worded carefully, with plenty of assurances that she was *just curious.*

The part where Claire asked for the dates of Aria's visits really bothered her. She was afraid the dates she gave her wouldn't add up. She had realized something in the weeks since she met her half-brother and sister. When Ethan and Claire talked about their mother's yearly absences, they always talked about *months.*

Aria never stayed in Victoria more than a month,

however.

Morgan could imagine how Ethan and Claire had felt when they learned their mother's shopping sprees in Europe were really visits to a daughter in Canada they didn't know she had. They must have felt betrayed—stabbed in the heart. It was a miracle they accepted her at all, let alone made friends with her, but their friendship meant more to her than she could ever express.

What if there were more secrets to find out about Aria Cruz? What if those secrets tore her new, precious family apart? Claire seemed bent on doing that herself.

What had Aria done with the rest of her time away from home? Had she actually gone to Europe and done some shopping?

Maybe.

Maybe not.

It was the *maybe not* that left her cold. Morgan hugged her arms across her chest. Could she possibly have another half-brother or sister out there? Could one Montana girl leave a trail of children across a continent or two?

In her darkest moments, that's exactly what Morgan pictured. But no—that would require lengths of time away from home that Aria simply hadn't spent. Claire said her year away during college was the only time Aria had been gone from Montana for so many months.

So no other children. *Probably.*

Morgan dropped a hand to her own flat stomach. No children for her, either. Claire had mentioned she and Jamie were thinking of trying for a child as soon as they got married. With Autumn already pregnant, Claire said she wanted to be sure their kids were of similar ages.

"That makes it so much more fun, don't you think?" she'd commented the last time they talked on the phone.

Yes. She did think that would make it more fun. Too bad she was stuck a thousand miles away, with no husband in sight, let alone a child.

Maybe she should say yes the next time Duncan hinted around about marriage.

Shivering with disgust at the thought of marrying her boss's son, she pulled her thoughts back to Chance Creek, the Cruz ranch, and Rob Matheson. Now there was someone she'd like to have a baby with. Tall, broad-shouldered, muscled in all the right places, with hands that set her skin on fire...

She stifled a laugh. As if that would ever happen. Everyone she met in Chance Creek took her aside at one time or another to tell her Rob was bad news. A lady's man with no desire to ever settle down. She'd told them all she could handle him, and she had. They'd made out a lot, but done nothing else. Every time he tried to take things further, she stopped him cold.

No way she'd lose her heart to someone so entirely off limits.

Except she kind of already had.

She glanced back down at Claire's text again, and resolutely clicked past it. Caterer. Party. Vintage.

She had far too much work to do to think about anyone back in Chance Creek.

"Buy me a drink, cowboy?"

Rob slid his gaze over to the curvy brunette who'd taken the stool next to his at the long, wooden bar in the Dancing Boot. He squinted a little. Georgette Harris, from the next town over. Where'd she work? The feed store, that was it.

"I'm outta cash," he lied. Truth was, he had a little money left in his pocket, but only enough to keep himself drunk tonight.

"I'll buy my own drink, then. Hope you don't mind the company." She smiled at him and leaned closer, all the better to flash him some cleavage.

Pretty impressive cleavage.

"Free country," he mumbled. He'd already consumed a hefty amount of alcohol, but the sting of the afternoon's confrontation at the airport was still sharp. *Some friends.* Not one of them had defended him. No respect at all.

She laid a hand on his arm. "I've got the night off."

He frowned, trying to work that one out. The feed store wasn't open past six. "Night off from what?"

"From my boyfriend, silly. From Jessie—you know Jessie Henry."

Sure. Maybe. But he couldn't bring the man's face to mind.

She leaned even closer, her breast brushing his arm as she whispered into his ear, "Thought I'd have a little fun while he's out of town. You know what I mean?" She dropped a hand to his thigh.

Yeah. He knew exactly what she meant. Rob

straightened a little and eyed her speculatively. "Why pick me?" he asked, surprising himself. Why even bother asking? Why not take the gift he'd been handed and show the lady a heck of a good time like he usually would?

"You won't be no problem tomorrow," Georgette said cheerfully. "Nor tonight. Some guys get squeamish about fooling around with another man's girl. Not you. And I know I won't get any phone calls next week wondering where I am. You'll be too busy chasing after some other guy's woman."

Wow. That was harsh. Suddenly he felt all too sober.

"Guys like you are handy," she said, as if sharing a confidence. "A girl can yank your chain, have her way with you, and kick you back into the closet when she's done. You're like a pair of high heels. Great now and then when you want a party, but useless for the day-to-day."

Rob blinked.

She must have caught his expression, because she rushed to add, "But pretty. You're real pretty, ain't you, Rob?"

"Fuck off." He stood up, slapped some cash on the bar and stalked toward the door, weaving a little before he got his bearings. Guess he was a little drunk after all.

Cab cut him off before he made it halfway across the room. He hadn't even seen the man enter the Boot.

"Tell me you're not driving," Cab said.

Rob pushed past him, into the still-warm Montana evening. Cab followed him outdoors. Aside from the music spilling out of the Boot with them, Chance Creek was already quiet. Most folks were tucked in for the night. Past nine o'clock this town shut down.

"Can't let you do that, buddy. Give me the keys."

For god's sake. His truck wasn't even in the lot—he'd taken a taxi here.

Unwilling to argue it out, Rob handed them over, and struck out on foot.

"Where you going?" Cab called after him.

"Nowhere."

Nowhere at all.

End of Excerpt

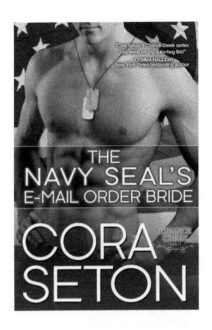

Read on for an excerpt of Volume 1 of
The Heroes of Chance Creek series –
The Navy SEAL's E-Mail Order Bride.

"BOYS," LIEUTENANT COMMANDER Mason Hall said, "we're going home."

He sat back in his folding chair and waited for a reaction from his brothers. The recreation hall at Bagram Airfield was as busy as always with men hunched over laptops, watching the widescreen television, or lounging in groups of three or four shooting the breeze. His brothers—three tall, broad shouldered men in uniform—stared back at him from his computer screen, the feeds from their four-way video conversation all relaying a similar reaction to his words.

Utter confusion.

"Home?" Austin was the first to speak. A Special Forces officer just a year younger than Mason, he was currently in Kabul.

"Home," Mason confirmed. "I got a letter from Great Aunt Heloise. Uncle Zeke passed away over the weekend without designating an heir. That means the ranch reverts back to her. She thinks we'll do a better job running it than Darren will." Darren, their first cousin, wasn't known for his responsible behavior and he hated ranching. Mason, on the other hand, loved it. He had missed the ranch, the cattle, the Montana sky and his family's home ever since they'd left it twelve years ago.

"She's giving Crescent Hall to us?" That was Zane, Austin's twin, a Marine currently in Kandahar. The excitement in his tone told Mason all he needed to know—Zane stilled loved the old place as much as he did. When Mason had gotten Heloise's letter, he'd had to read it more than once before he believed it. The Hall would belong to them once more—when he'd thought they'd lost it for good. Suddenly he'd felt like he could breathe fully again after so many years of holding in his anger and frustration over his uncle's behavior. The timing was perfect, too. He was due to ship stateside any day now. By April he'd be a civilian again.

Except it wasn't as easy as all that. Mason took a deep breath. "There are a few conditions."

Colt, his youngest brother, snorted. "Of course—we're talking about Heloise, aren't we? What's she up to this time?" He was an Air Force combat controller who had served both in Afghanistan and as part of the relief effort a few years back after the massive earthquake which devastated Haiti. He was currently back on United States soil in Florida, training with his unit.

Mason knew what he meant. Calling Heloise eccentric would be an understatement. In her eighties, she had definite opinions and brooked no opposition to her plans and schemes. She meant well, but as his father had always said, she was capable of leaving a swath of destruction in family affairs that rivaled Sherman's march to Atlanta.

"The first condition is that we have to stock the ranch with one hundred pair of cattle within twelve months of taking possession."

"We should be able to do that," Austin said.

"It's going to take some doing to get that ranch up and running again," Zane countered. "Zeke was already letting the place go years ago."

"You have something better to do than fix the place up when you get out?" Mason asked him. He hoped Zane understood the real question: was he in or out?

"I'm in; I'm just saying," Zane said.

Mason suppressed a smile. Zane always knew what he was thinking.

"Good luck with all that," Colt said.

"Thanks," Mason told him. He'd anticipated that inheriting the Hall wouldn't change Colt's mind about staying in the Air Force. He focused on the other two who were both already in the process of winding down their military careers. "If we're going to do this, it'll take a commitment. We're going to have to pool our funds and put our shoulders to the wheel for as long as it takes. Are you up for that?"

"I'll join you there as soon as I'm able to in June," Austin said. "It'll just be like another year in the service. I can handle that."

"I already said I'm in," Zane said. "I'll have boots on the ground in September."

Here's where it got tricky. "There's just one other thing," Mason said. "Aunt Heloise has one more requirement of each of us."

"What's that?" Austin asked when he didn't go on.

"She's worried about the lack of heirs on our side of the family. Darren has children. We don't."

"Plenty of time for that," Zane said. "We're still young, right?"

"Not according to Heloise." Mason decided to get it over and done with. "She's decided that in order for us to inherit the Hall free and clear, we each have to be married within the year. One of us has to have a child."

Stunned silence met this announcement until Colt started to laugh. "Staying in the Air Force doesn't look so bad now, does it?"

"That means you, too," Mason said.

"What? Hold up, now." Colt was startled into soberness. "I won't even live on the ranch. Why do I have to get hitched?"

"Because Heloise says it's time to stop screwing around. And she controls the land. And you know

Heloise."

"How are we going to get around that?" Austin asked.

"We're not." Mason got right to the point. "We're going to find ourselves some women and we're going to marry them."

"In Afghanistan?" Zane's tone made it clear what he thought about that idea.

Tension tightened Mason's jaw. He'd known this was going to be a messy conversation. "Online. I created an online personal ad for all of us. Each of us has a photo, a description and a reply address. A woman can get in touch with whichever of us she chooses and start a conversation. Just weed through your replies until you find the one you want."

"Are you out of your mind?" Zane peered at him through the video screen.

"I don't see what you're upset about. I'm the one who has to have a child. None of you will be out of the service in time."

"Wait a minute—I thought you just got the letter from Heloise." As usual, Austin zeroed in on the inconsistency.

"The letter came about a week ago. I didn't want to get anyone's hopes up until I checked a few things out." Mason shifted in his seat. "Heloise said the place is in rougher shape than we thought. Sounds like Zeke sold off the last of his cattle last year. We're going to have to start from scratch, and we're going to have to move fast to meet her deadline—on both counts. I did all the leg work on the online ad. All you need to do is read some e-mails, look at some photos and pick one. How hard can that be?"

"I'm beginning to think there's a reason you've been single all these years, Straightshot," Austin said. Mason winced at the use of his nickname. The men in his unit had christened him with it during his early days in the service, but as Colt said when his brothers had first heard about it, it made perfect sense. The name had little to do with his accuracy with a rifle, and everything to do with his tendency to find the shortest route from here to done on any mission he was tasked with. Regardless of what obstacles stood in his way.

Colt snickered. "Told you two it was safer to stay in the military. Mason's Matchmaking Service. It has a ring to it. I guess you've found yourself a new career, Mase."

"Stow it." Mason tapped a finger on the table. "Just because I've put the ad up doesn't mean that any of you have to make contact with the women who write you. If it doesn't work, it doesn't work. But you need to marry within the year. If you don't find a wife for yourself, I'll find one for you."

"He would, too," Austin said to the others. "You know he would."

"When does the ad go live?" Zane asked.

"It went live five days ago. You've each got several hundred responses so far. I'll forward them to you as soon as we break the call."

Austin must have leaned toward his webcam because suddenly he filled the screen. "Several hundred?"

"That's right."

Colt's laughter rang out over the line.

"Don't know what you're finding so funny, Colton," Mason said in his best imitation of their late father's voice. "You've got several hundred responses, too."

"What? I told you I was staying…"

"Read through them and answer all the likely ones. I'll be in touch in a few days to check your progress." Mason cut the call.

REGAN ANDERSON WANTED a baby. Right now. Not five years from now. Not even next year.

Right now.

And since she'd just quit her stuffy loan officer job, moved out of her overpriced one bedroom New York City apartment, and completed all her preliminary appointments, she was going to get one via the modern technology of artificial insemination.

As she raced up the three flights of steps to her tiny new studio, she took the pins out of her severe updo and let her thick, auburn hair swirl around her shoulders. By the time she reached the door, she was breathing hard. Inside, she shut and locked it behind her, tossed her briefcase and blazer on the bed which took up the lion's share of the living space, and kicked off her high heels. Her blouse and pencil skirt came next, and thirty seconds later she was down to her skivvies.

Thank God.

She was done with Town and Country Bank. Done

with originating loans for people who would scrape and slave away for the next thirty years just to cling to a lousy flat near a subway stop. She was done, done, done being a cog in the wheel of a financial system she couldn't stand to be a part of anymore.

She was starting a new business. Starting a new life.

And she was starting a family, too.

Alone.

After years of looking for Mr. Right, she'd decided he simply didn't exist in New York City. So after several medical exams and consultations, she had scheduled her first round of artificial insemination for the end of April. She couldn't wait.

Meanwhile, she'd throw herself into the task of building her consulting business. She would make it her job to help non-profits assist regular people start new stores and services, buy homes that made sense, and manage their money so that they could get ahead. It might not be as lucrative as being a loan officer, but at least she'd be able to sleep at night.

She wasn't going to think about any of that right now, though. She'd survived her last day at work, survived her exit interview, survived her boss, Jack Richey, pretending to care that she was leaving. Now she was giving herself the weekend off. No work, no nothing—just forty-eight hours of rest and relaxation.

Having grabbed takeout from her favorite Thai restaurant on the way home, Regan spooned it out onto a plate and carried it to her bed. Lined with pillows, it doubled as her couch during waking hours. She sat cross-legged on top of the duvet and savored her food and her freedom. She had bought herself a nice bottle of wine to drink this weekend, figuring it might be her last for an awfully long time. She was all too aware her Chardonnay-sipping days were coming to an end. As soon as her weekend break from reality was over, she planned to spend the next ten months starting her business, while scrimping and saving every penny she could. She would have to move to a bigger apartment right before the baby was born, but given the cost of renting in the city, the temporary downgrade was worth it. She pushed all thoughts of business and the future out of her mind. Rest and relax—that was her job for now.

Two hours and two glasses of wine later, however, rest and relaxation was beginning to feel a lot like loneliness and boredom. In truth, she'd been fighting loneliness for months. She'd broken up with her last boyfriend before Christmas. Here it was March and she was still single. Two of her closest friends had gotten married and moved away in the past twelve months, Laurel to New Hampshire and Rita to New Jersey. They rarely saw each other now and when she'd jokingly mentioned the idea of going ahead and having a child without a husband the last time they'd gotten together, both women had scoffed.

"No way could I have gotten through this pregnancy without Ryan." Laurel ran a hand over her large belly. "I've felt awful the whole time."

"No way I'm going back to work." Rita's baby was six weeks old. "Thank God Alan brings in enough cash to see us through."

Regan decided not to tell them about her plans until the pregnancy was a done deal. She knew what she was getting into—she didn't need them to tell her how hard it might be. If there'd been any way for her to have a baby normally—with a man she loved—she'd have chosen that path in a heartbeat. But there didn't seem to be a man for her to love in New York. Unfortunately, keeping her secret meant it was hard to call either Rita or Laurel just to chat, and she needed someone to chat with tonight. As dusk descended on the city, Regan felt fear for the first time since making her decision to go ahead with having a child.

What if she'd made a mistake? What if her consultancy business failed? What if she became a welfare mother? What if she had to move back home?

When the thoughts and worries circling her mind grew overwhelming, she topped up her wine, opened up her laptop and clicked on a YouTube video of a cat stuck headfirst in a cereal box. Thank goodness she'd hooked up wi-fi the minute she secured the studio. Simultaneously scanning her Facebook feed, she read an update from an acquaintance named Susan who was exhibiting her art in one of the local galleries. She'd have to stop by this weekend.

She watched a couple more videos—the latest installment in a travel series she loved, and one about over-the-top weddings that made her sad. Determined to cheer up, she hopped onto Pinterest and added more images to her nursery pinboard. Sipping her wine, she checked the news, posted a question on the single parents' forum she frequented, checked her e-mail again, and then tapped a finger on the keys, wondering what to do next. The evening stretched out before her, vacant even of the work she normally took home to do over the weekend. She hadn't felt at such loose ends in years.

Pacing her tiny apartment didn't help. Nor did an attempt at unpacking more of her things. She had finished moving in just last night and boxes still lined one wall. She opened one to reveal books, took a look at her limited shelf space and packed them up again. A second box revealed her collection of vintage fans. No room for them here, either.

She stuck her iTouch into a docking station and turned up some tunes, then drained her glass, poured herself another, and flopped onto her bed. The wine was beginning to take effect—giving her a nice, soft, fuzzy feeling. It hadn't done away with her loneliness, but when she turned back to Facebook on her laptop, the images and YouTube links seemed funnier this time.

Heartened, she scrolled further down her feed until she spotted another post one of her friends had shared. It was an image of a handsome man standing ramrod straight in combat fatigues. *Hello.* He was cute. In fact, he looked like exactly the kind of man she'd always hoped she'd meet. He wasn't thin and arrogant like the up-and-coming Wall Street crowd, or paunchy and cynical like the upper-management men who hung around the bars near work. Instead he looked healthy, muscle-bound, clear-sighted, and vital. What was the post about? She clicked the link underneath it. Maybe there'd be more fantasy-fodder like this man wherever it took her.

There *was* more fantasy fodder. Regan wriggled happily. She had landed on a page that showcased four men. Brothers, she saw, looking more closely—two of them identical twins. Each one seemed to represent a different branch of the United States military. Were they models? Was this some kind of recruitment ploy?

Practical Wives Wanted read the heading at the top. Regan nearly spit out a sip of her wine. Wives Wanted? Practical ones? She considered the men again, then read more.

Looking for a change? the text went on. *Ready for a real challenge? Join four hardworking, clean living men and help bring our family's ranch back to life.*

Skills required—any or all of the following: Riding, roping, construction, animal care, roofing, farming, market gardening, cooking, cleaning, metalworking, small motor repair…

The list went on and on. Regan bit back at a laugh which quickly dissolved into giggles. Small engine repair? How very romantic. Was this supposed to be satire or was it real? It was certainly one of the most intriguing things she'd seen online in a long, long time.

Must be willing to commit to a man and the project. No weekends/no holidays/no sick days. Weaklings need not apply.

Regan snorted. It was beginning to sound like an employment ad. Good luck finding a woman to fill those conditions. She'd tried to find a suitable man for years and came up with Erik—the perennial mooch who'd finally admitted just before Christmas that he liked her old Village apartment more than he liked her. That's why she planned to get pregnant all by herself. There wasn't anyone worth marrying in the whole city. Probably the whole state. And if the men were all worthless, the women probably were, too. She reached for her wine without turning from the screen, missed, and nearly knocked over her glass. She tried again, secured the wine, drained the glass a third time and set it down again.

What she would give to find a real partner. Someone strong, both physically and emotionally. An equal in intelligence and heart. A real man.

But those didn't exist.

If you're sick of wasting your time in a dead-end job, tired of tearing things down instead of building something up, or just ready to get your hands dirty with clean, honest work, write and tell us why you'd make a worthy wife for a man who has spent the last decade in uniform.

There wasn't much to laugh at in this paragraph. Regan read it again, then got up and wandered to the kitchen to top up her glass. She'd never seen a singles ad like this one. She could see why it was going viral. If it was real, these men were something special. Who wanted to do clean, honest work these days? What kind of man was selfless enough to serve in the military instead of sponging off their girlfriends? If she'd known there were guys like this in the world, she might not have been so quick to schedule the artificial insemination appointment.

She wouldn't cancel it, though, because these guys couldn't be for real, and she wasn't waiting another minute to start her family. She had dreamed of having children ever since she was a child herself and organized pretend schools in her backyard for the neighborhood little ones. Babies loved her. Toddlers thought she was the next best thing to teddy bears. Her co-workers at the bank had never appreciated her as much as the average five-year-old did.

Further down the page there were photographs of the ranch the brothers meant to bring back to life. The land was beautiful, if overgrown, but its toppled fences and sagging buildings were a testament to its neglect. The photograph of the main house caught her eye and kept her riveted, though. A large gothic structure, it could be beautiful with the proper care. She could see why these men would dedicate themselves to returning it to its former glory. She tried to imagine what it would be like to live on the ranch with one of them, and immediately her body craved an open sunny sky—the kind you were hard pressed to see in the city. She sunk into the daydream, picturing herself sitting on a back porch sipping lemonade while her cowboy worked and the baby napped. Her husband would have his shirt off while he chopped wood, or mended a fence or whatever it was ranchers did. At the end of the day they'd fall into bed and make love until morning.

Regan sighed. It was a wonderful daydream, but it had no bearing on her life. Disgruntled, she switched over to Netflix and set up a foreign film. She fetched the bottle of wine back to bed with her and leaned against her many pillows. She'd managed to hang her small flatscreen on the opposite wall. In an apartment this tiny, every piece of furniture needed to serve double-duty.

As the movie started, Regan found herself composing messages to the military men in the Wife Wanted ad, in which she described herself as trim and petite, or lithe and strong, or horny and good-enough-looking to do the trick.

An hour later, when the film failed to hold her attention, she grabbed her laptop again. She pulled up the Wife Wanted page and reread it, keeping an eye on the foreign couple on the television screen who alternately argued and kissed.

Crazy what some people did. What was wrong with these men that they needed to advertise for wives instead of going out and meeting them like normal people?

She thought of the online dating sites she'd tried in the past. She'd had some awkward experiences, some horrible first dates, and finally one relationship that lasted for a couple of months before the man was transferred to Tucson and it fizzled out. It hadn't worked for her, but she supposed lots of people found love online these days. They might not advertise directly for spouses, but that was their ultimate intention, right? So maybe this ad wasn't all that unusual.

Most men who posted singles ads weren't as hot as these men were, though. Definitely not the ones she'd met. She poured herself another glass. A small twinge of her conscience told her she'd already had far too much wine for a single night.

To hell with that, Regan thought. As soon as she got

pregnant she'd have to stay sober and sane for the next eighteen years. She wouldn't have a husband to trade off with—she'd always be the designated driver, the adult in charge, the sober, wise mother who made sure nothing bad ever happened to her child. Just this one last time she was allowed to blow off steam.

But even as she thought it, a twinge of fear wormed through her belly.

What if she wasn't good enough?

She stood up, strode the two steps to the kitchenette and made herself a bowl of popcorn. She drowned it in butter and salt, returned to the bed in time for the ending credits of the movie, and lined up *Pride and Prejudice* with Colin Firth. Time for comfort food and a comfort movie. *Pride and Prejudice* always did the trick when she felt blue. She checked the Wife Wanted page again on her laptop. If she was going to pick one of the men— which she wasn't—who would she choose?

Mason, the oldest, due to leave the Navy in a matter of weeks, drew her eye first. With his dark crew cut, hard jaw and uncompromising blue eyes he looked like the epitome of a military man. He stated his interests as ranching—of course—history, natural sciences and tactical operations, whatever the hell that was. That left her little more informed than before she'd read it, and she wondered what the man was really like. Did he read the newspaper in bed on Sunday mornings? Did he prefer lasagna or spaghetti? Would he listen to country music in his truck or talk radio? She stared at his photo, willing him to answer.

The next two brothers, Austin and Zane, were less fierce, but looked no less intelligent and determined. Still, they didn't draw her eye the way the way Mason did. Colt, the youngest, was blond with a grin she bet drew women like flies. That one was trouble, and she didn't need trouble.

She read Mason's description again and decided he was the leader of this endeavor. If she was going to pick one, it would be him.

But she wasn't going to pick one. She had given up all that. She'd made a promise to her imaginary child that she would not allow any chaos into its life. No dating until her baby wore a graduation gown, at the very least. She felt another twinge. Was she ready to give up men for nearly two decades? That was a long time.

It's worth it, she told herself. She had no doubt about her desire to be a mother. She had no doubt she'd be a great mom. She was smart, capable and had a good head on her shoulders. She was funny, silly and patient, too. She loved children.

She was just lousy with men.

But that didn't matter anymore. She pushed the laptop aside and returned her attention to *Pride and Prejudice*, quickly falling into an old drinking game she and Laurel had devised one night that required taking a swig of wine each time one of the actresses lifted her eyebrows in polite surprise. When she finished the bottle, she headed to the tiny kitchenette to track down another one, trilling, "Jane! Elizabeth!" at the top of her voice along with Mrs. Bennett in the film. There was no more wine, so she switched to tequila.

By the time Elizabeth Bennett discovered the miracle of Mr. Darcy's palace-sized mansion, and decided she'd been too hasty in turning down his offer of marriage, Regan had decided she too needed to cast off her prejudices and find herself a man. A hot hunk of a military man. She grabbed the laptop, fumbled with the link that would let her leave Mason Hall a message and drafted a brilliant missive worthy of Jane Austen herself.

Dear Lt. Cmdr. Hall,

In her mind she pronounced lieutenant with an "f" like the Brits in the movie onscreen.

It is a truth universally acknowledged, that a single man in possession of a good ranch, must be in want of a wife. Furthermore, it must be self-evident that the wife in question should possess certain qualities numbering amongst them riding, roping, construction, roofing, farming, market gardening, cooking, cleaning, metalworking, animal care, and—most importantly, by Heaven—small motor repair.

Seeing as I am in possession of all these qualities, not to mention many others you can only have left out through unavoidable oversight or sheer obtuseness—such as glassblowing, cheesemaking, towel origami, heraldry, hovercraft piloting, and an uncanny sense of what cats are thinking—I feel almost forced to catapult myself into your purview.

You will see from my photograph that I am most eminently and majestically suitable for your wife.

She inserted a digital photo of her foot.

In fact, one might wonder why such a paragon of virtue such as I should deign to answer such a peculiar advertisement. The truth is, sir, that I long for adventure. To get my hands dirty with clean, hard work. To build something up instead of tearing it down.

In short, you are really hot. I'd like to lick you.

Yours,
Regan Anderson

On screen, Elizabeth Bennett lifted an eyebrow. Regan knocked back another shot of Jose Cuervo and passed out.

End of Excerpt

The Cowboys of Chance Creek Series:

The Cowboy Inherits a Bride (Volume 0)
The Cowboy's E-Mail Order Bride (Volume 1)
The Cowboy Wins a Bride (Volume 2)
The Cowboy Imports a Bride (Volume 3)
The Cowgirl Ropes a Billionaire (Volume 4)
The Sheriff Catches a Bride (Volume 5)
The Cowboy Lassos a Bride (Volume 6)
The Cowboy Rescues a Bride (Volume 7)
The Cowboy Earns a Bride (Volume 8)
The Cowboy's Christmas Bride (Volume 9)

The Heroes of Chance Creek Series:

The Navy SEAL's E-Mail Order Bride (Volume 1)
The Soldier's E-Mail Order Bride (Volume 2)
The Marine's E-Mail Order Bride (Volume 3)
The Navy SEAL's Christmas Bride (Volume 4)
The Airman's E-Mail Order Bride (Volume 5)

The SEALs of Chance Creek Series:

A SEAL's Oath
A SEAL's Vow
A SEAL's Pledge
A SEAL's Consent

About the Author

Cora Seton loves cowboys, country life, gardening, bike-riding, and lazing around with a good book. Mother of four, wife to a computer programmer/ eco-farmer, she ditched her California lifestyle nine years ago and moved to a remote logging town in northwestern British Columbia. Like the characters in her novels, Cora enjoys old-fashioned pursuits and modern technology, spending mornings transforming an ordinary one-acre lot into a paradise of orchards, berry bushes and market gardens, and afternoons writing the latest Chance Creek romance novel on her iPad mini. Visit www.coraseton.com to read about new releases and learn about contests and other events!

Blog:

www.coraseton.com

Facebook:

www.facebook.com/coraseton

Twitter:

www.twitter.com/coraseton

Newsletter:

www.coraseton.com/sign-up-for-my-newsletter

4-19

DISCARD

Maynardville Public Library
Maynardville, TN 3780?

CPSIA information can be obtained
at www.ICGtesting.com
Printed in the USA
LVHW041520090419
613523LV00003B/499